THE SUMMER ARRANGEMENT

PART OF THE SUMMERS IN SEASIDE SERIES

AMANDA SHELLEY

Visit my website at
www.amandashelley.com

CONNECT WITH AMANDA SHELLEY

Want to be the first to know about upcoming sales and new releases? Make sure you sign up for my newsletter as well as connect with me on social media and your favorite retail store.

Website:
www.amandashelley.com
Newsletter:
https://geni.us/AmandaShelleyNL
Facebook:
https://www.facebook.com/authoramandashelley/
Instagram:
https://www.instagram.com/authoramandashelley/
Reader's Group:
https://www.facebook.com/groups/AmandasArmyofReaders/
Tik Tok:
https://www.tiktok.com/@authoramandashelley
Amazon:
https://www.amazon.com/author/amandashelley
Goodreads:
https://www.goodreads.com/author/show/19713563.Aman
da_Shelley
Book Bub:
https://www.bookbub.com/profile/amanda-shelley

ABOUT THE BOOK

One, two, three—it's all down to me.

As the youngest and only single Lancaster, I'm eager to spend my summer in Seaside, Oregon, with my sisters. It's something I've looked forward to all year, and I'm determined to make every minute count. After all, I've only got one year before I graduate from college and have to adult for real.

However, if I want to graduate debt free, I need to work. I have a lead on the perfect summer job with the nanny agency I've spent the last three summers catering to.

I just have to win over an adorable three-year-old and convince her single dad I'm the right one for the job.

Simple enough, right?

Except when I show up at his door, I'm shocked to find he's the guy I hooked up with last semester.

This cannot be happening.

I need this job. There's too much on the line to walk away.

Maybe we can put the past behind us and make some sort of summer arrangement?

Chapter 1

Lizzy

"Mrs. Kruse will see you now," The receptionist in front of me stands and guides me to a conference room.

My heart races, and I force myself to take a steadying breath.

I can do this. I've worked for several families. I have what it takes to nanny a three-year-old. Hell, I've done it a million times. My references are stellar, and the agency has assured me that I'm among their top candidates. I just need to get through this.

Focus.

Read the room. Be myself.

That's all I can do.

Gah, why the hell are my palms sweaty?

It's not like I've never done this before. Why the hell am I so nervous?

Uh—Maybe because the stakes are higher?

I can't afford to choke and blow this opportunity.

I've got so much riding on this.

If this works out, so long second summer job. I'll easily be able to cover next semester's tuition—and I can spend quality time with my sisters this summer, if I play my cards right.

Inconspicuously wiping my palms down the sides of my pants, I follow the receptionist into the large conference room.

Immediately, an older woman dressed in a dark-gray pantsuit stands from the large table and greets me. "Welcome, Ms. Lancaster. I'm Dianne Kruse. I'm sorry my son can't be here with us. He's away on business. Since I'm only in Seaside this week, I must get preliminary interviews out of the way, so things are settled before I leave."

Her smile is warm as she grips my hand in hers, then gestures for me to have a seat adjacent to the one she'd left. Pointing at the table along the wall, she offers, "Would you like anything?"

Glancing at what has been set out, I notice there's an assortment of cookies, bottles of water, and a few sodas. All of it looks amazing, but my stomach can't handle anything like that until I get this interview over with, so I politely decline. "No, thank you. I'm good for now."

"Well then," she says, taking her seat. "Let's get started. Your resumé says you're attending Portland State University, double majoring in psychology and elementary education, but you're here in Seaside for the summer?"

"Yes, I'm spending the summer with my family and if all goes as planned, I'll graduate next spring."

She glances at my resumé next to us and nods. "Oh, that's right. Did you grow up here?"

"Yes and no," I admit. "My grandmother lived in Seaside. My dad is in the Air Force, so technically, we lived in several places, but this is where I feel most at home, even without Nana."

Shit. Why did I say that?

When Mrs. Kruse's expression turns quizzical, I rush to explain.

"Nana passed just over four years ago. But her place will always be home. In fact, we're all here again this summer. It's what we do every year... though I guess Lanie lives in Seaside with her husband Ryan year-round."

For fuck's sake, she didn't ask for your life story. Stop rambling already.

"All of you? I take it you have a big family?"

Exhaling slowly, a smile creeps onto my face as I admit. "Not really, though I do have three sisters... and with each of them now married or on their way to be, I guess our family is growing. Dad is stationed at Lewis-McChord, and my mom is a traveling nurse who currently works for a family in New Hampshire. Both will come out at some point this summer, I'm sure."

"That's wonderful. I'm traveling with my sister this summer, too. I'll miss Emilia like crazy, but I'm looking forward to spending time with Judy on a European cruise. It's something we've dreamed about for years. Time with family is precious."

"Nothing could've kept me away from my sisters this summer. I've missed them while I've been in school," I admit.

"I'm sure you do..." She trails off with a smile, then her face and tone turn serious. Clearing her throat, she asks, "Will tending to my granddaughter keep you from your family? The agency informed you that my son's schedule won't be the typical nine to five. Of course, we will ensure you have at least two days off each week, but the days and times may vary, depending on his workload."

Crap. That's not what I meant.

"Oh, it won't be a problem," I rush out. How do I ensure her this job won't get in the way? Hell. Even if I did work around the clock, I'd still have more time with them than I did last summer when I practically worked two full-time jobs.

When she still isn't convinced, I add, "I assure you, my sisters all have busy lives of their own. Some of them travel for work and honestly, I'm just grateful we're spending the summer in the same vicinity."

Her demeanor relaxes, and I'm relieved when she changes the subject. "Tell me more about what you enjoyed here as a child while visiting your grandmother."

With that simple request, a huge weight lifts, and I'm put at ease. I launch into my countless memories about summer adventures with Nana. I tell her about trips to the aquarium, walking along The Promenade, making sandcastles by the shore, going to the local library and bookstores, and baking endless amounts of treats in Nana's kitchen.

Seamlessly, our conversation flows from one topic to the next. She tells me about her granddaughter Emilia's favorite foods, stories, and love for all things about the ocean. I quickly learn that if I get the job, they've recently signed Emilia up for swim lessons.

I'll be responsible for taking her to the aquatic center in Astoria and encouraged to practice those new skills at home with her, should I feel comfortable. Apparently, her son has rented a house with a pool this summer, so it's a new feature for them. With easy access to both the pool and the ocean, it's crucial her granddaughter learns to swim.

Though even if she becomes the best swimmer, I assure Mrs. Kruse I have no intentions of letting her get anywhere close to the ocean without being right beside her. She's still young, and the waves are far too unpredictable.

When she asks about my previous experience, our conversation quickly morphs from water safety to our love of children and books. My experience as a previous nanny and working at

Booked at the Beach, our local bookstore, gives us many things to talk about.

Before I know it, the interview comes to an end. Mrs. Kruse thanks me for coming and lets me know she'll be in touch after she finishes the rest of the interviews and consults with her son.

Just as I'm about to leave, she adds, "Thank you so much for coming today, Elizabeth. I've enjoyed getting to know you. Please know, *if* you make it to the next round, it will be with my son and granddaughter. We need to ensure you get along well with Emilia and her father as ultimately, he'll make the final decision."

"Of course. Thanks again for your time. I look forward to hearing from you."

Chapter 2
Lizzy

Later that night at dinner, as my oldest sister Lanie passes me the salad dressing from across the table, she asks, "Any idea when Raven and Finn will arrive? Surely, they're done with the open house."

"I assumed they'd be here by now, though I haven't heard from her all afternoon," I admit, pouring dressing on my tossed salad.

Raven and her boyfriend Finn are looking at a place to rent for the summer. Sure, they could stay with us in Nana's house, as there is plenty of room. But Finn insists they get a place of their own. He's joked several times about family being like fish, and we're not meant to spend more than three days together.

Obviously, that's not true since he and Jax just came off a long music tour with Ruby Frax. They had spent months together traipsing across the country, and my sisters hardly ever missed a show. Touring with Riser put Ruby Frax on the map, and their momentum continues to grow as a band. After hearing some of the album they're releasing later this summer, I'm certain they'll soon be the ones headlining.

"Hopefully, this means they've found something they like," Sloane adds, passing the plate of bread to her fiancé Jax. Letting out a loud breath, she adds, "Some amazing places just went on the market."

Raising a brow, Jax pauses mid-scoop with the cheesy lasagna still strung to the dish. "See any you like in particular?"

Sloane plucks her garlic bread from her plate and rips off a piece of it. "The house next door just went up for sale. It's super cute, and I've always loved it, but I'm not sure they're looking to purchase anything."

"Really?" Lanie perks up. "Which one?"

"Harriet's place." Sloane sighs and shakes her head. "I can't imagine it'll be on the market long. She just remodeled her kitchen and has done several upgrades."

Harriet was one of Nana's good friends. Even though she was at least twenty years younger than Nana, the two of them loved spending evenings together drinking wine and catching up.

Recalling our conversation from a few days ago, I add, "Her daughter Elise lives in Maine and will have her second baby later this summer. She was on the fence about leaving Seaside. I guess she finally decided to make the move."

"That makes sense. Family is important." Lanie nods, then raises a brow in my direction. "Speaking of family... I think we've *all* waited long enough. How did the interview go? I've been dying to ask since you got home."

Sighing heavily, I admit, "I think it went as well as it could. Once my nerves settled, I felt like we were on the same page... but who knows?" I shrug. "They'll call me in the next few days if I get the second interview."

Lanie quickly asks, "How soon will they hire someone?"

"One way or the other, I'll know by the end of the week."

"I'm sure you'll make it to a second interview." Sloane smiles encouragingly.

Leave it to my older sisters to be my biggest cheerleaders.

Lanie nods at Sloane. "I agree. So, what's the next step when they call you back?"

"Oh..." I exhale heavily and attempt nonchalance. I know better than to get overconfident and jinx myself. "Only win over both the three-year-old and her dad, of course."

I'm surprised when it's my brother-in-law Ryan who chimes in. "You're amazing with kids. I watched you wrangle the Spencer twins last summer." Shaking his head, a laugh escapes. "Those two were *wild,* and you had them towing the line without breaking a sweat."

I shake my head at the memory. "Oh, there was plenty of sweat, trust me."

Travis and Trent made me earn every penny last summer. Apparently, I was the only one who could keep those seven-year-olds out of too much trouble. With their dad traveling for work and their mom working different shifts at the hospital, I was first on the list when their parents needed a sitter.

"You made it look easy to me," Jax adds. "Emily watched those boys only once a few years ago, and that was enough for her."

Emily is Jax's younger sister. She's about my age, and like Jax, a local to Seaside. She's been away at college since Sloane and Jax got together, so I haven't spent much time with her, but after my time with the boys last summer, I'm sure he's not wrong.

Before anyone can say another word, the front door to the house bursts open, and my sister Raven's voice gleefully fills the room. "Honey... we're home!"

"We're in here..." Lanie calls back. "Hope you're hungry. I've made plenty of food."

"Thank God. I'm starving," Finn grumbles as he comes into sight. "This woman," he points with his thumb to my sister beside him, "had me traipsing all over town for hours. There wasn't a vacant house in this vicinity we didn't look at."

"You're the one who insisted on doing this *all* today," Raven reminds him. "I'm not the one who's hell-bent on finding a place of our own immediately."

Plopping down in a chair, he reaches for the plate next to him and fills it with lasagna, salad, and bread. Before saying another word, he places it in front of my sister. "Eat. Hangry Raven isn't good for any of us."

"Uh-oh," Sloane says under her breath. "I take it you didn't have any luck?"

Sloane and Raven stare at one another for a moment, and they have some sort of unspoken conversation between them. It's quite useful to them being twins, but as their younger sister, I get frustrated when I'm not invited to the conversation.

After Finn dishes up a plate for himself, he says, "Yes. We found a few actually."

"So, what's the problem?" I ask when I can't figure out what's got my sister in such a grumpy mood.

"First, she hasn't eaten all day. Second, I may or may not have told her I'm not interested in renting after seeing what was available."

"And third, this idiot just put an offer on a house," Raven spits out.

"What?" I can't have heard her right.

The room erupts in several conversations at once, however, my attention ping-pongs from Raven to Finn. Simultaneously, his face breaks out into a triumphant grin while hers purses as if she's just bitten into a lemon.

It's Sloane who finally gains the focus of the room. "I don't get it. Why is this a bad thing?"

Raven's nostrils flare. "This... this... annoyingly perfect man just bought my dream house... like... paid for it out right... who the hell does that kind of thing?"

All eyes turn to Finn, and he simply shrugs. "What? Fiduciary planning people... Did you think I've blown all my adult money just because I'm a rockstar? I've worked my ass off for the last ten years, living well below my means and doing what I love. God knows being a musician isn't always steady work... In my early days, I made day trading my bitch and put that business degree my mom insisted I get as a backup to great use."

The moment Finn reaches for Raven, her features soften, and it's suddenly as if they're the only two in the room. "What's really going on here, babe?"

"I... I'm... just in shock. Who the hell goes out to look at *rentals* and comes back a homeowner? Since it was a cash offer, we close on it *next* week." Looking to the room for help, she asks, "Who the hell does that?"

Cupping her cheek in his hand, he asks, "Do you not like the house?"

Pulling back with wide eyes, Raven gasps. "Of course, I do. It's been my freaking dream house since I was a kid. But it's so much... and *all* your family is in South Carolina. Are you sure you want to buy a place in Seaside?"

"Raven..." he says sternly. "You're here. Your family's here, and it's time we put down roots *here... together.*"

Oh, my freaking heart. *Did he really just say that?*

"Roots..." she whispers as tears fill her eyes.

My sister never cries, so this must have some hidden meaning for them.

My gut clenches, and I hold my breath waiting to hear what he says next.

"I told you... you're it for me..." Finn pauses for a moment and glances around the room briefly before mumbling, "Fuck it.

I had something extravagant planned, but this can't wait another minute. I love you, Raven Marie Lancaster. I need to spend the rest of my life with you. You're the fucking sun, the moon, and stars for me. Where you go, I go. Let's call Seaside our home base. Let's make a life *here* together... Let's start forever right now. What do ya say..."

He pushes out his chair and suddenly is on bended knee before her, pulling something from his pocket.

Holding out a black velvet box between them, he asks, "Will you marry me?"

Tears streak down Raven's cheeks as she repeatedly whispers, "Yes. Yes, I'll marry you."

As the room erupts in hoots and hollers, I feel my phone buzzing in my pocket.

Glancing at the caller ID, I ignore the celebration of my family and quickly dart away from the crowd, to answer it in a quieter place.

Pushing open the sliding glass door, I step out onto our deck. "Hello?"

"May I speak with Elizabeth Lancaster?"

"This is she," I quickly respond.

"This is Dianne Kruse. My son and I would love to have you join us for a second interview. Would you be available tomorrow?"

Relief floods through me, and I quickly agree to the time and place.

Before I know it, I'm back inside, celebrating more than my sister's unexpected engagement. The night flies by, leaving me little time to worry about what tomorrow may bring.

Chapter 3
Cameron

It's been a shit day, and I'm late.

Every single meeting throughout the day went longer than expected, and now I'm rushing across this *supposedly* small town. I swear, Seaside feels more like rush-hour traffic in Portland, than driving through a lazy beach town along the coast when you're in a hurry. Out of nowhere, it's as if every pedestrian comes out of the woodwork. They suddenly *need to* cross the street in random places, stop traffic to practice parallel parking because clearly no one can successfully do it the first time, and every light in this town must turn red, as if it senses my car approaching.

As I stop for yet another pedestrian, I look to the overcast sky and pray for the love of all that is holy, the woman I'm interviewing is as competent as my mother makes her out to be. I've already met with two others today and since this is Mom's favorite, I've chosen to meet with her last to ensure I give my top three picks a fair chance.

Although the first candidate came with good references, there was something off about her when we met in person. She made it through my preliminary interview without Milli, but when Mom brought Milli in to interact with us, Suzie seemed far more interested in continuing our conversations than getting to know my daughter. That was a big turnoff. Milli's only three, so of course she's shy at first around new people. But once she gets to know you, she's quite outgoing. The fact that this woman made no effort toward my daughter is a hard pass.

The second candidate didn't even make it to meeting Milli. Again, her references were good, and she checked the boxes Mom and I had talked about. But when we started talking about my need for flexible hours due to the music festival I'm organizing, she suddenly got starstruck. No matter how hard I tried to steer the conversation back to my daughter—the reason she was there in the first place—all conversations led back to the possibility of meeting famous musicians in Seaside.

Sure, Smashing Waves Records hosts the Summer Music Festival. And yes, Jax Cartwright, the lead singer of Ruby Frax, made his start at this very festival. With their recent success while touring with Riser, they've become a household name. I can't even say I blame her.

However, that isn't why she was here.

Clearly, all thoughts of my daughter jumped right out the window. Upon realizing this, I quickly shut the interview down and sent her on her way.

Now, I'm down to one candidate.

Mom leaves in less than a week, and I'm screwed if I can't find a nanny.

Instead of meeting at my office, Mom set up the meeting at the house, so Milli can get her nap in this afternoon. I'll admit I'm a little leery after the last interview, but Mom insists she's found the one. It's who she wanted in the first place. Hopefully, I'll feel the same.

I'm extremely protective of my daughter. She's the greatest

thing I never knew I needed in my life. She's had the keys to my heart since the moment our eyes met. Although I've hated uprooting her from the only home she's known, Milli's young and resilient. If I can find someone to help watch her, this summer will be a great experience for both of us.

The only way I'll ever get to see my daughter this summer is by renting a place in Seaside. Commuting two hours each way just isn't an option, after putting in a full day's work. I'm bound and determined to find someone who can help lift the load of being a single parent and manage the ins and outs of the festival.

I'm a good father—or at least I try to be. I've somehow managed to balance being a solo parent and working my way up at the label, into this new position. If this summer goes well, it'll allow me to travel less in the coming year, which inevitably allows me to spend even more time with Milli.

Rushing into my driveway, I don't even bother parking in the garage. Throwing my vehicle into park, I quickly grab the resumé sitting in my passenger seat and look it over once more as I make my way to the front door.

As soon as I realized I would be late, I called Mom. She assured me she'd let this third candidate know about the setback in my schedule. She knows how important it is for Milli to feel comfortable in her surroundings and promised me she would use this time to see how the candidate interacts with my daughter. Unfortunately, Milli has swim lessons in about an hour, so my time to see for myself how Milli responds is limited. Mom and I decided if the interview should proceed, she'd take Milli to swimming lessons, and I'll finish the interview—if it gets that far.

With my track record, I'm not holding my breath.

From the moment I open the door, I can hear laughter coming from the family room. Milli's high shrills are mixed in with Mom's and someone I don't recognize. Typically, Milli's the first to greet me when she hears me enter the house. She's clearly distracted, so I use this time to pause in the hall and listen intently.

"Again... again," Milli gasps between giggles.

In a deep growl of a voice, I hear, "Somebody's been sleeping in my bed."

Milli guffaws, and the obvious story the stranger is reading continues. I'm quite familiar with Goldilocks and the *Three Bears*. It's one Milli enjoys reading quite often. I'm certain I could recite it in my sleep; I've read it so many times.

As the stranger's voice changes with each character, my daughter giggles in anticipation of what's to come, much like she does when I read it.

My heart races at the possibility of this candidate being a good fit. Milli is clearly relaxed and happily enjoying this experience. I'm impressed this person can put my daughter at ease in such a short time. Not wanting to disturb them or change the energy in the room, I hang back and listen as the story is finished before making my presence known.

When I walk in to join them, my chest squeezes at what I witness.

The two of them are on the couch, with their backs to me. Mom's standing in the kitchen sipping her water with a wide smile on her face as she watches her granddaughter with our potential nanny. Milli's shyness has clearly disappeared as she has wormed her way onto the practical stranger's lap. I haven't seen her do this with anyone but family before. With her trusted blanket squeezed in her chubby hand, she points at the pictures in the book with her other.

"This book now..." my daughter insists, picking up another book beside her. Without skipping a beat, I watch the woman pick up our well-worn copy of *the Barnyard Dance* and enthusiastically start the words I know so well. "Stomp your feet…"

The rhythm and cadence she adds brings so much more to the story than my version. Milli sighs heavily and leans in to rest her head against the woman's side. I can't see her face, but her body language alone has my nerves relaxing as well.

Glancing at my mom to see if she's witnessing this too, she reassures me with a nod and mouths, "She's great with her."

I couldn't agree more. I haven't even spoken to the woman on the couch, but clearly, she's got a gift with children. This definitely puts bonus points in her favor. Hopefully, she'll pass the rest of the interview with flying colors as well.

When the story comes to an end, Milli asks for "More."

But before anyone can respond, I make my presence known. "Milli, I think that's enough for now, don't you?"

My daughter practically bolts off the couch and yells, "Daddy!" as she runs toward me.

Scooping her up, I squeeze her tight. "How was your day, baby girl? Were you good for Gammy?"

Nodding heavily, she says, "Uh-huh. And for Iz."

"Is?" I question and look toward my mom at the same time Milli shouts, "Her!"

Mom quickly rushes out, "She couldn't say Lizzy."

My eye catches motion as the stranger on my couch quickly stands, smooths her hands down the front of her clothes, and quickly walks around the couch to greet me.

The moment our eyes meet, she halts abruptly.

Her eyes widen as round as saucers, and her jaw drops for the slightest of moments, before she quickly pulls her lips together tightly.

My breath freezes in my lungs as I stare in disbelief.

This cannot be happening.

The universe must hate me.

I rapidly blink, hoping my mind is playing tricks on me.

How. The. Fuck. Is the only woman I've connected with since Milli was born standing in my living room?

But I read the resumé. This woman—well, girl if we're being technical—is only twenty years old.

"Cameron?" my mother asks, concern laced in her voice.

Milli chooses this moment to squirm, so I quickly put her on the floor.

I kid you not, my shy daughter runs up to Lizzy, takes her hand, and pulls her toward me.

"Dis, is Iz. She gonna watch me when Gammy goes."

Oh shit.

My heart thunders in my chest.

All I can do is stare into my beautiful daughter's eyes as she silently pleads with me to make her request come true. Clearly, this woman has made an impression on her.

You and me both, kid.

Fuck... what the hell am I supposed to do?

Glancing at the resumé still in my hand, I read the name once more. Slowly, a question rolls off my tongue, "*You're Elizabeth Lancaster?*"

Chapter 4
Lizzy

As I stare into the eyes of the sexiest man I've ever seen, I remain frozen in place. My ears pulse with the sound of my racing heart, and my legs feel like they might buckle at any moment.

I know from personal experience, under that white button-down shirt is a chest with pecs for days. I've freaking kissed every muscle along his happy trail, had my hands roam along his sculpted body, and I've experienced what it feels like to have this glorious man fill me from the inside out.

How the hell is *he* of all people standing in front of me?

The one who's starred in *all* my recent fantasies.

The one I was instantly attracted to the moment we met.

The one I broke all my rules for and had my first one-night stand with because I didn't want to regret *not* being with him.

Our chemistry was off the charts. Sure, he's a bit older than the guys I typically date, but when we were together, none of that mattered. He made me feel as if I was the only one in the universe. Our attraction was more than physical though. He was charming, and fate had a way of making our paths continually cross when we least expected it.

With both of us leaving town, we couldn't commit to anything. But I couldn't walk away without knowing what it was like to be with him. Our chemistry was so combustible, and I will *never* regret the hottest experience of my lifetime.

To protect my heart, I did make some mental boundaries. I purposely made a point in not exchanging numbers or revealing much about my personal life—once I realized our time was limited. I knew there wouldn't be any point. It couldn't go anywhere.

Has it really only been three weeks?

His unreadable expression fills me with unease as he glances to the paper in his hand, then back to me. "*You're* Elizabeth Lancaster?"

"Yes, but everyone calls me Lizzy."

Clearly, he knows that. It's the name the barista called at the coffee shop by the university each time we ran into one another. I frequent there because it's just far enough away from the college crowd, I was able to focus on my studies—that is until he stole my attention.

Squeezing my hand, Emilia adorably draws my attention to her as she obliviously states, "Iz is my friend."

Looking to the daughter I never knew he had, Cameron asks, "Is that so?"

Emilia nods fervently. "Ya. She reads my favorite books." (Though she pronounces the v in favorite with a b instead, making her even more adorable.)

Cameron's body shifts, and he leans in and bops his daughter on the nose. "Is that right?" Turning to me, he grumbles, "She's a sucker for anyone who reads to her nonstop. It's *also* how she always stays up *way* past her bedtime, if I'm not paying attention."

Emilia grins widely, but it's her grandmother who says, "Who can blame her? A girl and her books are nothing to be messed with."

When Emilia shrugs as if saying, *yeah, what Gammy said,* the room fills with laughter.

Blood still courses through my veins, and every nerve ending in my body remains on high alert, but as the laughter dies down, it feels as if some tension in the room has been released.

"Has she been to the library yet?" I ask with curiosity. I loved going to our local library as a kid.

Cameron's expression is still unreadable as his head cocks to the side. "No, we haven't been there. We've spent the last few weeks getting settled, as we just moved out here."

"They're from Portland," his mother adds for my benefit. "The two of you may have crossed paths without even knowing it. Cameron works not far from the University of Portland."

Oh, trust me, Dianne. Our paths have crossed.

Cameron's silence speaks volumes. Obviously, he doesn't want his mother knowing that he does indeed know me—intimately at least. We never quite made it past our carnal needs to go far beyond our casual flirting that led to our one date.

Focusing his attention on the resumé in his hand, he asks, "So you're a student at U-P. You're double majoring in psychology and elementary education?"

Okay... so we're doing this.

Clearing my throat, I straighten to meet his eyes when they return to me. "Yes. I've got two more quarters of classes, then I'll be placed for student teaching in the spring."

"Clearly, she's got a talent for working with kids. Just look at how attached Emilia is to her already," Dianne chimes in.

Crap. Looking down, I realize she's still holding my hand. There's no way I would drop hers, even if my instincts say to do so. I can't do that to an innocent child. Her grandmother told me she doesn't warm up to people easily, so I'd never purposely push her away.

However, her getting attached to me could be disastrous in so many ways if shit goes sideways between her dad and me. Not only could it mean I never get this job, but even if I did, could I handle working for someone I've slept with?

Fuck. I'm so confused.

Yes, I wanted to run into him again. But I never in a million years expected it to be today.

Glancing back to Cameron, his expression remains stoic.

I thought I could read him so well in our weeks spent flirting. But hell, I didn't even know he had a kid. Clearly, I don't know him at all.

"Tell me about your experience as a nanny in previous summers."

Taking a steadying breath, I force myself to relax.

"I've worked for a variety of families. I was on call whenever the agency needed me. I did everything from being a glorified Uber driver for preteens to staying overnight for families who worked or had other commitments. I've watched kids from as young as four months old to teens who just needed someone to hang out with them to keep them out of trouble with so much time on their hands. You name it, I've probably done it. I've been babysitting since I was twelve."

Narrowing his eyes, he asks, "And just how many years ago was that?"

Before I can answer, he holds up a hand and shakes his head. "Wait. Don't answer that. You're obviously experienced in this field, and I won't discriminate against you by asking."

"I... uh... respect that." The words fly out of my mouth before I can think better of it.

There's an obvious age gap between us, so he likely wants

to know on a personal level as well as professionally. But it says a lot about his character that he's trying to remain professional.

This can't be easy on him either. Finding me here certainly wasn't on his bingo card.

"Look…" he starts, but his mom interrupts.

"I think we'll leave the two of you to finish this interview…"

Suddenly, she's beside us, reaching for Emilia. I've been so distracted by seeing Cameron again, I'd forgotten she was even in the room.

Reaching out, she pats Cameron on the chest, before she calmly says, "It's time for Emilia to get ready for swim lessons."

"Swimming?" Emilia's excitement fills the room. "I go get my soup."

And just like any three-year-old, she runs as fast as she can down a hallway and disappears.

Chuckling, Dianne shrugs. "I'd better go help. It was great seeing you again, Lizzy." Glancing between the two of us, she adds, "I hope everything works out as it should."

Cameron and I watch his mother disappear down the same hall as his daughter. Within seconds, we hear the sound of feet, and Emilia comes running back to us. She flings herself into her dad's outstretched arms, who has somehow gotten to her level and crouches to envelop her in a hug.

"Bye, Daddy. I go swim with Gammy."

"You be good and listen to your teacher," he warns lovingly.

The moment he releases her, she flings herself at my leg and squeezes me as tight as a toddler can. "Bye, Iz. I play with you next time."

Before I can say a word, Dianne calls her to what I assume is their garage door, and they're gone.

Tension remains strong, and there's a long moment of silence.

Suddenly, Cameron breaks it by barking out a loud laugh as he asks, "Is this really happening?"

Chapter 5
Cameron

Elizabeth's mouth drops and for the longest time, it's as if she's been stunned into silence.

This situation is awkward enough, and there's no need to prolong it.

Gathering my swirling thoughts, I go with an obvious one. "So... Seaside's where you're spending the summer."

Soon after meeting, we quickly found we were both leaving Portland. I was persistent in wearing her down to even consider a date. We had one amazing night together. Expecting there to be no future, we both agreed to just enjoy that night—and fuck, it was one of the best nights of my existence—even though we clearly didn't know much about each other's personal lives.

Hell, I didn't even know she was still in school. An image of our dinner pops into my mind. I clearly remember her asking for a soda instead of wine.

Ohmigod! I knew she was younger than me, but fuck, is she even legal?

Running a hand down my face, I need confirmation. "Uh... Let's pause this interview for a moment."

"Okay," she says, pulling her lower lip into her teeth.

Sighing heavily, I realize there's no polite way to say this. Abruptly, I blurt out, "Please tell me it was legal for me to be with you."

Her beautiful laugh fills the room. "I'm not legal..." She pauses, and I nearly have a heart attack. But then she adds with a mischievous grin, "To drink..."

Seeing the look of horrification on my face, she shakes her head and pats me on the shoulder. "Relax, Gramps. I turn twenty-one next month."

Sighing heavily, I nod. "Okay." That's a relief. Then another thought hits me. "Wait. Did you know this interview was for a job with me?"

A mixture of relief and nerves wash over me as she shakes her head. "No. I truly had no idea. I just know you as Cameron, the charming, sexy man I kept running into at the coffee shop."

Sexy. She thinks I'm sexy. That's never a bad thing to hear.

Fuck, man, get it together. You need her to take care of your child, not make your wildest fantasies come true.

Her cheeks darken, and she pushes her hair behind her ear before adding, "I guess... We... uh... didn't get into many details on our date."

"That's true," I admit, feeling foolish for asking. "I'm just as guilty in that respect, I suppose."

Elizabeth closes her eyes, and her spine straightens as she braces herself for impact before she locks her gaze on me. "Look, I'm not sure what you think about me, both personally or professionally. This..." She looks around the room. "Well, this... is beyond awkward... I'm completely out of my depth for how to proceed."

"So am I," I admit as a million thoughts zip through my thoroughly fucked brain like a hummingbird on speed.

Personally, I still think she's the most beautiful person in the fucking world.

My attraction to her goes beyond the physical though.

She's funny, charismatic, and has the most generous heart.

From the moment I laid eyes on her in that coffee shop months ago, she's always had my attention. If I'm being honest with myself, that hasn't changed. I'm still as attracted to her as the day we met.

Professionally, fuck—I'm at a loss, too.

Watching her now with my daughter before I even knew about our connection, I know without a doubt she is a great fit for this job.

It's clear Emilia likes her.

Hell, it took her weeks to have smooth drop-offs at preschool this year. I've never seen her so taken to anyone. I'm not sure I'll ever be able to find anyone who's won over my daughter in such a short time.

But given our history, as brief as it was—*can I really go through with hiring her?*

If everything goes to hell in a hand basket, like it usually does in my relationships, can I take the risk of hurting Milli like that?

"Look, Elizabeth," I start, but she cuts me off.

"It's Lizzy. I only use my government name for resumés and official documents, Cameron."

God, I love how she says my name.

Memories of our night together flash through my mind. The way she called out my name as she fell apart was such a turn-on. The way she—

Focus, dipshit. She's talking.

"We clearly know each other well enough for you to call me Lizzy. But beyond that..." She looks to the window beside us as if it will give her the words she's looking for. "Beyond that, I'm gonna be real with you. I need this job. When I got the call from your mom for this second interview, I was beyond thrilled to know I'd only be working with one family this year, rather than random people the agency assigns. I already told Booked at the Beach I won't be returning, but... maybe they haven't filled the position just yet."

She trails off for a moment, then pins me dead in the eyes and somehow manages to slay me with her next thought. "I get it if you don't think I'd be a good fit for Emilia, given our brief history. But if you choose to hire me, I give you my word that I *can* be professional. My focus will be on *her*. I'll be the best damn nanny you could hope for."

Fuck... how does her conviction both make me proud and devastate me at the same time?

I shouldn't feel this way for someone I've known for such a short time. I shouldn't feel such a sense of loss for her insisting she'll be professional.

"You're the only person Milli's grown this comfortable with in such a short time," I say before I can think better of it.

But what does this mean?

Do I really want to hire someone I'm this attracted to?

Fuck, even as she stands there staring at me, I'm recalling how good it felt to be inside her. How the taste of her lingered on my tongue long after we parted. If I'd known that I'd see her again, I probably would've pushed for things to continue.

I haven't felt this way about anyone since being a father became my number-one priority. Can I really push all these feelings aside?

Is it even possible to keep things strictly professional?

Can I do it for Milli's sake?

I have always put Milli's needs above my own. She is my top priority.

However, Lizzy's the only one we've interviewed who even

came close to meeting the qualifications. Not only does she have what it takes on paper, but if I put my feelings aside, I'm not the only one she's made a connection to.

Milli freaking hugged her before she left.

Can I take this new connection away from my daughter?

Lizzy breaks my inner monologue when she asks, "What's going on in that head of yours?"

"Where do I even begin?" I sigh.

God, it's like I no longer have a filter around her. What the hell is wrong with me? I'm an executive at a major recording studio. I keep my private thoughts to myself.

Her expression softens, and her shoulders relax. "The beginning's a great place. I'm sure, like me, my presence is a bit of a curveball."

Thank God, she's willing to address the elephant in the room.

"Truth? I feel like I'm stuck between a rock and a hard place. Hands down, even without another word from you, after talking with my mom and looking into your references, I know without a doubt you're the most qualified candidate for Milli."

She nods once but doesn't say anything.

"But we obviously have a past. I can't let that past get in the way of Milli's care."

Lizzy's hands punch her hips, and she juts out her chin in challenge. "I can be *professional* if you can. You and I both know I made a true connection with your daughter. I'm more than qualified to care for her and frankly, you'd be a fool not to hire me. Don't get me wrong, there are others you can find through the agency, but I wouldn't be here if I weren't at the top of your list."

God, her tenacity turns me on.

But she's right. When I checked her references earlier today, I knew all I needed to offer her the job. The only thing holding me back was waiting to see how her interaction with Milli went.

Thoughts of my starstruck interview pop into my head so I ignore her comment and counter with, "How are you with handling celebrities?"

Confusion crosses her features as she asks, "What do you mean?"

"A previous candidate got starstruck when I mentioned my job. As the main organizer of the music festival this summer, will I have to worry about you trying to use me to get to any of the acts?"

It seems petty, but it's the only real reason I could come up with on the fly to ensure all my worries from the idiots I've interviewed set her apart.

Her brows pull together, and her mouth drops open. "Wait... you work for Smashing Waves Records?"

Crossing my hands over my chest, I brace myself for what's coming. "I do."

Lizzy's beautiful hazel eyes widen as she sucks all the air out of the room. "I... uh... think we might have another problem."

Chapter 6
Lizzy

Fuck. My. Life.

This cannot be happening. Not only did I sleep with the man who could potentially be my boss, but I literally slept with not one—but two of my sisters' boss. Don't even get me started on the fact that *both* of my future brothers-in-law are signed with Smashing Waves Records.

Trying to bring some levity to this situation, I throw out, "Ever hear the phrase, *The world is an incredibly small place?* Well... I think it just got smaller."

Now it's Cameron's turn for confusion. "What do you mean? I'm not following you."

Glancing at my resumé on the table beside us, I suggest, "Look at my resume, *again.*"

He picks it up from the table nearby and looks it over. My pulse beats like one of Finn's drum solos as I wait for him to read it over.

When his eyes warily return to mine, he asks, "What am I missing?"

I clearly have the shittiest luck—in all of history.

"I'm. Elizabeth. Lancaster." I punctuate each word, hoping he'll make the connection.

"Okay..." he draws out, clearly missing my point.

Fuck, maybe he doesn't know?

"Not one, but *two* of my older sisters work at the label. Raven's a freelance graphic designer, but Sloane acquires new talent. I'm pretty sure you work closely with her, or at least you will this summer during the festival. Oh, and as of this week, *both my sisters* are engaged to members of Ruby Frax."

He draws in a slow breath as his brows reach his hairline. "It's an incredibly small world... How did I not put the connection together?" he asks more to himself, than to me.

A nervous laugh escapes as I warn, "Being the youngest, they're all extremely protective of me." More than they should, if I have any say over it.

My dad may be an intimidating pilot in the Air Force, but I've always been more afraid of what my sisters will do or say to the guys I've dated. Not that I'm dating Cameron.

No—he's my boss—or could be my boss—if I haven't FUBARed everything.

Clearing his throat, Cameron looks to the floor. His jaw ticks as he processes the bombs that keep dropping between us today.

What are the fucking odds? How does this keep happening?

When he looks up, there's a lopsided smile trying to escape as he asks, "Is there anything else you care to share? Got any long-lost cousins, ex-boyfriends, or children I should know about?"

"You're the one who kept having a kid from me," I quickly counter, trying to make light of our situation.

Shrugging, he rolls his eyes. "Do you blame me? I haven't dated much since Milli was born, so I'm not exactly in the habit of giving my whole life story on a first date."

"I don't blame you," I agree. "But speaking of Milli? Or should I call her Emilia? What do you want to do?"

"Since it's usually just her and me, I've gotten in the habit of using her nickname regularly. She answers to either, but I reserve her *government name*, as you call it, for when I'm being serious, or she's in trouble."

God, he's adorable when he's mocking me.

"Good to know... but..."

Shit. How do I say this?

"But???" he draws out, waiting for me to finish my thought.

"I guess the question we need to figure out is whether or not we should work together."

His pensive expression is unreadable, and I have no idea what he'll decide. His eyes drift to the floor, and he stares for a long moment, as the wheels spin in his head.

I have no clue what it's like to be a parent, but I imagine finding childcare is a huge feat. Given the tangled web that surrounds us and our brief history, it's truly a lot to consider. My family shouldn't be a factor, but truth be told, because of them, no matter what's decided today, I'm certain Cameron's and my paths will cross again. Seaside may be a tourist town, but it's not that big.

I'm so lost in my thoughts, I'm startled when he claps his hands together and says, "I'll tell you what... Let's put the past behind us... for now. Why don't we sit down and truly talk through the details of you working as Emilia's nanny. If we both come to a mutual consensus at the end, then the job is yours."

With that, he leads me back to the sitting area where I read to Emilia. He sits on the edge of the sofa, and I take the armchair beside him.

Noting he doesn't fully relax into the couch, neither do I.

Planting my feet solidly on the floor in front of me, I lean forward and treat this just like any other interview. Instead of waiting for him to ask the first question, I flip the script and ask, "So, what exactly are you looking for in a nanny?"

I ignore the way his navy-blue eyes sparkle but enjoy that his shoulders visibly relax. This tiny motion puts me at ease, and I feel the stiffness of my body loosen. Sighing heavily, he admits, "Unfortunately, I'm expected to work a lot of long hours this summer. I'll do what I can at nights and on the weekends when Milli's sleeping. But with planning for the festival in full-swing, I might need to be onsite more often and won't always have a predictable schedule."

He pauses to see if we're on the same track. When I nod in agreement, he continues, "Until the week of the actual festival, I might put in some long hours, but you should... in theory... have Saturdays and Sundays off. If things change, I'll try to work from home to give you two days off each week. During the festival itself, I'll need to find someone else to also help with Milli, as I'll be working round the clock at that point."

"We'll figure it out when the time comes," I offer. "Not everything needs to be hashed out today."

He nods, then proceeds to tell me Milli's schedule for the summer. My heart goes out to him as a single parent. His desire to be there for Emilia resonates deeply, especially as a daughter whose dad was often deployed for long periods of time throughout my childhood. Cameron clearly knows the value of time, and Milli is fortunate to have a dad like him.

As he talks, my nerves nearly disappear. Relief flows through me as I find we see eye to eye on most scenarios when it comes to expectations for Milli. Besides the elephant in the room regarding our personal past, if I were to get this job, it feels like we'd work well together to have Milli's best interest in mind.

All is well until he asks, "What kind of vehicle do you drive?"

"I... uh... have my license. However, my Camry took its last joy ride a few months ago. I never really used my car in Portland, and with student teaching next spring, I decided not to replace Lola and save some money. During the summer, I typically use my sisters' cars to get around, when I can't walk where I need to go. Will that be a problem?"

He hesitates for a moment longer than I feel comfortable. "I've got a car you can use. Milli's car seat is already installed and inspected. Do you live far? Sometimes my meetings will run later into the evenings."

"This is Seaside. Everything is *fairly* close," I quickly remind him. "Besides, like I said, I've got plenty of family around. They'll give me a ride if necessary."

He purses his lips, and I'm certain he isn't impressed.

Please don't let *this*, of all things, be the reason I don't get this job.

He surprises me when he says, "I don't really like the idea of you walking alone after dark. But... as you say...we can cross that bridge when we get there."

Our conversation quickly flows into further details of the day-to-day expectations of this position. Cameron adamantly insists my primary job is caring for Milli. I can expect to cook and clean up after her, including do her laundry if necessary. When he asks if I'd feel comfortable taking her swimming regularly, I smile. His mother and I had discussed this earlier, however I could tell he was surprised to know I'd been on the swim team in my youth.

By the end of the interview, I feel confident the job is mine.

That is until he says, "Just one last thing before we discuss salary. I've never had to ask this of any employee, but... I need to know your honest thoughts. Are you *really* okay working for me... given our history?"

I stare into his eyes for a long moment to gauge my true feelings.

Will it be awkward to work for the only man I've had a one-night stand with?

Yes.

But can I handle it?

Also, yes.

My head swirls with a mirage of what-ifs. *So many things could go sideways—but does that mean it will?*

Sighing heavily, I release the pent-up tension quickly growing within me.

I must trust my gut instinct.

Squaring my shoulders, I sit up straighter and speak my truth.

"Look. I've never been in this situation either. It's truly an interesting predicament. But the truth is, I really like your daughter. Please know, if you choose to hire me, I will always put her needs first. I'm honest and hardworking. I'm great with kids, and you can trust me to care for her the best way I know how. Will I be perfect? No. But I don't think anyone who works with children is. But I promise I'll give my best effort to whatever situation I find myself in with her. She and I will have trials and errors as we navigate our relationship, as working with any toddler will be."

"I already know you're a good fit for the job," he states pointedly. "That's not what I'm talking about, and you know it."

Rolling my eyes, I try my best to lighten his mood. "It's okay, Cam. We're both adults. Sure, you've got this sexy older man thing going for you, but I can control myself and *not* behave like a teenager who's discovered her first crush."

"Hey, I'm not that much older," he cuts in, with a grin forming on those sexy lips.

Raising a brow, I question, "Just how much older are you than me anyway?"

"I just turned twenty-eight in January," he admits sheepishly.

"Good to know." Again, my words roll off my lips before I can think better of them.

When his eyes bulge, I quickly add, "Honestly, Cameron, I can handle it. But at the end of the day, it's you who must decide. The real question is, *can you?*"

His eyes pin mine, and I can tell his wheels are spinning.

The silence that lingers between us is thunderous.

Sweat forms on the back of my neck, as I wait for his response.

I feel the tension rolling off him in waves.

This can't be an easy decision for him.

Our chemistry has always been undeniable, but at the end of the day, I really do need this job. I know I can put whatever feelings I have for this man aside. After all, I'm only here for the summer.

How hard can it be?

He exhales heavily and, once again, looks to the floor. Then he levels me with a serious stare. "The only question I have left is... when can you start?"

Chapter 7
Lizzy

Three days later, I'm up at the crack of dawn. I'm ready for an adventurous day with Milli, and I'm eagerly walking the quarter mile to their house. I've brought my *Mary Poppins* bag, and I'm certain I'm prepared for anything this toddler throws at me.

It's barely six thirty in the morning, and although I'm not expected until seven, I need Cameron to know I'm taking this job seriously. Experience has told me it's always harder for parents to leave on their first day with a new sitter. He needs to feel confident he's leaving his daughter in good hands by the time he steps out that door. My promptness is just a step in that direction.

Not wanting to wake Milli, I knock quietly and wait.

I should've known better, as the sound of stomping feet quickly approaches.

The lock on the door disengages, and my tongue nearly sticks to the roof of my mouth when I'm greeted by a shirtless Cameron. Thankfully, I don't get a chance to ogle or make a fool of myself, as Milli practically throws herself at me in excitement. I'm suddenly too busy catching my balance.

"Iz... You here!"

Doing my best to ignore my body's response to Cameron, I force my focus on the eager girl before me. Patting her on the back, I match her enthusiasm. "Yes! I get to spend the day with you."

"Yay!" With puppy dog eyes, her long lashes bat at me as she asks, "We swim and read books?"

Ohmigod. This girl is absolutely adorable.

"Of course. You have swim lessons, right?"

Nodding profusely. "Yep. I see Cora."

Not fully following, I finally glance at Cameron for assistance, "Cora?"

When I meet his eyes, he smiles wide and nods. "Yes, Milli. You're swimming with Cora today."

To me, he says, "Cora's her swim instructor."

"Yay!" Milli squeals, as she fists her hand and pumps it in the air. "I'm hungry, Daddy. Bacon?"

The moment Cameron nods, she's off like a rocket into the house, leaving the two of us to stare after her.

Shaking his head, Cameron turns to me. "Have you eaten? I've got omelets... shit... speaking of which, I've gotta get those..."

I follow him as he strides to the kitchen.

"Sorry, I'm not ready. I wasn't expecting you so soon."

"Uh, I'm from an Air Force family. Early is on time. On time is late." I can't help it. It's been engrained in me since before I could make the choice for myself.

This earns me a devious grin. "Good to know..."

Once in the kitchen, he efficiently plates three large omelets and readjusts the temperature on the griddle. "Uh... if you'll excuse me. Milli's orange juice won out against my shirt just as you arrived, and now I need to...uh..." His brows raise, and he looks to his chest for explanation. "Find something else to wear."

Reaching for what I now recognize as a shirt on the counter, he adds, "Please... help yourself. I've made plenty."

Without another word, he dashes out of the room, and I'm left staring for far longer than I'll ever admit.

Why world—of all people—why him?

Why does he have to be the only person I've been able to think about since the day we met?

Why couldn't he be some random single dad in Seaside?

I need this job.

I can be professional.

But Gah—That man makes my panties melt with just a simple smirk.

Gah, get it together, Elizabeth.

This isn't the time nor the place.

I've got a job to do and even if Cameron's the only man who's lit my body on fire from the inside out, I need to put any feelings I might have for him aside—for now.

He can star in every single one of my fantasies—*when I'm off the clock.*

Damn him, for being a DILF.

Oh, my fucking god. I've never been into *any* dad I've worked for.

Look what he's turned me into.

This is one-hundred percent Cameron's fault—and mine for agreeing to go out with him in the first place.

Why did I break my rules for him?

Focus. You're here to do a job.

Speaking of job—where's Milli?

Shit! I can't lose her in the first five minutes on my very first day. I'll be fired before he can even leave for work.

Frantically looking around the room, I find her obliviously sitting at the kitchen table. She's got a crayon in one hand and is diligently coloring her own picture on a piece of construction paper, while chomping on a long piece of bacon from the other. Thank God she's so focused on her drawing, she doesn't even notice I'm having an existential crisis.

"Hey, Milli, you ready for an omelet?"

She's so focused on her drawing, she doesn't even look up. Face down, she mumbles something that sounds like, "Uh-huh."

Needing to make myself busy so I'll stop thinking about Cameron in the other room changing, I focus on Milli's needs. Walking to the stack of plates set out on the counter, I can't help but grin at the stack of bacon sitting next to a large pile of omelets.

Geeze, these omelets are enormous. Who the heck is he planning to feed this morning?

There's no way Milli can eat one on her own. Taking the spatula propped against the griddle, I split one in half, then add another slice of bacon to her plate. Not seeing any forks set out, I make myself at home. After two failed attempts, I find the silverware drawer.

"Want some help cutting this up?" I offer, setting her plate beside her.

Milli's so engrossed in her drawing, she doesn't even react. That is until Cameron unexpectedly breaks the silence in the room a few seconds later.

"Mills, it's time to put the drawing aside and eat."

His no-nonsense tone has her setting the crayon down and looking eagerly for her plate as if she had no idea I'd put it beside her in the first place.

As Cameron approaches, I catch the faint scent of his cologne. My mouth waters, and tingles spark up my spine as flashes from our night together pop through my mind. Needing to keep my sanity, I clear my throat and force myself to breathe through my mouth.

Focus your attention on Milli, Elizabeth.

Quickly holding up her fork, I ask, "Want me to cut this up for you?"

Beautiful blue pleading eyes that match her father's level me. Add in the tilt of her head and the most adorable "Please," rolling off her lips, my heart completely melts.

From my years of working with children, I can tell there's not an ounce of manipulation behind this request. Clearly, Milli has manners—or at least the adults around her have worked with her on this.

From my peripheral, I spot Cameron grabbing an omelet for himself at the counter. "Have you eaten?"

"Not yet. But I brought something in my bag," I admit, placing Milli's plate in front of her.

"You're welcome to anything we have here. Milli was extra helpful in helping me break eggs this morning, so please eat. Otherwise..." He grins knowingly at his daughter before adding, "We might have omelets for breakfast and dinner... reheated eggs turn rubbery." His faux-horrified expression is hilarious.

"Well, we wouldn't want that now," I say on a laugh.

Without another word, he piles food onto two plates, grabs utensils, and brings them to the table. Placing a plate in front of me, as if it's something he does every day, he walks to the chair on the other side of Milli and eats.

As I bite into the cheesy goodness, I notice there's not only bacon but mushrooms, along with some seasoning that makes me eager to eat more. Once I finish chewing, I remember to thank the cook. "This is delicious. Thank you."

"It's not a problem. I don't get to do breakfast like this every morning, but I try when I can. You'll find Milli's not too picky when it comes to food."

"That's good to know. Do you have a specific meal plan for Milli?" Some families are rigid, others are lax. I'm more of a mood eater but I can adjust to whichever suits their needs.

Cameron shakes his head. "Nope. My fridge and pantry are stocked, so help yourself. I've got a little of everything. I'll get you a credit card to use when we're done eating in case you have any expenses while you're out and about together."

"Okay," I say, taking another bite. This is standard. Many families I've worked with often hand me a card to use for expenses while spending the day with their children.

"I've got a few meetings today, so if you need anything small, a text would be best, unless it's an emergency. I'm never too busy for my daughter."

"Is the number you originally called me from your cell?" I ask, making sure I have his most direct line of communication.

"Yeah. You can text me anytime if you have questions. I'll try to get back to you as quickly as I can. Service out here at the beach can be spotty, so I'll text you the land line, should there be an emergency."

"Oh, I've already got it, unless there's a different number I should call. Since Sloane has worked there, I've had the studio's main line."

"Ah..." A slight grin tugs at his lips. "I keep forgetting how small our world is. If you call the main line, they'll put you through to me.

"Milli's swimming class is at nine this session. She's got multiple suits, so I find it best to let her have a choice if you want to arrive on time. You may pride yourself on being early, but I swear, toddlers have no concept of minutes ticking by."

"Oh, I'm fully aware. Trust me."

Eyeing his daughter, he says, "She's mostly potty trained, but we're still using swim diapers and Pull-Ups at nap time. Milli, will you tell Lizzy if you need to go?"

"Uh-huh." She grins and puffs her chest. "I'm a big girl."

"Yes. You. Are," he drags out with a grin and bops her on the nose, making her giggle with delight.

To me, he continues, "Her bag is well stocked with everything you should need. She'll need reminders if she's too engrossed in her activities. As you could see with her drawing, she's extremely focused when she's engaged. She waits until she's ready to burst, then rushes to the bathroom, which unfortunately results in accidents."

"That's to be expected," I assure him. "She just turned three, right?"

"Yep. When's your birthday, Mills?"

A grin splits across her face. "June eleventh," though it sounds like elebenth. Holding up three fingers in my direction, she adds, "I'm three now."

"That's right," Cameron agrees. "Even big girls need help sometimes, so if you need anything, you be sure to tell Lizzy, okay?"

She rolls her eyes and huffs. "Hmph... Daddy. I can't do it *all* myself. I only three."

"Three going on thirteen," Cameron grumbles under his breath.

Covering my mouth to hide my reaction, I do my best not to laugh at their interaction. Without thinking, I add, "I'm the youngest of four girls. What can I say? She's not wrong."

"Lord help me when she's a teenager." He rolls his eyes, and my belly flips at the sexy smirk thrown my way.

He's your boss, Elizabeth.

Forcing myself to stay professional, I clear my throat, then ask, "I know your schedule can be unpredictable at times, but should I feed Milli dinner if you're not home by a certain time tonight?"

Closing one eye, he stares at his plate of food for the briefest of moments. "I think I have a light afternoon. I can double check my schedule, but if she's hungry, feed her and yourself for that matter. *No one* wants to see hangry Milli, trust me."

"Hangry isn't a good look on anyone." *Me especially,* I almost add, but he doesn't need to know that, just yet.

Pivoting back to Milli, I quickly add, "I forgot to ask earlier. Does Milli have any special toys or blankets she uses for comfort... especially at N... A... P time?" I spell it out in case naps happen to trigger her. There's no way I'm starting the morning off on a bad foot if I can help it.

"She's usually pretty good, especially if she's swimming this morning. She'll be exhausted. She couldn't wait to see you today. She's been up since five thirty."

"Wow. Is that what time she usually wakes?"

His head shakes before he tussles her hair. "Nope. This girl *usually* sleeps in 'til nearly seven."

This gets her attention. A wide smile spreads across her face. "I play with Iz today! We're gonna swim and read!"

Oh, my heart. Milli is the cutest.

Matching her enthusiasm, I exclaim, "Yep, I've even brought some of my favorite books!"

"Oh..." Cameron says on a laugh. "You're gonna be her new best friend. She'll never let you go home now."

"Oh, she'll tire of me. I'm sure," I insist. "They always do eventually, especially at nap time."

"Speaking of nap time," Cameron draws out. "I'll admit,

we've gotten a little out of our routine since being out here at the beach. But typically, at bedtime, she'll snuggle with her green blanket that's on her bed, and I'll read her a book or two before she falls asleep."

No kid is ever that easy *all the time.* "Does she nap as easily, too?"

Wincing, Cameron quickly adds, "Don't judge me... but we're flexible when it comes to napping. The reality is, sometimes I'm traveling, and she sleeps in the car. Other times, we'll snuggle on the couch or in my bed, and I'm not stupid enough to move her. Desperate times call for desperate measures as a single dad. I can't always be home, but she usually naps between noon and three, so she'll sleep at night."

Thank God, he's down to earth. I can only imagine how crazy his schedule is, but above all, it's obvious he puts Milli's needs first. There's nothing worse than parents who fail at this simple task. His flexibility will help her adjust to changes in her routines.

"I can work with that."

Before either of us says another word, Milli springs from the table. "I gotta go potty!" And just like that—her little feet scurry out of the room down the hall.

The moment she disappears, he sighs heavily. "I'll get this one, then head off to work... Little Miss Independent still needs help, whether she wants it or not."

Standing, he rinses his plate, then loads it in the dishwasher. "Besides, it's only a matter of minutes before I'm beckoned."

As if on cue, "Daadddyyy... I'm done!" echoes through the house.

"On my way," he answers, then turns to me. "In case I forget to tell you, I *do* appreciate you being here... Even under our unusual circumstances, you really are the most qualified candidate. Milli's lucky to have you, and I couldn't be more grateful to have her with someone I trust."

"That's the whole point," I say without a thought.

Though I'm not sure who I'm talking to—him or myself.

With a quick nod, he turns and disappears down the hall.

Apparently, I'm not the only one challenged by our circumstances.

Chapter 8
Cameron

My desk phone buzzes from my assistant Merna. "Cameron, I just got a call that your eleven o'clock with Tara needs to be pushed to tomorrow. Her flight has been delayed and won't make it today."

Ever since I've taken over this project in Seaside, Tara and I hold weekly meetings so we can keep each other up to date with what's happening on both coasts. Her focus is creating music festivals much like the one here in Seaside, along the East Coast, while I take the Pacific Northwest. Tatum and I divide our coast, since California is a beast all on its own.

When Emilia came into my life, I needed something predictable. Rather than being out in the trenches for the label and traveling around the world at a moment's notice, I'm stuck in countless meetings behind a desk. Sure, I still work with many musicians behind the scenes, but it's not nearly as glamorous as one might think.

I love my daughter and would make this choice over again, without looking back. But sometimes, I miss that carefree life. I miss being able to call up the woman I like and spontaneously take her out.

Hell, when was the last time before Lizzy I even went on a date?

Fuck, stop thinking about your kid's nanny—you have a job to do.

Clearing my throat, I focus on my call. "Thanks for the update. Do you know if those mockups for the marketing proposal are done? I'm waiting to hear back from Raven so I can push those campaigns."

Raven and I have been working together for the better part of a year since I transitioned into Tara's position here and taken over the Seaside Music Festival.

How the hell did I not make the connection to her sister?

And now, I've gone exactly two seconds without thinking of Elizabeth Lancaster.

Fuck, I can't believe how small this world is.

I knew Raven and Sloane were sisters—who wouldn't— they're twins and with their case of mistaken identity that went viral last year, the entire world knows it, too. Apparently, I've never taken the time to get to know either of them beyond work events. Not only do both of them work for the label, but they're engaged to members of Ruby Freaking Frax—our hottest hitting talent, who tops all the charts.

Those guys are going places. With their next album coming out soon, I can only imagine how popular they'll become on the worldwide stage. We're still working out the details, but if all goes well, they'll be on tour again by next summer with more international stops.

How the hell did I not know the Lancasters had a younger sister?

Am I so self-absorbed? Or did it never come up?

Sure, there was a sense of familiarity when I met Lizzy at the coffee shop. Could that have been it?

No, I've never felt that strong of a connection toward anyone.

I certainly wasn't thinking about Raven or Sloane when we met.

"Did you see her latest email?" Merna breaks me out of my thoughts of Lizzy. "I think it came through this morning while you were on the phone with Colin."

"I am just sitting down to go through emails," I admit, opening the app on my laptop. "Thank you."

"Well... I'm here if you need me. I don't see anything else scheduled in your day, so I'll let you be."

With that, the intercom turns off, and the room is quiet once more.

That is, until my stomach rumbles so loud, I'm certain Merna can hear it from her desk outside my office.

Checking the time, I see it's almost eleven.

Maybe I'll go home for lunch. I can eat *and* check in.

Two birds. One stone.

That *is* the benefit of having my daughter here for the summer, right?

This has *nothing* to do with spending more time with Lizzy.

Without allowing myself to overthink my decision, I grab my laptop, shove it into my messenger bag, and then head home.

Maybe I'll catch Milli before nap time.

*****

Instead of hearing the sounds of running feet to greet me, I'm met with silence as I walk into the house.

That's strange. The car is here. Where are they?

"Hello? Anyone here?" I call out, letting them know I'm home.

No response.

Walking through the house, I see the kitchen is cleaned from breakfast, and toys are put away from this morning, but no one is in sight.

Maybe they went swimming again?

When the realtor first showed me the house, I wasn't sure if I'd like an indoor pool. However, I quickly found it is one of the best decisions I made this summer. The weather in Seaside is so mild compared to southern California, it's almost necessary to be inside. Milli and I use it all hours of the day and never get cold or sunburnt. That's a win in my book. I've taken to swimming laps early in the morning or late at night once she's sleeping.

To make sure I'm not missing anything, I open the door and go inside the pool room.

Nope. Not here.

Where could they be?

The car is in the garage. Maybe they're at the beach or going for a walk?

I pull out my phone to call but think better of it.

They're obviously enjoying their first day together, and I'm not expected home.

Sure, I want to see Milli as often as possible, but it's also important she builds a bond with Lizzy, too. After all, they're the ones spending the summer together. Besides, I'd hate for Lizzy to think I don't trust her.

Flopping onto the couch, I stare at the wall. The unusual silence of my home is deafening, and nervous energy flows through me. There are a million things I *should* be doing, but my concentration is shit now that Lizzy's back in my life.

Images of our time together flash through my mind. It was one of the hottest nights of my existence. Before Emilia, I had my share of playing the field. But I swear, I've never had more of a visceral connection to anyone than Elizabeth Lancaster.

Hell, from the very first time I laid eyes on her, she's captivated me.

Obliviously, I'd been standing in line at the coffee counter, minding my own business when the barista called her name. I didn't think anything of it. But when Lizzy turned and accidentally bumped into me, my world tilted.

When our eyes locked, all the air from the room disappeared. I still remember the feel of her hand on my chest and the way her cheeks darkened as she looked at me in shock.

She was mesmerizing.

Of course, I immediately apologized. But I couldn't move to get out of her way for the life of me. Hell, I don't even know how long I stared. I must've looked like a complete idiot.

Just standing there, blocking her way.

Eventually, she broke eye contact and went back to her table.

Having already made a fool of myself, I grabbed my coffee then walked out the door, kicking myself the entire way back to my office for being such a tool.

I kept berating myself because I'm freaking twenty-eight, not twelve.

I know how to talk to girls.

Hell, I wasn't even interested in dating, but for some reason, I couldn't get my mind off her the entire night.

The next day, I was running late thanks to Milli's unwillingness to get dressed. I stopped in mid-afternoon for a pick-me-up to get through the day. Imagine my surprise seeing that same gorgeous girl suddenly behind me as I ordered.

The moment I turned around and our eyes met, a playful grin swept across her face. She wasn't wearing any makeup that I could tell, but her long, dark lashes lined the most stunning hazel eyes I'd ever seen. "We've gotta stop meeting like this."

"I sure hope not," I admitted. "It's been the highlight of my day."

Yes, I was cheesy as hell, but it was sincere.

My morning had been a shitshow and seeing her in that moment, made it all worth it.

We chatted until her peppermint latte was ready. She was a spitfire, and I pushed right back. Even in that brief conversation, our chemistry sizzled. I don't remember the specifics of what we talked about, but I distinctly remember the way she made me laugh. Thankfully, I brought my A-game, but I was late for a meeting, so I had to cut the conversation short.

I left her with a promise I'll never forget.

"Unfortunately, I'm due at a meeting, but I'll tell you what... *if* we happen to meet again, would you let me sit with you and buy you something more than coffee?"

"Hmmm... *If* we were to randomly meet again, maybe the third time will be the charm?"

It soon became our thing. We didn't meet every day, but we did bump into each other often over the next few weeks—which led to our one and only official date.

Suddenly, my stomach growls in hunger, drawing me out of my trip down memory lane.

Fuck, I came home for lunch, not to reminisce about Lizzy.

Dude, you're sitting here like a fucking creeper.

If she comes in, what are you gonna say? *Don't mind me, I'm just stalking in my living room, waiting to see you again.*

Fuck, man, get it together.

You'll see her plenty—she's your daughter's freaking nanny.

The only one who was remotely qualified for the job. You'll see her plenty of times in the coming months—don't fuck this up on the first day.

Making a snap decision, I do something I rarely experience.

Go out to eat.

Alone.

Chapter 9
Lizzy

With Milli's love of books, I had to take her to story hour at Booked at the Beach. Having worked there for the last few summers, I know the effort Sophie, the owner of the store, takes into creating the experience for children of all ages. Since it only happens a few times a week, today is the perfect day to start our new summer routine.

As soon as we returned from her swim lesson in Astoria, I quickly grabbed a snack for Milli and loaded her into her stroller. With some brisk walking, we made it just in time to see Sophie start the story.

Today's book is about a frog princess who lived in a castle by the sea. Sophie had a frog hand puppet dressed as a princess, and she brings the story to life with her fabulous voices for each character.

My heart fills with joy watching Milli roar with laughter at Sophie's dramatic storytelling. After reading with Milli during my interview, I knew Sophie would have the adorable child beside me eating out of the palm of her hand.

Sophie never disappoints.

Wide-eyed Milli sits beside me the entire time, completely engrossed in everything Sophie says. She cackles at the humor, gasps with the drama, and tries to warn the princess of danger like the rest of the children when the dark moment comes. My heart nearly bursts with joy watching Milli cheer on the frog princess when she doesn't wait for a smelly old prince to save her. No, this frog princess uses her bravery and courage to save not only herself, but the entire town.

As the story comes to an end, I realize I'm more entertained from watching Milli's reactions than Sophie's theatrics. This girl loves her books, and I'm happy I found an activity we'll both enjoy this summer.

Hopefully, Cameron can make it to story hour because his daughter's enthusiasm for books is priceless. I'd hate for him to miss something this memorable.

Once the story is done, I stand and offer, "Want to look around the store before we leave?"

"Uh-huh." Milli nods quickly and darts in the direction of the children's books.

Before I can say anything, she gasps, "Look, that's the story!" when she spots the exact book Sophie read to us. "We get it for our house?"

I'd already planned on letting her pick out one book today.

Who goes to a bookstore and doesn't come home with at least one?

"Are you sure this is the one you want? There's a lot of other ones we can choose from," I counter, letting her know she has options.

"No. I want this one. I llooovvee Princess Thea!" The smile she beams my way as she hugs the book against her chest is the spitting image of her father.

"So do I, Mills. Let's go pay for this, then go home for lunch."

Milli hugs the book and bounces from foot to foot as we wait in line to pay.

This girl loves reading. Who am I to get in the way? It's one obsession I can get behind. Most of my books are electronic now, and now that school's out for the summer, I hope to get plenty of reading in myself.

As we exit the store, I ask, "Do you want to walk or ride in the stroller?"

Placing the book in the basket beneath her seat, she proudly states, "I walk."

"Hold onto the handle and help me push then," I suggest so she won't get separated on this busy street. Tourists are out in full swing, even for a weekday.

The moment her chubby little hand grasps the stroller, I ask, "What sounds good for lunch?"

"Grilled cheese?"

"I think I can do that. Hold on tight; we're about to cross the street," I warn as we approach a light.

As soon as we cross, Milli shouts, "Daddy! Look, there's Daddy!"

Chills run down my spine, as my eyes follow the direction she's pointing. Sure enough, the man sitting at an outside table at the next restaurant is indeed Cameron.

Reaching for her hand so she won't run ahead, I notice he's alone. Hopefully, we're not interrupting anything important. He mentioned something about meetings today.

Milli's energy is palpable, and I swear it ricochets through me just as much. Tugging on my hand, she can barely contain her excitement. As if I'm not getting the message, she shouts, "Daddy! Daddy! Let's go see Daddy!"

Her shouting gets his attention, and he darts his eyes around to find her. The moment Cameron spots Milli, his eyes widen, matching her energy. Standing quickly, he closes the distance between us and scoops her into his arms. "Hey, Mills. Fancy meeting you here!"

Pointing at her stroller, she squeals, "Look, Daddy. I got a new book!"

"A new book? I don't think we have any of those at our house. What are books?"

Her brows adorably pull together, and her lips purse. "Daddy! We have lots of them!"

"But do you think we *really* need one more?"

Rolling her eyes as if it's the most ridiculous thing she's ever heard, she says, "Uh... yeah. This one is about a frog princess who's strong and brave and saves the day! We heard the bestest story! You missed it!"

"I did, did I? You'll have to tell me all about it," Cameron asks as he looks toward me. "Have you eaten?"

"She had a snack earlier, but we're on our way home for lunch."

"I just sat down. Care to join me?"

"Grilled cheese?" Milli asks hopeful, looking between us.

"I'm not sure it's on the menu, but we'll find something. I think I saw some chicken nuggets. I know you like those if grilled cheese isn't an option."

To me, Cameron asks, "Are you okay with lunch?"

Knowing his time with his daughter is limited, I offer, "Are you sure you don't want it to just be the two of you?"

"And what are you going to do? Sit in the corner and *watch* us eat? I don't think so. There's plenty of room, and I've only just ordered."

"I'll never pass up a meal from Hop's." I grin widely and follow him to his table.

Once I'm seated, I state, "Fun fact... did you know *this* is where Jax Cartwright got his start?"

A low chortle escapes as Cameron's head shakes. "Nope. I knew Sloane found him locally but had no idea where."

"Yep, my oldest sister Lanie worked here that summer... so Sloane pulled some strings with Joe, the owner, to get him some stage time before the competition."

Before he can say anything further, I lean in and pretend to cover one side of my mouth conspiratorially, "Don't let Joe know you know anything about Jax... or Ruby Frax for that matter. I'm not sure if he's working, but we'll never hear the end of it. He's pretty proud he "Found" Jax ..." Yes, I use air quotes to punctuate my point before adding, "You and I both know... Jax's road to his musical success was all Sloane's doing."

With his voice full of wonder, Cameron states, "Could our worlds get any smaller? I swear it's a wonder our paths never crossed before they did."

"No kidding." I laugh.

Before I can add anything further, the waitress comes. She offers Milli some crayons and a kid's menu to draw on. When Milli finds she can indeed get a grilled cheese sandwich, she squeals with delight, "I llloooovvve grilled cheese! Thank you."

Once the waitress finishes with our orders, she dashes off to her next customer.

Needing to fill the silence before things get awkward, I say the first thing on my mind. "Milli's got eyes like a hawk. I'm not sure I would've seen you had she not pointed you out."

"She notices everything. Trust me. Not much gets past her. I think it's all those times we play I spy in the car."

"We played that and the alphabet game when we rode with Nana... She loved road trips."

"I only have one. I can't imagine trying to entertain four girls at once. Your nana must've been a saint. Did you travel often?"

"Every summer, we went on at least one trip. Her goal was

to drive in every state around the US. It didn't faze her one bit, to hop in a car full of kids and drive. Once my sisters went off to college, Nana and I flew to a random destination and would road trip from there during my spring break. I think it helped my parents because Mom worked long hours as a nurse and well... Dad was busy being a pilot."

The waitress returns with our food, and the next few minutes is filled with silence as we enjoy our meal.

Eventually, Cameron stops eating and leans his corded arms on the table and lifts a brow. "So... Did she make it to all fifty states?"

"Technically..." I draw out for suspense. "She's been *in* all fifty states."

His thick brows pinch together. "Technically?"

"Well, my dad likes to tease she never really drove in Alaska. She was there on a cruise. It was an inside joke between them."

"Did you inherit her love of traveling?"

"The teenager in me would say, there's a reason some states are *fly-over states*. But honestly, I wouldn't trade my time with Nana for the world. She always had a way of making things memorable."

"Have you traveled much outside of the States?"

"Does visiting my dad while he was stationed overseas count?"

This earns me a sexy smirk. If the situation were different, I'd kiss that expression right off this gorgeous man's face. "Yes... I suppose it does."

Shit, where did that come from?

Milli, focus on Milli.

Forcing myself to flip the script, I ask, "What about you? Have you traveled much?"

Exhaling heavily, he leans back in his chair and studies me.

"When I was younger, yes. I got my start at Smashing Waves Records much like Sloane. I toured all over the country, promoting various bands. I also spent a lot of time overseas. I love seeing new places. It was invigorating waking up in different countries all over the world."

"So... what changed? How did you end up in Seaside?"

Looking at his daughter, he explains it with one word, "Emilia."

Duh... I should've known this. *Why the hell did you ask him that?*

He mistakes my silence as judgement.

"Emilia is hands down the best thing that's ever happened to me. I know my time with her is precious, so when she came along, I took the more stable route and focused on working my way up at the label."

I'm dying to ask about her mom but think better of it, especially in front of Milli. That's a conversation for another day.

Quickly changing the subject, I ask, "Speaking of work, how did you manage to be here of all places today? I thought you were booked with meetings."

That devilish smirk that melts my panties with one glance returns. "A man's gotta eat..." With the way his eyes roam over me, I could swear he's talking about something else entirely.

My body flushes with heat in reaction to his smoldering navy blues being sent my way. Millions of thoughts swirl through my brain like a hurricane, and none of them are appropriate—especially with his daughter right here, obliviously coloring beside me.

This man is dangerous.

Leaning in like I did, before he cups his hand on one side of his mouth, he admits, "Fun fact... I actually went home for lunch, but you weren't there."

Snap.

Just like that, he breaks the sexual tension that had been building between us.

"Seriously? Why didn't you call?"

An impish expression flits across his features, and he looks to his hands for the briefest of moments. "I uh..." He darts his eyes to his daughter and back to me before adding, "Guess... I... didn't want you to think I didn't trust you. It's hard enough being away from her, but I knew you needed to form your own bond together and didn't want to interrupt."

"That's..." Ridiculous... sweet? I love that he thought of me, but this summer isn't about me, it's about Milli.

What the hell do I even say?

"Well... that just won't do. You said your hours are going to get crazier as it gets closer to the festival. If you're free during the day, you're welcome to join us on any excursion I might have planned."

"Good to know..." He nods, then squeezes an eye shut. "But sometimes I won't have a lot of notice if a meeting is canceled and who knows where you'll be in town."

"Are you such an old man that you forget technology exists?"

The hard lines of his jaw drop open in shock. "Wha..."

But I cut him off, and it's my turn to smirk. "Uh, there's an app for this... *Grandpa.*"

"He's my *daddy*, not a Papa, Iz!" Milli admonishes me, and we both burst out laughing.

"You're right, Mills. I may be *old*, but I'm certainly not *that* old. I think I may have heard a thing or two about a tracking app."

This only makes me laugh harder.

When I finally get myself under control, I reach for my phone, quickly open my locked screen, and tap out a text with a link to share my location.

"There. Now you'll never have to wonder where we are," I state matter-of-factly. "I can't believe I didn't think of it earlier. I should've offered it this morning."

Our eyes lock, and he holds my gaze for the longest of moments.

His eyes darken, and my body heats.

And just like that, the tension between us is back.

His darts his tongue out to wet his lips as a slow grin forms.

"Thanks. Now, I'll never have the excuse of not knowing where you are."

Oh, boy, this man is dangerous.

Chapter 10
Lizzy

Later that week, I couldn't believe my eyes as we passed a garage sale on our morning walk. There in the corner of the yard was a practically new balance bike, built specifically for toddlers Milli's size, for only ten bucks. I wouldn't be Nana's granddaughter if I didn't stop.

As luck would have it, upon further inspection, there sitting on a table right next to the red balance bike is a brand-new helmet. Not only is the helmet in perfect condition, but it still has the tag on it. Clearly, it hasn't been used and is perfect for Milli. My pulse speeds up as I look the bike over with care. No scratches or paint chips. I'm not even sure this bike was used either.

Last summer, I nannied for a little girl about Milli's age. I know firsthand how amazing a balance bike can be for teaching someone her age to ride. Without the hassle of learning how to pedal, Emma quickly learned how to balance and soar down The Promenade. By the end of summer, she was riding a regular bike with no training wheels, thanks to the balance bike her parents started her on.

Channeling my inner Nana, I walk to the lady in charge of the garage sale and do what she taught me to do—barter. Acting as if I'm not interested in the purchase, I casually ask, "If I buy the bike, will you throw in the helmet for the same price?"

Holding my breath, I watch as the woman, not much older than my mom, looks carefully from me to Milli and back. Of course, she's already watched me have Milli try out both the bike and helmet for size, so I'm fully prepared to pay full price for both items. They're fairly priced, but it wouldn't be a yard sale if I didn't attempt to haggle.

When the lady asks Milli, "Have you ever ridden a bike before?" I'm not sure where she's going with it.

Milli shakes her head, and the woman's stoic face morphs into a smile.

"Well…" the woman sighs. "It looks like you're the proud owner of both now."

To me, she adds, "I just bought that helmet, but my grandbaby's head is far too big for that thing, so his loss is your gain. Besides, it's the last day for our sale. You'll get far more use out of them than our storage shed. Oh, while we're at it, why don't I throw in these knee and elbow pads I bought the same day, too. I'd hate for her little legs to get banged up."

Quickly, I pull out my cash and thank her for her generosity.

Before I know it, Milli and I are on our way to The Promenade. This famous cement pathway parallels the beach near the center of town. It may only be a little over a mile long, but it's the best place to learn. The sand lining is the perfect place to land, and it's away from any moving vehicles. My sisters and I all learned to ride on this very pathway as Nana's house borders it.

*****

"There you go... You've got this!" I exclaim, jogging beside Milli.

I'm still holding the seat of the balance bike, but she's figured out how to keep her head over the handlebars and work her feet in the short time we've been practicing. I'm not sure who will be more tired when we're done, but she's determined to keep going.

"Yay!" Milli shrieks as she runs over a small bump in the sidewalk. Unfortunately, the wheel jerks, and she loses control.

"Whoa," I warn, swooping my free arm around her just in time for the bike to veer off the path. If I hadn't been holding onto the seat, she would've toppled onto the ground and crashed into a bush.

"Everything okay?" a familiar male voice approaches, laced with concern.

Turning, I see Lanie with her husband Ryan, walking from our deck to the pathway.

"Guess what, Milli? This is my sister and her husband Ryan."

Milli's arms grip around my leg as an unusual shyness sets over her as Ryan's six-foot-four frame approaches.

Ryan immediately notices and stops a few feet back from us. My sister however comes closer and squats to her level as she says. "It's nice to meet you, Milli. I've heard you love coloring and reading books. I love reading, too."

This perks Milli up. "Books? I love reading my new book with Princess Thea! My Iz gave it to me. We went to story time."

"You went to story time with Sophie?" Ryan asks knowingly. "Did she use puppets?"

This earns Ryan an enthusiastic nod, and she apparently forgets all about her shyness as she steps closer. "Uh-huh. The frog princess saved the day."

Ryan reaches down and picks up the forgotten balance bike from the bush it's currently leaning against.

"My Iz got me dat today."

Raising a brow, Ryan asks, "Wow. Lanie and I were watching you from the kitchen. You're picking this up fast."

Lanie's brows knit together. "Where on earth did you find a thing like that?"

"A garage sale, of course." I smile. "I even got them to throw in this protective gear all for the tune of ten bucks."

Ryan's jaw drops as he guffaws, "Dude, you stole this!"

"No. Iz not steal." Milli's voice suddenly is stern as she points a finger in his direction. "She paid. Stealing is bad."

Oh, my heart. This girl.

As we all fight to stifle a laugh, Ryan somehow manages to regain control. Dropping to her height to look her in the eye, he calmly says, "You're right, Milli. Stealing *is* bad. I know Lizzy *paid* for your things. I'm teasing her. I'm sorry if you thought otherwise."

Milli's expression is hard to read as she stares at Ryan with her lips pursed.

Ryan points to her bike and asks, "Wanna show me how you ride this?"

And just like that, everything is forgotten.

Reaching for the handle, she grins adorably at him. "Run beside me?"

"I think I can do that," he says, glancing to me for permission.

The moment I nod, he stands and helps Milli get settled on the bike.

"Hold onto the back of her seat," I warn. "She hasn't quite mastered the balance part yet."

"She's getting there though," Lanie encourages. "We've been watching from the house."

"You ready?" Ryan asks once she's settled.

With a single nod, Milli tightens her hold on the handles.

"Chin over the handlebar," I remind her as she pushes off with her feet.

My breath catches in my throat with her wobbly start, but after a few strides, she seems to get her rhythm, and I finally breathe again.

Lanie and I follow the two of them as Ryan does his best to keep her upright. "Keep it steady, squirt. Look straight ahead."

This works for a few strides, then Milli's head drops, and the bike wobbles once again.

"Focus on what's in front of you," Ryan encourages. "I won't let you fall."

"Chin over the bar, Mills," I call out, thankful for the reprieve from chasing her.

Ryan's a saint. I was just about to suggest a break, and he's clearly saving the day. Milli's having a blast. His white knuckles grip the seat, and I know he's the one doing all the balancing in this endeavor, but he encourages her to go further. "You've got this, squirt. Watch out for that bench."

"Iz, look at me. I'm doing it!" Milli shouts when she finally stabilizes again.

Lanie claps beside me as we jog to keep up. "You are! You're such a big girl!"

Her little tongue pops out the side of her mouth as she pushes the bike faster with her feet.

She must truly be balancing because suddenly, Ryan's grip relaxes, and his hand hovers inches from the seat behind her.

"Woo-hooo! You're doing it, Mills!" I shout, getting caught up in the moment.

As if I jinxed her, she suddenly looks down, and the bike wobbles once again.

Ryan's quick and grabs her seat just as she tilts to one side.

Cringing, I watch as he does his best to settle her. With inches to spare, he hoists her with his other hand and somehow hurdles himself over the bike as it falls. Fortunately, she never grazes the pavement below her.

Whew, crisis averted.

Her bike isn't as lucky. As it clatters to the ground, I cringe at what could have happened.

Milli isn't fazed in the slightest as she pumps a fist into the air enthusiastically. "That's fun! Let's do it again!"

"All right, squirt. Let's do this!" Ryan says, once her feet are back on the ground.

The two of them spend the next twenty minutes roaming back and forth along the path. Once I realize Ryan's got things handled, I stand near the path to our house, out of their way.

When Ryan's just far enough not to hear, I lean into my sister and whisper, "You've got quite the catch there. He's amazing with her."

He towers over her but never is more than inches from her seat. It's almost comical how he contorts to match her size. But the reality is, he's spending his lunch hour making a practical stranger's day.

"Oh, I know he's gonna be a great dad," Lanie agrees. "This right here... is just one of many reasons I love that man."

Our conversation stalls as we watch him pick her up, bike and all, and turn them to come back toward us. Once Milli moves again, Lanie says, "Can you keep a secret?"

Raising a brow at her audacity, I state, "You have to ask?"

"I know, you're the keeper of so many secrets in *our* family. But we're thinking about trying to start a family of our own soon."

"That's incredible!" I start, but she shushes me and pulls me in for the hug I desperately want to give her.

"Secret... Liz..." she reminds me but quietly matches my enthusiasm.

"Why are you hiding this?" I ask once I'm in control of the volume of my voice.

"In case we don't get pregnant right away." She sighs. "I don't want the added pressure of people asking, ya know? It'll happen when it happens."

Milli interrupts all conversation when she yells my name, "Iz! I need to potty!" Ryan immediately halts her bike.

When her wide eyes meet mine, I sprint in her direction. She's held it for way too long. I should have reminded her, but we both were distracted with this bike.

"I've got you, girl," I say on the run. "Let's go inside and take care of this!"

Thankfully, the bathroom isn't far from the beach, and we make it inside just in time. I'm not sure how long she'd been holding it, but I make a mental note to check in with her more often. This was way too close of a call.

Once we've washed up and are back in the living room, we find both Ryan and Lanie waiting for us. Through the window, I can see her bike leaning against a chair out on the deck.

"Are you hungry, Milli?" Ryan asks, reaching into the fridge for something.

"Uh-huh." She nods.

"Let's take off your gear, and we'll have lunch at my house today."

"You lib here?"

"I do for the summer." I grin, pulling off her elbow pads. "I spend every summer here in Seaside. This was my Nana's house."

"You have a nana?" she asks innocently as she looks around. My heart squeezes at her connection.

Shit, how do I explain death to a child?

Going with the truth, I say, "My nana lives in Heaven. My sister Lanie and Ryan live in this house all the time, and I get to visit when I'm not in school."

A perplexed expression crosses her features, but thankfully, her lack of filter doesn't make me wonder what she's thinking for long. "You sleep here?"

"Yep." I chuckle at her cuteness. "My room is upstairs."

"I see it?" she asks eagerly.

"Why don't you two go check it out, and I'll help Ryan with lunch," Lanie suggests, pointing at the stairs. "Any allergies?"

"Nope. But her favorite is grilled cheese," I offer as a suggestion as I reach for Milli's hand.

Milli's eyes widen in shock. "You have grilled cheese?"

"Yes, we do, squirt," Ryan teases, pointing a spatula our way. "Once you're done checking out Lizzy's room, we'll get you one."

"Let's go, Iz!"

There's not much to see, but Milli's entertained by my over-stuffed bookshelf. She manages to find one of my favorite picture books from my childhood called *A Princess Wears Hiking Boots*. When she asks if she could lie down in my bed to read it, I worry she might fall asleep, but surprisingly, she stays awake.

When we return downstairs, she's ravenous. She eats her entire sandwich and some grapes Lanie has set out. Realizing I should get her home for a nap, I ask my sister, "Mind watching her while I use the restroom? We should get going."

I swear I was gone for less than five minutes, but when I return, I find Milli sound asleep on the couch. Chuckling, I ask my sister, "How the heck did that happen?"

A light laugh escapes as she shrugs. "I think we broke her. I helped her wash her hands, then we sat down on the couch to wait for you. Ryan has a meeting at one with a contractor, so I walked him to the front door. When I returned, she was conked out."

"She's exhausted. I think we'll just stay here until she wakes up. I didn't bring her stroller on our walk and passed out like that, she'll be like carrying a sack of potatoes. I don't think I can carry both her and her new bike all the way to their house."

Reaching for a blanket beside the couch, I cover her. She doesn't even stir.

My sister walks into the kitchen and pours herself a glass of iced tea. "Want some? I'm gonna hang out on the back deck for a bit. Care to join me? It's been forever since just the two of us hung out. You've been so busy this summer."

Once we're outside and settled on the deck chairs looking out at the ocean, my sister unknowingly asks a loaded question. "So... what's the deal with Milli's dad? What's he doing here in Seaside that's got you working so many hours?"

Chapter 11
Lizzy

I'm not sure if it's the way she's asked or the fact that I've been extremely tightlipped when it comes to all things Cameron. But suddenly, my cheeks heat, and I feel the need to look anywhere but at her.

Being the oldest sister, she knows my tells better than anyone—And apparently, my silence speaks volumes.

"Oh..." she gasps, and her brows practically fly off her forehead.

In a singsong voice, she says, "The great secret keeper apparently has some of her own. Is her dad hot or something? Why are you suddenly acting so weird about this?"

Hot doesn't even begin to describe Cameron. He is hands down the sexiest man I've ever laid eyes on. Every time he's in the room, my body lights up like it's the friggin Fourth of July.

"Or something..." I finally admit when I make eye contact with her.

"What's the deal? He's treating you well, right? That girl is the sweetest thing. I can't imagine her dad being an asshole to you."

"Oh, he's *not* an asshole in the slightest," I say on a sigh, still not sure how to explain everything. I mean, where do I even begin?

"So... what gives?" My knowing sister persists. Lanie's like a dog with a bone; when she wants information, she'll press until it's released.

Jumping to conclusions once again, Lanie quickly asks, "Elizabeth Renee Lancaster, do you like him or something?"

"Shhh... could you maybe not yell that? Geez, his daughter is sleeping right there in that room. God forbid the rest of the family find out anything. As if our world isn't small enough, we don't need Mrs. Buzzard down the street spreading gossip. You know Nana still has friends who love to spread all the tea... everywhere!"

In a much lower tone, she asks, "So something has happened?"

"Yes... and no... not in the way you're thinking... Shit... yes in the way you're probably thinking with your eyes bugging out like that, but not since being Milli's nanny."

"What the hell are you talking about?"

"I met Cameron, Milli's father, a few months ago at school."

"Okay, so you knew him *before* you started working for him? If that's the case, why were you so nervous about the interview process?"

"Again... yes and no." How exactly do I explain this?

Taking in a huge breath to steady myself, I let the words pour from my mouth.

"Yes, we met and *ohmigod*, let me tell you our chemistry was off the charts! So much so, I gave into all my rules and allowed myself to give into my feelings for one night. Hell, he'd been the man who'd been starring in every one of my fantasies for the past few months. We were both leaving town, so we never let things get too serious. I made him promise we'd enjoy our one incredible night, with no strings attached. Hell, we never even exchanged numbers." Or last names for that matter.

"I swear, I had no idea it was him when I interviewed for this position. I didn't even know he had a kid or was in Seaside of all places... but fate is twisted when she's got plans we're unaware of. Hell, even if I wasn't his nanny, I'm sure our paths would've crossed this summer since he's Cameron Kruse... You know... the guy who took over Tara's job at the label."

"No shit!" Lanie says on a sigh. "No wonder you're so tightlipped. You've not only slept with *your* boss, but apparently, everyone else's boss, too. You sure know how to step in it... big time, little sis."

Rolling my eyes, I agree wholeheartedly. "No kidding."

"But how did you of all people become his nanny without knowing about it?"

"With him being an exec at the label, he's extremely busy. So... his mother of all people interviewed me."

For the next few minutes, I unload the entire situation on Lanie, including where Cameron and I left things. "I can't afford to turn this down. With my student teaching next spring, I need all the cash I can earn now to survive."

As a teacher herself, Lanie of all people knows I get to *pay* an entire semester's tuition so I can work more than full time—at a job I one day merely hope to have. I've worked throughout college, but I can't next spring. My focus needs to be on finishing my degree.

"Okay... but you know this secret won't contain itself. You're gonna have to let everyone know you're working for Cameron." One look in my direction has her backtracking quickly. "You don't have to tell them all the details but since two-thirds of our family technically work for the man, you may want to clue them in."

"I don't think either Jax or Finn will have a problem with it, as long as they never learn about our past," I admit.

"Liz..." Lanie sounds exasperated as she heeds a warning. "Even if you're grown, you're still the baby of *our* family. Record label or not, if that man hurts you, I wouldn't put it past either of the twins *or their fiancés* to let it slide. Hell, Cameron won't need to worry about Dad, who's an active member in the Air Force, if Sloane or Raven hear word of this."

"That's why I'm *only* telling you, Lanie," I forcefully remind her. "You can't tell anyone about my past with Cameron. There's just too much at stake to let it slip."

Exhaling heavily, Lanie nods in agreement. "I suppose you're right."

"It's not like I'm working for him forever. Summer will be over before I know it. Then I'll go back to school, and things can return to normal. Sure, Cameron works for the label, but it's not like he's anyone's direct boss... but mine."

"Oh, girl," my sister says on a knowing laugh. "You've got it bad... and I hate to say it, if you don't play your cards right, you'll be screwed every which way from Sunday. Tread carefully, my friend."

Glancing at her watch, she sighs heavily. "Look, I'm meeting up with a friend from work in a bit. You know I may bust your chops, but I'm here for you. That girl in there is incredible, so focus on her. As for everything with her dad... well, that will have to work itself out. I wish you all the luck, because... let's face it, you need it."

"Don't I know it," I mumble to myself as she walks away.

Chapter 12
Cameron

The moment I enter the house, the sound of pounding feet greets me. Pair that with Milli's excited shouting, "Daddy, you're home!" and all my stress from the day melts away. I barely make it down the hall before she crashes into me. Scooping her up, I squeeze her tight and revel in the few seconds she hugs me in return.

This right here is everything.

"God, I've missed you," I admit, snuggling her close. She smells of innocence and the fresh ocean breeze. Leaning back to look her in the eye, I ask, "Did you play outside today?"

"Yep, and I got a surprise for you!" She giggles.

With that one little grin, I may as well be putty in her hands.

Lord help me when she's a teenager.

Bopping her on the nose, I tease, "You do, do ya? What kind of surprise?"

When she wiggles, I take the hint and return her to the floor.

Instantly, she reaches for my hand and pulls me toward the kitchen. "We *have* to eat first. Iz said so. Then I show you."

Milli's usually quick to let the cat out of the bag, so I choose not to press her.

Walking into the kitchen, my senses go on overload, and my mouth waters for more than what's cooking.

Lizzy's wearing a dark tank top and a pair of *really* well-fitting shorts.

I know this because her ass is wiggling in the air as she bends over to get something out of the oven.

Fuck. My. Life.

Why did I have to walk in and see this of all things?

It's hard to stay professional when that fuckable ass is on display.

Oh, the things I want to do to her.

Lizzy places the pan on the stove, shuts the oven, then turns my way, a smile tugging at her lips.

Yep, she totally caught me checking her out.

I should feel ashamed, but the glorious color her lightly freckled cheeks turn is completely worth it. It's the exact shade of pink she turned when she fell apart while I was buried deep inside her.

I may not be able to act upon my thoughts, but I certainly can replay these fantasies when I'm alone at night.

"Cameron?" she says, peering at me suspiciously.

Shit. She's waiting for a response, and I have no idea what was said.

Now, it's my turn to blush. "Sorry, I was..."

God, get it together, dipshit. Pull your head out of your ass and focus on her actual words—not the fantasies flowing through your head.

"I was lost in thought," I finally manage to spit out.

There—That's not a total lie.

Her laughter fills the room, and that beautiful voice makes my chest squeeze tighter. God, I miss her laughter. Our friendly banter drew me to her in the first place.

"Obviously..." Shaking her head at my ridiculousness, she says, "I was saying I hope you like ribs. I also sautéed some mushrooms and asparagus. Milli helped make mashed potatoes, as well."

Then, my other senses hit me, and my stomach growls in anticipation. "Mmmm... It smells delicious. If you're not careful, we'll get used to this special treatment."

"Oh, it's not that special, trust me. They happened to be on sale when I stopped at the store earlier."

"Daddy, I set the table. Let's sit down. Iz says we *must* eat before the surprise."

"Now I'm really curious." I dart my focus from Milli to Lizzy and back.

Both are grinning conspiratorially, but Lizzie holds up her hands in surrender, when I stare at her a moment too long. "Don't look at me. It's her surprise, and *we're* keeping it until *after* dinner," she emphasizes more for Milli's reminder than mine.

Milli shakes her head and punches her fists into her hips. "I told you, Daddy, *after* dinner."

"Okay... okay. I'll wait." Turning to Lizzy, I ask, "Need any help?"

"Just grab whatever you want to drink and have a seat. Your arrival is timed perfectly." Placing two large serving dishes piled with food onto the table, she states, "Dinner is served."

Once seated, I reach for Milli's plate, but Lizzy beats me to it by placing a scoop of vegetables on it before it can be lifted. I suddenly find myself in disbelief in this simple gesture. As Milli's sole provider, I'm used to being the one who does everything for her. No one besides my family has ever stepped into that role. The next thing I know, Lizzy places a scoop of potatoes with a rib alongside it, leaving me nothing to do.

How can she be so effortlessly thoughtful?

"Iz!" Milli suddenly chastises Lizzy, and I frantically search for what she's clearly upset about.

Lizzy is just as clueless as me because she quickly asks, "What's wrong, Mills?"

Milli's brows have a deep crease, her lips purse as disgust fills her features. "Iz," she warns, her voice raising in anger. Fisting her tiny hands beside her, she spits out, "I'm *not* a doggy!"

"Wha..." Lizzy starts, but my very determined daughter interrupts her.

"I'm not a doggy!" she repeats louder than before, then pushes her plate away before adding, "I don't eat bones!"

Oh. My. Fucking. God. I'm dying.

Did she really just say that?

I'm at a complete loss for words, and I know better than to laugh at her expense in this moment.

Thankfully, Lizzy once again comes to my rescue.

"Oh... sweet girl," she says, quickly grabbing her knife and Milli's plate. "None of us are eating bones for dinner. Here, let me cut the meat *from* the bone for you."

Milli crosses her arms and skeptically watches as Lizzy slices the meat away from the rib. When she's done, she looks from me to my daughter. "Have you never had ribs before?"

"I'm certain we have... but maybe she's too young to remember." I shrug as if that should explain everything.

Milli just stares suspiciously at her pile of food.

Lifting a rib from my own plate I take a bite. "Mmmm... This is delicious, Lizzy." I may have exaggerated at first, but then, the actual flavors register, making me moan for real. "Well, if you don't want to eat these, I guess it means I can eat yours after you have your *no, thank you bite,* to make sure you don't like it."

Emilia knows the rule. It's something my mom instilled in me as a child as well. I never force her to eat, but she is required to take at least one bite before declining.

My daughter stares me down but knows I won't budge on this.

Slowly, she reaches for her fork and pokes at the meat in front of her. I swear my child never blinks as she holds my gaze defiantly. Slowly, she brings her fork to her lips. Once the food is in her mouth, she finally closes her eyes and chews.

Then her eyes pop open, and she smiles jubilantly at Lizzy. "Mmmmm... This is good, Iz. I like it!"

Lizzy's lips twitch but somehow, she manages not to laugh at my daughter's antics. "I thought you might. Have you tried the potatoes you mashed?"

And just like that, the drama is forgotten, and we're all devouring this scrumptious meal together.

This right here is something I could get used to.

During our first week of working together, Lizzy tried to leave just as I arrived home one night. She had just set the table for herself and Milli, so I insisted she stay and eat—if she didn't have other plans. After all, if I hadn't arrived when I did, she would have eaten with Milli and enjoyed the fruits of her labor. Ever since, she's taken to eating with us if I arrive in time, and I, for one, will never turn down her company.

After a few minutes, I break the silence by asking, "What did the two of you do today?"

I catch my daughter's eyes widen and dart toward Lizzy as her mouth exaggeratedly clamps shut.

Lizzy covers her mouth with a hand, too. I'm not sure if it's to finish chewing or for covering a smile, but she rotates her other hand in a circle, gesturing for me to move on from this subject. "Next question…"

"But…" I protest, and she shakes her head.

"It'll ruin the surprise. You'll find out soon enough. Why don't *you* tell us about *your* day?"

"Sheesh… Okay… Point taken. Hmmm… Let me see… I spent most of my day either on the phone or in meetings. Besides being here with you, the highlight of my day was probably dropping by the studio and listening to Ruby Frax as they worked on their newest song."

"I haven't heard much from this new album, but the guys have certainly been putting some time in the studio. I've hardly seen them since they've been off tour."

"I'm certain they'll have another hit on their hands, if today's session is anything to go by."

"I know I'm biased," Lizzy shrugs, "but honestly, I've never heard a song I didn't like from either Jax or Ruby Frax for that matter. I'm looking forward to seeing them play again this summer."

"Yeah," I agree. "Don't get me wrong. I think Jax is incredible as a solo artist, but when he started playing with Finn and Ryker, their talent as a band grew exponentially. They feed off one another and push each other to limits that far exceed expectations. Their ability to pull in crowds from all ages makes them in high demand for future shows. Speaking of shows, did you catch any of their stops while on tour?"

"I made it to their Seattle and Portland stops but never got to travel beyond that due to my class schedule."

"They killed it in Portland! I was there…" I trail off as it hits me that our paths crossed once again mere weeks before officially meeting that day in the coffee shop.

Damn, this world is small.

"I watch Frax, too?" Milli bounces in her chair with excitement.

I don't exactly switch my playlist when Milli's around. In fact, I'm not sure I've ever purposely listened to children's music just for her. Obviously, she has great taste in music. But a three-year old at a full-length concert? That might be pushing it.

"Uh... I'll see what I can do," I start but stop myself before promising something I won't follow through with. Instead, I hedge, "They're in Seaside for the summer, Mills. Maybe I can bring you into a practice session."

"Or... maybe you can come to a family bonfire," Lizzy cuts in. "The guys are known for singing at those."

Milli's eyes bug out, and her jaw drops into an O. "You like Frax, too?"

"Yep... I sure do." Lizzy grins. "Do you have a favorite song?"

Suddenly, she belts out, "I never knew I could be free... Just being me."

"Oh, I love that one." Lizzy grins.

Milli nods in agreement. "I know... my daddy plays it in the car." Milli takes one last bite of food and pushes her plate away. "All done! Ready for your surprise, Daddy?"

*****

"Can I come out yet?" I holler from the mudroom. Whatever these girls have planned, it's happening in the garage. For the life of me, I can't figure out what they're doing in there. Originally, I thought they might've baked dessert or created an art project.

"Not quite," Lizzy quickly responds on a grunt.

When the outside garage door opens, my fingers itch to turn the knob in front of me. I'm on pins and needles as I wait to be summoned. Milli loves surprises. She's three, so I can usually sniff them out a mile away before they're revealed. Today, I'm clueless.

"Okay, Daddy!" Milli shouts. "I'm ready!"

Opening the mudroom door, I expect to see her on the other side, but all I see are my two vehicles. Walking out to the driveway, I hear my daughter shout, "I'm ready, Iz! Let's go!"

"Okay, chin up," Lizzy says as they come into view. "You've got this!"

My heart stops as my daughter glides toward me on a red bike.

She's wearing a matching helmet and protective gear on her knees and elbows. Lizzy's jogging right beside her, holding onto the seat.

Wait... that's not a bike. Where are the pedals?

Milli's deep in concentration as her tongue slips from the side of her mouth, but the minute she spots me, she shouts, "Daddy! Look at me!"

She wobbles slightly, but Lizzy quickly reminds her, "Chin over the handlebar, Mills. You've got this. Let's show him what you've learned!"

That's all it takes for Milli to straighten and keep gliding my way. Her feet push along the pavement, and she steers right past me on the sidewalk in front of our house.

From behind, I watch as Lizzy's hand hovers closely behind her seat. Holy shit, she's doing this all on her own!

"Ohmigod, Mills, you're riding a bike!"

Not wanting to miss out on the action, I jog and quickly catch up with them. Milli squeals with delight as she goes faster and faster.

With the sidewalk coming to an end, my stomach clenches when Lizzy warns, "Whoa, Mills. Slow down."

Of course, my daredevil of a child ignores her.

Lizzy's calm but firmly states, "Milli, we need to slow down...You don't know how to turn yet."

Lizzy's pace picks up, and she grabs hold of the bike seat with one hand, while reaching for the handlebar with the other. "Emilia, it's time to stop pushing."

The use of her full name does the trick. Milli slows, just as the sidewalk nearly comes to an end.

Instead of having my daughter get off the bike to turn around, in a well-practiced move, Lizzy warns, "Hold on," and literally picks her up along with the bike and spins her in the opposite direction.

Once back on the ground and steady, Milli asks, "Go again?"

"Holy Moly, Mills! You've been holding out on me. Where did this bike come from?"

"My Iz got it for me!" My daughter beams.

"She did, did she? Just how long have you been practicing?"

Punching her hip, she looks at me as if I should already know the answer. "She got it *today*, Daddy."

I glance between my daughter and Lizzy.

"Yep. I found it on the way back from our walk at a garage sale! Can you believe it?" Lizzy boasts. "Milli's picking it up like a champ!"

"You taught her to ride, *today*?" I ask in disbelief. "How is that possible?"

"A lot of running back and forth," she deadpans.

"Here in the driveway?"

"We ride at the beach!" Milli explains.

What? That doesn't make sense. There's no way she could ride this in the sand.

Before I can say anything, Lizzy cuts in. "The Promenade runs right in front of my house. It's where I learned to ride as a kid. The path is wide, but the sand is a great place to land when you need to bail."

Milli pushes again, and all conversation stops as we jog alongside her. Again, once she gets going, Lizzy lets go, and Milli rides solo until it's time to turn around. In the same move as before, Lizzy flips her in the opposite direction with ease.

My chest tightens seeing my daughter giggle with glee. For her entire life, I've been the one to help her with her firsts. In a matter of hours, Lizzy's gone out of her way to teach Milli something I've never considered. Who knew a three-year-old could learn to ride like this?

"We're gonna wear out the pavement if we keep this up," I tease when we turn around and return down the sidewalk. I've only done this for a few minutes. I can only imagine how tired Lizzy is from chasing her all day. Even at three, I know first-hand how determined Milli is when learning something new. She doesn't stop until she gets it or drops from exhaustion.

If only there was a place wide enough to turn, I think Mills could probably do this on her own.

When we reach the edge of the sidewalk once more, I jokingly suggest, "We should find a place where she can work on her turns."

With a sly grin, Lizzy nods in agreement. "I think I know just the place, if you're up for it."

Chapter 13
Cameron

"Hop in, Mills," I encourage, reaching for a cart at the grocery store.

Shaking her head, she grins adorably and counters, "I walk, Daddy."

It's the weekend and although I'd love nothing more than to get through the store, I'm not in a hurry. I give in and go at her pace. "Okay, but hold onto the cart so I don't get lost."

The trick with toddlers is to give them something to do. If she has a job, then I rarely need to worry about her wandering off. We're only popping into the store for a few things and at this hour, the tourists are hardly ever up.

"Want some cereal?" I ask, turning down the cereal and coffee aisle. I'm here for coffee, but we may as well stock up while we're here.

Her little feet rush down the aisle, stopping where her favorite leprechaun sits on a shelf at her height. She plucks the box off the shelf, then runs back, reaches up onto her toes, and pushes the box into the cart. Once it plops inside, she's eager to help again. "What's next, Daddy?"

"Let's pick up some eggs and milk," I suggest, turning the corner.

Hmmmm… What else do I need? Maybe I should pick up some Gogurts and some of that coffee creamer I know Lizzy likes while were in this section, too?

The way Lizzy lit up when she saw the peppermint creamer in my fridge makes it worth my while to pop by the store when we're running low. I may not be able to date her, but there's nothing wrong with going out of my way to earn a smile from her, is there?

Pointing across the aisle, I add, "I'll grab the eggs if you want to get some Gogurts."

"Yay!" She scurries to one side of the aisle, while I open the refrigerator door on the other.

If you'd asked me pre-child if I'd be buying yogurts in a pouch, instead of family-sized containers like I had as a kid, I would've laughed in your face. But those little snacks are worth their weight in gold. First, she eats the entire thing. Next, when I put some in the freezer, she thinks she's getting a special treat when I pull it out. Third, she can get it for herself when needed. That right there is priceless.

While I'm checking to see that all the eggs are intact, I hear Milli shout something excitedly, but I don't fully catch it over the fan with my head inside the fridge. I turn back in time to catch my daughter jump up and down and throw herself at a man's leg in a bear hug.

What the actual fuck?

My body's suddenly on full alert.

Why is she hugging a complete stranger?

Standing to my full height, I quickly approach them.

This man is huge and muscular and towers over my six-foot frame. But he's got another thing coming if he messes with my baby girl.

My sudden rage dissipates a little when his words register.

"Hey, squirt." The stranger laughs out, ruffling her hair as she clings to him. "Fancy seeing you here."

"Emilia?" comes out as I shorten the distance between us, making my presence known.

My daughter is as shy as they come with strangers. Clearly, she knows him.

Or she thinks she does?

Fuck, what the hell is going on?

She's grinning at him like he's hung the moon, and I've never seen this man in my life.

As I approach, the tall man my daughter's still holding onto reaches out his hand. "Hi, I'm Ryan. You must be Cameron Kruse, Milli's dad."

Slowly, I reach out and shake his hand, darting my focus from my daughter to him.

Obviously, she knows him. But how?

When she still doesn't let go, Ryan laughs once more. "I met this little squirt the other day while she learned to ride her balance bike," as if that should explain everything. To her, he looks down and asks, "Have you figured it out yet?"

"Uh-huh." Milli nods proudly. "I can turn, too. My Iz and Daddy help me."

"Your Iz?" Ryan nods knowingly. "She's a pretty special lady, isn't she?"

"You know Lizzy?" I clarify, forcing my brain to connect the dots.

It's not every day my daughter hugs strangers, but if he knows Lizzy, he can't be too bad.

But that doesn't mean I have to like him.

Eyeing him speculatively, I realize he's closer to Lizzy's age than mine. Maybe she's met someone this summer? I mean—it's possible. She *is* from Seaside. Maybe they've reconnected now that she's returned. After all, she's young, single, and extremely attractive.

Hell, she's more than that. She's the total package.

When I hired her as Milli's nanny, we agreed that we couldn't keep seeing each other, but does that mean she's moved on?

Why does the thought of her dating someone make me want to throat punch him?

Instinctively, my hands curl into fists as I wait for his response.

"Yeah." Ryan nods slowly, looking me over with care. When his eyes land on my tightly clenched fists, he quickly adds, "I'm her brother-in-law. I've married the *only* Lancaster that *doesn't* work for you... apparently."

"Work for me?" I repeat.

Damn, my brain is slow on the uptake.

Thankfully, I finally register his actual words—*in-law*.

Relief washes through me, and the stress I didn't know I'd been holding onto dissipates.

God, I'm an idiot.

Ryan continues, thankfully clueless of my internal struggle. "I'm Lanie's husband. I'm not sure when the others will be married, but apparently, almost our entire family works for you."

"It *is* a small world," I admit as all our invisible strings connect in my mind.

"No kidding," a woman who resembles Lizzy states as she joins us. "Hey, Milli. How's it going?" To me, she holds out her hand and introduces herself. "I'm Lanie, Lizzy's oldest sister. You must be Cameron, the proud father of this pint-sized peanut."

Her smile replicates Lizzy's as she points to my daughter—who has yet to let go of her husband.

"Yep. I most certainly am," I say, puffing my chest proudly.

Milli finally releases Ryan's leg and looks around. "Where's my Iz?"

"Oh, she's at home sleeping... I think," Lanie muses.

"Not everyone gets up at the crack of dawn like you," I tease my daughter.

Lanie clears her throat, and I catch her nodding knowingly at her husband.

He agrees to her unspoken message with a nod.

She suddenly turns and asks, "Do the two of you have plans today? We're barbequing and having a bonfire at the beach."

My daughter squeals, "We see my Iz?"

"Oh, I wouldn't want to impose."

Batting a hand in the air, Lanie shakes her head. "Don't feel obligated, but honestly the more the merrier. My sisters, their fiancés, and Ryker are joining us."

Milli puts her hands together and pleads, "Please, Daddy? I wanna see my Iz."

"Honey, it's her day off," I warn, not wanting to intrude.

Lanie quickly assures me, "Oh, she won't mind. Besides, you're new in town. You've already met everyone, and we'd love to have you."

"If you're sure," I draw out, wondering what Lizzy will think of our sudden invasion.

"Perfect. Why don't you pop by the house anytime after three this afternoon. You have our address, right?" Lanie asks.

Nodding, I admit, "I do. Should I bring anything?"

"Nothing but yourselves. We've got everything covered. We're picking up last-minute things now."

"If you change your mind and need something, let me know. I can easily pop into a store if needed," I offer.

"You've got a tiny human to care for. I'm sure being at the store once in a day is more than enough. Besides..." Her brows waggle as she looks to her husband. "We've got plenty of other gofers to fetch anything we'd need. Just bring hoodies and warmer clothes for when the sun goes down."

Compared to California, the weather in Seaside is much cooler. I swear it's hoodie season all summer. However, it's unusually warm this week, or so I'm told. I'll pack appropriate things for Mills and myself, beyond her usual diaper bag.

We say our goodbyes and get back to shopping. Just as they reach the end of the aisle, Ryan turns and asks, "Can Milli bring her bike? I'd love to see her riding solo!"

Milli beams in excitement, and I'm certain Ryan's just become her new favorite person.

*****

Milli is so eager to see "Her Iz" as she refers to Lizzy, that I can hardly get her down for a nap. Of course, that means she is out cold when it's time to finally leave for the barbeque. Knowing she'll never sleep tonight if she doesn't get up soon, I opt to wake her instead of letting her rise naturally. As I approach her door, I pray to the toddler gods, she won't be cranky.

The moment she hears the door snick open, my worry is forgotten as she bolts out of bed and gasps with excitement, "Is it time to see My Iz?"

"Yes, baby girl. Let's get you ready."

The moment her feet hit the floor, she bolts to the bathroom and changes from her Pull-Up. While we're in there, I convince her to let me brush her hair and teeth. In a well-practiced move, I quickly pull her hair back into two braids to keep it from being a tangled mess from the ocean breeze. The moment we're done, Milli shouts, "Let's go, Daddy! I wanna see My Iz."

You and me both, kiddo.

I'm not sure if it's Milli's eagerness or the mere thought of spending the evening with Lizzy that's got me amped up as well. As weird as things started, we've settled into a routine. She shows up before I need to be at work, I join them in any activity they have going on if my schedule allows, and she goes home at night. I know my daughter thinks she's incredible, but I'd be lying if I said I didn't miss her on days we don't see her either.

For the last week or so, I've taken to working late at night once Milli's asleep, just so I can catch an outing at the aquarium or the bookstore with the girls during the day. Sure, I want to spend time with my daughter, but I'd be a liar if I didn't admit Lizzy factors into my new late-night work routine.

Pulling into her driveway, my pulse quickens.

I've tried keeping things professional between us, and I truly hope our coming today isn't a mistake. But there's no way I could disappoint Milli—or myself for that matter if I'm being honest. Even if I can't act upon my feelings, I find myself drawn to Elizabeth Lancaster in a way I've never experienced.

Fuck, that right there is why *I shouldn't* be looking forward to seeing her.

She is Milli's nanny, dipshit.

Milli's obvious attachment to "her Iz" *should* be reason enough to keep my distance from Lizzy. I've never seen her bond with anyone like this—my family included. I can't afford to fuck up our arrangement. We agreed to put things on ice for the sake of this job.

But what about when the summer ends?

Geez, man, get it together.

You have no business thinking about Lizzy like this. She's your daughter's freaking nanny. Hell, who am I kidding? Seeing how she interacts with my daughter makes her more intriguing than when I joked around with her at the coffee shop. I look forward to spending time with her any way I can—even if it is with her *entire family* at this freaking barbeque.

By the time Milli knocks on the door, my nerves are fried.

Why the hell did I agree with this?

When the door flies open, Jax puts my nerves at ease, "Hey, man! It's good to see you." Reaching out to shake my hand, he pulls me in for a man hug and thwacks me on the back before turning his attention to my daughter. "You must be the infamous Milli! I've heard so much about you."

"My Iz here?" Milli asks, looking around his legs into the house.

"She sure is!" Jax beams. "I hope you've brought that bike of yours. I need to see for myself how fast you can ride that thing!"

"Is that you, Mills?" a voice I recognize as Ryan's calls from inside.

That's all the invitation she needs.

My sprite of a child darts by Jax into the house, clearly making herself at home.

"Apparently, she knows where she's going." Jax chuckles. Turning to me, he asks, "Do you need help bringing anything in?"

"Nah, I'm good. But I'd better get her bike, or I'll never hear the end of it." I chuckle. "That girl has been on a mission all day. No one had better get in the way of seeing 'Her Iz.' She's had a one-track mind since receiving the invite."

"I sure hope Lizzy knows how much Emilia has taken to her," I say more to myself than to Jax as I watch her disappear around the corner.

Jax pats me on the arm and says, "Oh, I'm certain the feeling's mutual. Liz raves about her any chance she gets. Go get that bike. I hope you brought your appetite." He thumbs over his shoulder. "They've been cooking all day."

Chapter 14
Lizzy

The hairs on the back of my neck tingle, and I know Cameron's arrived.

I have no idea how I sense it, but the next thing I know, there's a commotion at the door, and Milli's bursting into the living room. That girl has two modes—full speed ahead or hyper focused on her task at hand—well, three. She also sleeps.

She's always on a mission, and at the moment—her sights are set on me.

The second her eyes meet mine, she squeals, "My Iz," and launches herself into my open arms. Scooping her up into a hug, I spin us in a circle. Her giggle is infectious and before I know it, I'm laughing right along with her.

It's hard to believe someone I've known for such a short time can bring me so much joy.

She clings to me like I've seen her do with Cameron after a long day at work. When I stop spinning, her chubby hands cup my face to look me in the eye. "I come for dinner." She beams. "Daddy says I have ta be good... I miss you." She throws her arms around my neck, squeezes me tight, and I gladly return her hug.

"I missed you, too, Mills," I admit. It's only been a day, but this little girl has wormed her way deep into my heart. I find myself thinking of both her and her father much more often than I should on my days off.

"Is this the infamous Mills?" Finn asks, stepping closer to us.

"Yep! She's the one I'm lucky enough to spend the summer with." I beam at my future brother-in-law. I dart my eyes around for Cameron but no such luck.

Milli gasps, drawing my attention to her, then points to one of Finn's tattoos peeking out from his shirt. "You like to draw?"

Chuckling, Finn pulls up his sleeve so she can see the entire tattoo. "Uh, not really. But I like meaningful tattoos. I prefer making the music I've got inked here."

"You make this?" Milli's lips purse together as she reaches for the music notes he has inked on his upper arm and traces a note with her finger.

"It's the opening notes to a song I wrote for Raven," Finn admits, giving his fiancée a knowing glance before returning his attention to us.

Turning to me, she asks, "Your sister?"

Of course, I've told her all about my family. We've spent countless hours together in these past few weeks, and I swear, once this girl's curiosity is piqued, she relentlessly garners all the information she can until she's satisfied. She's precocious for a three-year-old, but then again, what else would you expect from an only child?

As if on cue, Raven steps up beside us. "Hi, Milli. I'm Raven." Pointing across the room, she adds, "That's our sister Sloane. You've already met our oldest sister Lanie."

Milli looks from Raven to Sloane, then back to me.

"She looks like her," Milli observes, pointing at the twins.

"She sure does," I whisper conspiratorially. "But once you get to know them, they're easy to tell apart."

Milli's eyes bounce back and forth between the twins, and I'm certain she's about to say more, but Jax and Cameron enter the room with Milli's bike in tow, and all focus on my family is forgotten.

Squirming in my arms to get down, she pleads, "I ride now?"

"Not yet, squirt," Ryan says before Cameron responds. "Dinner's ready, and you're a speed demon. We need energy if we're gonna stand a chance of keeping up with you later."

A smile plays on his lips as Cameron darts his attention from his daughter to Ryan, then to me. Once his eyes land on mine, I feel a weight I didn't know I'd been holding lift. I've been on edge since Lanie mentioned they might come today. I'm not sure what I've been so worked up about but seeing him here in this moment makes everything right once again.

My heart races when I inhale a faint scent of his cologne. *Mmmm. He smells amazing.*

How does this man both simultaneously excite me and put me at ease?

I don't get to contemplate my response because the next thing I know, my arm is being tugged. "We eat?"

Just like that, Milli's joined my entire family with ease.

*****

True to his word, Ryan does indeed take a turn chasing Milli as she relentlessly rides her bike along The Promenade. At first, it's just Cameron or myself, but then my sister Raven steps up and insists we grab ourselves something to drink and relax and let the others take over. It'll get dark soon, and we'll head to the beach when she can no longer ride.

As Cameron and I walk up the back deck and grab a drink

from the cooler, I can't help but glance back at all three members of Ruby Frax gleefully chasing that precious girl down the path.

"Do you think she knows she's hanging out with one of her favorite bands?" I ask, handing Cameron a beer, while grabbing myself a Pepsi.

"I doubt it," Cameron guffaws. "With my line of work, she'll meet plenty of famous people in her lifetime. I want her to get to know people for who they are to her, not for their notoriety or what they are to the public."

"So, you've given this some thought? I wouldn't have the slightest clue how to handle fame as a parent."

"Yes... and no. It's how I treat everyone—I try not to let reputations precede anyone, good or bad. I focus on getting to know them personally before casting judgement. As for parenting, full disclosure... I make that shit up as I go."

His sexy laugh sends tingles down my spine, and it's all I can do to not close the distance between us. If I didn't already like this man, this right here would be why I could easily fall for him.

"I'm certain that's what everyone does," I admit on a laugh.

"Wanna head out to the beach and start the bonfire?" I suggest. "The guys already brought some wood down to our favorite place, but we may as well go out there and get things started. Does Milli like s'mores? Lanie bought things to make them."

Looking to Milli, Cameron sighs. "Sure, I think she's covered for now."

Slinging a blanket over my shoulder, I grab one of the folded chairs we've set out on the deck and motion for Cameron to grab another for himself.

I don't get more than a few steps before Cameron suggests, "Here, let me get that for you."

I could totally handle it myself, but his *don't be difficult* expression has me giving the chair up with ease.

It takes a few minutes of walking along the path through the seagrass before the ocean comes into view again. Cameron sighs heavily and pauses to look around. "Wow... You got to experience this view every summer? This sunset is gorgeous."

"It's the same in the winter, too," I admit. "Seaside is one of my favorite places in the world. The view from the house is amazing, especially upstairs from Lanie's room. But nothing beats the unobstructed view from the dunes."

"I've spent years in LA. Don't get me wrong, I love their beaches, but I love the simplicity of Seaside—even if it barely gets warm. Wait..." He points to the cove. "Are they surfing over there?"

"Yes, the cove's great for morning rides."

"Wait... you surf, too?" Cameron's mouth drops open.

"We all do... Raven and I can be found out here most mornings when we're not working. Do you surf?"

"I've only gone out a few times. The ocean in Oregon is way too cold for me."

"Duh, that's what dry suits are for," I cut in. "You can go out in your sweats and never get cold."

"Fair point," he muses. "That would make a difference, I'm sure."

When we reach the crest of the next hill, we find Ryan's beat us out here. His back is to us, stoking the fire. The moment the kindling he's placing lights up with flames, he stands and grabs more wood.

"I told you I'd take care of this," I warn when we finally get within earshot.

"I know, but you all looked like you were having too much fun with Mills." To Cameron, he grins. "She's great, by the way. You've got one hell of a kid on your hands."

Cameron nods in agreement. "I can't complain. I got pretty lucky having her come into my life."

The way he says it reminds me of an earlier comment.

What happened between Cameron and Milli's mom?

He always talks as if Milli is a blessing—which she rightfully is, but as far as I can tell, her mom has nothing to do with them. Did something happen to her? I can't imagine walking away from that precious girl—or him for that matter.

As much as I'm dying to know, I won't ask such a personal question in front of Ryan.

Technically, it's none of my business, and I need to remember this.

Besides, if he wants to share the details, he will in his own time.

"So have we." Ryan beams. "She sure knows how to keep you on your toes. I nearly died when Lizzy told us how she thought she was eating bones the other day."

This draws laughter from us all.

"I felt so bad for her," I gasp. "I had no idea she thought I was feeding her dog food."

"She was a hoot when I helped her ride that first day, too." Ryan shakes his head at a memory, then adds, "That girl doesn't know the meaning of giving up. I've never seen anyone more determined to ride a bike... all in one day."

Cameron turns to me. "Lizzy must've been wiped out by the time she went home that night. I know I was... and I barely spent an hour running beside her."

"Her smile made it all worth it," I admit. "But keeping up with Mills has me in the best shape of my life. Between swimming each afternoon and walking all over Seaside, I'll never need a gym membership."

"Kids will do that to you, I suppose," Ryan muses and from the far-off look on his face, I'd bet my next paycheck he's thinking about having his own one day. He would be an incredible dad.

"You guys ready for us?" Raven shouts as she crests the last hill. "We've got a girl who's hoping there will be s'mores and music soon."

"Come on down," Ryan calls back.

My family ascends, and it's blissful chaos.

We're loud, boisterous, and full of opinions.

I wouldn't trade it for the world. It's hard to believe but when I'm on my own at college, I truly miss the noise.

After setting up our chairs and blankets, I settle in and watch the commotion ensue. Milli flits from person to person, chatting them up. My family isn't one to put on airs, so I know their smiles are genuine when she tells them one story or another. Even Ryker is enamored when she uses her whole body to explain how she jumped off the high dive at swim lessons this week.

Eventually, she spots the sand toys I brought out for her earlier, and she settles in the small space between her dad and Ryan and plays in the sand.

"Did anyone see the sign on Harriet's place changed to sold?" Lanie asks the group once we're finally settled around the fire. "I've been so busy, I haven't even noticed anyone touring it."

"Really?" Sloane says on a sigh. "I wanted to see it again. I loved that place when we were kids. It hasn't even been on the market that long."

"I'm sure Harriet would let you see it one last time before the new owners take over," Lanie suggests. "Her number is in that notebook Nana kept by the landline."

Even though she and Ryan live in the house full time, there are still subtle reminders of Nana everywhere—a landline being one of them. Between winter storms and cell reception far too unpredictable, it's something we've kept since Nana passed. I'm not sure any of us were ready to give up the number we'd memorized so diligently as kids, either.

"I sure hope our new neighbors use it for themselves, rather than as a vacation rental," Ryan mutters. "I love how quiet this place is most of the year."

"I never understood why Nana wanted to be here year-round, but I totally get it now that I live here as an adult," Lanie admits.

"Hey now," Jax challenges. "I'll admit I couldn't wait to leave this small town as a kid..."

"No kidding," Ryan chimes in. "I couldn't wait to get out of here either... and look where that got me."

"Exactly," Jax guffaws. "We've both found our way back home—one way or another. You're building your family's business and although the band will likely be on tour again soon, it's where the Lancasters have landed, and you and I both know where they go, we'll be right behind them."

"Guilty as charged," Finn coughs, making us all laugh.

Raven cups her fiancé's cheek knowingly and teases, "Look at you... putting down roots in this town, too."

"I told you, love." He leans in and presses his lips to hers. "Where you go, I go."

My heart melts watching their intimate moment. With Finn's career, he's traveled the world several times over and always has focused on his music—that is until Raven came and stole his heart.

Gah, I want a man to look at me like that someday.

"It's a good thing the two of you bought a house so close," Sloane teases. "I'm not sure I could be *that* far from my partner in crime."

"Oh, please." Raven swats at the air between them. "You

left me at college for a *whole* year while you went off and lived your best life with Jax at the start of his first tour."

"I'd never say living on a tour bus is my best life," Sloane cuts in. Looking to each of the guys in the band, she scrunches her nose and says on a laugh, "Don't get me wrong... I love you all... truly, I do, but I've learned more about each of you than I ever thought possible. There are some things..." She shakes her head in disgust. "Ewww... Just no... It's a good thing you're family, or I might have throttled you a time or two."

Ryker pipes in, "I'm not family. Does that mean you don't love me?"

Ohmigod, that's the most pathetic voice ever. It's a good thing he can sing because his acting sucks.

"Of course, I love you, Ryker. We'll have to work on finding you someone here in Seaside this summer, so you'll want to stick around, too. We can't have the band breaking up because you fall in love with someone in Timbuktu."

Ryker claps his hands together and rubs his palms. "Oh, really... Just who..."

"The point is..." Raven clears her throat. "We're back in Seaside... Together."

"Yes, we are." Sloane beams. "And I, for one, couldn't be happier."

"Oh, I can think of one thing that might make you happier..." Jax challenges and reaches for Sloane's hand.

Sloane's brows knit together. "What's that?"

Where is he going with this?

"Well... I may have done something... Well... It's more of a gift for us... Really... But I've been keeping something from you."

"Jax Cartwright, what have you done?" Sloane jumps in the air and stands to face him. Her hands punch into her hips, and her expression is stern.

Yep, serious Sloane is quick to action when things are left out of her control.

He should know better by now. He's been with my strait-laced sister for nearly two years.

Reaching for her hand, Jax stands. "If you'd like, I can give you a tour of that place as soon as tomorrow?"

"Wha... What do you mean?" Sloane sputters, trying to put the pieces together.

Then it hits me as I replay his words in my head.

Holy fucking shit.

Did he do what I think he did?

My stomach clenches in anticipation as I wait on bated breath for him to drop his bomb of a surprise.

"It's ours, Sloane," he says, barely loud enough to hear over the ocean breeze. But the words are freaking there! Then he adds, "We can move in as early as next month." Suddenly, my entire family is out of their seats, screaming with joy as we rush them for a hug.

Once we pull apart, Ryan says, "Welp, I guess we won't have to worry about *that kind* of annoying neighbors. We'll just have to deal with the two of you."

Chapter 15
Cameron

Watching Lizzy with her sisters makes me wish I had a bigger family of my own. Sure, I have a sister who's six years older than me, but Megan and I aren't as close as the Lancasters. My dad was never around, and Mom's finally enjoying her retirement. Megan's due for another visit soon, but with her busy schedule as an airline pilot, we only meet up when she has a long layover in the area where I'm staying. Now that we live in Seaside for the summer, it's next to impossible for her to get out here unless she schedules a vacation.

"Anyone want a s'more?" Ryker asks, breaking into the bag of marshmallows.

"What's a s'more?" Milli asks as she pops up from playing in the sand beside me.

"Cameron," Lanie gasps. "You've never given this sweet child a s'more?"

"I... Uh... Don't think I have. I tend to keep her away from roaring flames," I tease.

As everyone busts my balls for holding out on Milli, Lizzy reaches for her hand and says, "A s'more is a roasted marshmallow, placed between two graham crackers with a piece of melted chocolate inside."

Milli licks her lips and smiles. "Yum."

"It sure is." Ryker laughs. "Want me to make you one?"

Milli darts her eyes to mine for approval, and she beams. "Yes, please!"

"Why don't you sit on my lap, and we'll watch Ryker roast it for you," Lizzy offers. "The fire is hot, and I'd hate to see you get burned."

And just like that, she's once again proactively putting my daughter's needs first and effortlessly keeping her out of harm's way. My chest squeezes at her natural instincts when it comes to Milli.

Milli climbs into her lap faster than he can get the white glob onto his roasting stick. Ryker quickly puts two marshmallows onto the metal prongs and places the rod closer to the fire.

"Anyone else want one?" Finn asks, roasting two at a time over the red-hot coals.

"See, Milli," Lizzy points out, "look how it's turning golden-brown. Once the whole thing turns that color, it'll be done."

"Ooooh. It's workin'." Milli points excitedly.

"Marshmallows are a fine art," Finn explains. "If we're not careful and put them too close to the flame, they'll catch on fire."

Mills gasps, and Finn continues, "If this ever happens to you, don't panic or shake your stick. It could fly off and burn you."

As if on cue, one of Ryker's catch on fire, and Milli's eyes turn round as saucers.

"Just pull it up slowly and blow on it like this," Ryker demonstrates, and the flames disappear, leaving one blackened marshmallow behind.

Milli's mouth drops into a pout thinking her snack has been

ruined, but I quickly point out. "Don't worry, Mills. Burnt marshmallows taste just as good sometimes."

"That's where we'll have to agree to disagree," Lizzy counters. "*Some* people like them that way, but I much prefer the golden-brown ones roasted to perfection."

"Here, here!" Sloane chants, and we all burst into laughter.

"So... What's this I hear about you having a birthday next week?" Ryker asks Lizzy after handing my daughter an assembled s'more with the less burnt mallow inside.

"It's your birthday?" Milli asks in excitement.

"Yep, the baby of our family is *finally* turning twenty-one next Saturday. We're all gonna be there to help her celebrate!"

"Well, count me in!" Ryker exclaims. "I'll never miss a twenty-one run!" He's quiet for a moment, then he says, "Hey, with you being the only single one in this bunch of love birds, you can count on me as your wingman for the night."

Instantly, I see red.

The thought of him "helping" her while she's drunk is unacceptable.

Lizzy chuckles. "Oh, Ryker. I'm happy to have you join us, but..." Glancing to me, she says, "I do just fine on my own, thanks."

"I go, too?" Milli pipes in, and my scorching-hot rage simmers to a slow burn.

I'm being a jealous asshole, and there's no way I'd ever let my daughter see this side of me in action. Taking in a deep breath to calm myself, I point out, "Sorry, Kiddo. Twenty-first birthdays happen in places where only grown-ups can go. Maybe we can celebrate Lizzy's birthday on another day instead?"

Milli's face drops into a pout, then she gasps and points a finger in the air. "Can I make a cake?"

Lizzy's light laughter is a direct shot to my heart. "Of course you can, sweet girl."

As the conversation around us flows into their father coming for a visit soon, I'm sure details are mentioned, but my focus remains on Lizzy holding my beautiful daughter. Now that the excitement of cake has worn off, I notice Milli's eyes drooping, and she pulls one of Lizzy's arms around her.

When the breeze kicks up, Lizzy effortlessly leans forward and pulls the blanket she had draped over her shoulders around the front of them. Before I can even offer to help, she has them covered and snuggles Milli closer.

Milli visibly relaxes and surprisingly, so do I. With one hand, she fists the blanket and leans further into Lizzy's chest. The moment Lizzy starts patting Milli's back, I know she's a goner. It's a trick I've learned long ago that makes my daughter fall asleep faster than the speed of light once she's relaxed.

I'm not sure how long I get lost in watching the two of them, but one thing is certain—Elizabeth Lancaster is not only the G.O.A.T when it comes to caring for Emilia, she's quickly becoming someone I'm not certain I can live without either.

Chapter 16
Cameron

My phone buzzes in my pocket, and I quickly pull it out to make sure it's not Lizzy. I've been so swamped with work. It's only Tuesday afternoon, but I feel as if the week has been a month long already. Hopefully, Lizzy won't mind staying late again tonight. There's no way I'm finishing what needs to be done at a decent time—and unfortunately, none of this particular project can be done at home.

> Megan: Hey little bro—I've got a few days off this week. Can I swing by and pick up my favorite niece to take her to Disney on Ice?

I'm twenty-eight... and there's nothing little about me I almost type... but think better of it. This is my sister we're talking about, so I point out the obvious.

> Me: There's no swinging by when it comes to Seaside. You know that, right?

Megan: Semantics. I'm renting a car (with a car seat), and I'll pop out Thursday afternoon. I'll stay in your guest room for the night, then drive to PDX. Mills and I will have a spa day on Friday. See the show on Saturday afternoon and come back sometime Sunday. I'm scheduled to fly out Monday evening.

Hi to you, too, Megan. So nice of you to *ask* me if I'm okay with this.

Me: Do I get a choice in this? Or are you being my bossy big sister again?

Megan: Wise ass… can I take my favorite niece or what?

If I thought my schedule was full, Megan's is even busier. I'd never deny her time with Emilia, but I'm her younger brother. It's my duty to be difficult.

Me: Is that all I am to you? The one who supplies your baby fixes?

Megan: Of course. She's the best baby fix in the world. But seriously, smartass… I know you're putting in a lot of hours. With Mom still in Europe, I also know you could use a break. Give me my baby fix, and you'll get your break. I'll spend time with your ugly mug—if I must. Someone's gotta show me around your new town.

Me: Gee, thanks. I feel so loved.

I do—but again, this is Megan. I wouldn't be her favorite pain in the ass brother if I didn't throw shade her way. Of course, I'm her only brother, and I love her fiercely. Our banter is how we've always shown affection.

> Megan: What can I say, I miss you and Emilia like crazy. Let me do this for you. Stop being a PITA and accept my help for the weekend. It's the least I can do.

> Me: I can't wait to see you Thursday.

> Megan: Love you, little bro—see you soon!

With Emilia suddenly having plans for the weekend, I'd better let Lizzy know the change in schedule. I'm sure she'll enjoy a few extra days off, and it'll be an added bonus for her birthday weekend.

Pulling up her contact information, my thumb hovers over the text icon. But wanting to hear her voice, I opt to call instead.

She picks up on the third ring out of breath. "Cameron? Is everything okay? You usually text to check in."

Shit. That's what I get for being selfish.

"No... everything is good. My sister just informed me she is coming into town and taking Mills to Portland for a long weekend."

"Okay..." Lizzy draws out. "What exactly does that mean for me? Do you need me to do anything while she's gone?"

Shit, she's counting on every penny she earns for tuition next year.

"Well, I guess it means you get an extra-long birthday weekend." I muse. "Since this wasn't a part of our schedule, I'll pay you of course."

"That's uh... not necessary."

"Think of it as a birthday bonus. I'm not negotiating this, Liz."

I can hear the smile play on her lips. "Well, if you insist, I'll certainly enjoy the extra time off."

*****

Tonight is my first kid-free Saturday in—hell, I don't know how long.

I should be thrilled.

I should feel relaxed.

I should be doing *anything*—but here I am, staring at my phone, feeling like a fucking creeper.

In my defense, it started with an innocent notification.

Stalking's not entirely my fault.

Thinking it might be a text from my sister, I pick up my phone, and my heart stops in my throat.

Nope. I could only be so lucky.

This notification has nothing to do with Megan or Emilia for that matter.

Lizzy is approaching your destination.

My pulse spikes at the thought of her stopping by.

But why would she come here?

She's supposed to be out celebrating her birthday with her family.

Why does the thought of her stopping by send a rush of adrenaline through me?

I know I shouldn't look, but I can't help myself.

I'm like a moth to a flame when it comes to Elizabeth Lancaster.

When I open the tracking app she insisted I download so we can be notified if we're near one another, my heart sinks to my stomach.

She's now moved past my house and is currently heading downtown.

I know she's got an evening planned with her family—and that presumptuous fuck, Ryker.

Until now, I've always found him to be a decent guy.

But fuck it all if I want him around Lizzy when she's vulnerable and drinking.

The more his words from the bonfire last weekend roll through my head, the more on edge I become.

"Hey, with you being the only single one in this bunch of love birds, you can count on me as your wingman for the night."

Then Sloane's words strike like a lightning bolt, ripping a hole through my chest cavity. *"We'll have to work on finding you someone here in Seaside this summer, so you'll want to stick around, too."*

Sure, Jax and Ryan are from Seaside. But just how many single women in this town are *available* for Ryker? Narrow that small list even further for him to find someone who wouldn't be out for more than a quick claim to fame.

Yes, that was a topic of concern.

I know this for a fact because I heard it with my own ears when I walked into the studio between takes earlier this week. Ryker claimed he isn't interested in something serious. But that didn't stop Jax and Finn from subtly reminding him that neither of them were looking for love when it walked up and smacked each of them respectively in the face.

Look at them—they're both freaking engaged to their very own Lancaster.

Gah, who am I kidding?

Lizzy's the perfect candidate for Ryker.

She's beautiful, witty, and full of life. Best of all, she could give two shits about him being famous.

Fuck, wouldn't that be some positive PR for the band?

I can see the headlines now. "Another Lancaster steals the

last man standing from Ruby Frax, giving a whole new meaning to *family affair.*"

Fuck. My. Life.

Why of all nights didn't she turn off her location?

Does she even know she's left it on?

When her blinking location stops at Pop's Hops, I'm certain it's where she'll stay for a while. The guys talked about Pop's being one of the only places where they can hang out and still be themselves. Who wouldn't want great food, drinks, and live music?

If I didn't feel like such a creeper for knowing her location, I'd stop by myself.

There's only so many places to go in Seaside.

Would it be so bad if I joined them?

And say what exactly?

I... Uh, tracked you here because tonight of all nights you had your location on.

Or better yet—*You insisted I follow you so we could meet up this summer; surely this still applies, right?*

I can see it now.

Not only will Ryan, Jax, and Finn kick my ass. They'll likely sic their significant others on me as well. Lizzy's warned me how protective her sisters are. According to her, they're feral and take no prisoners when it comes to sticking up for those they love.

But—Will that apply to me?

I mean, Lanie herself invited me to that barbeque last weekend.

Yeah—probably because she doesn't know about your past with Lizzy.

Speaking of Lizzy—the way her face lit up when I arrived last weekend was worth all the turmoil I endured as I drove to her house.

She wanted me there. I could feel it deep within my soul.

But would she want me there tonight?

Not allowing my indecision to paralyze me further, I stand and grab my keys and wallet from the kitchen counter.

Fuck it—I deserve a night out, too.

Chapter 17
Lizzy

"You go, girl!" I shout, watching Raven dance around Finn.

We're still waiting for our meal, but the band has started playing "Teenage Dirtbag," and my sister pops out of her seat faster than a bullet and beelines it to the dance floor. Finn is on her heels in an instant. Not only are they belting out the lyrics to the song, but they're putting on quite a show for the rest of us as they dance circles around the crowded floor.

Sloane leans in conspiratorially. "This is the song that started it all for them. Just look at how happy she is. Finn is perfect for her. You know... he's one of the few who knew the difference between us in record time."

"Hey now..." Jax warns. "I can, too."

Leaning in, Jax squeezes her leg, then quickly kisses her on the lips.

"Though if he hadn't called her out for impersonating you..." he shakes his head, "I'm not sure what I would've done."

"Thank God, that shit show is behind us," Sloane huffs out on a laugh. "The paparazzi was insane last summer. Now that we're old news, it's far easier to just be us again."

Raven and Finn had hooked up that first night. Let's just say there was one hell of a case of mistaken identity between my sisters when the photogs caught Raven leaving his hotel room the next morning. To be fair, they're identical twins. The world was going crazy with Jax leaving a solo career to form Ruby Frax. The announcement of him being engaged crushed many a fan's heart—or so I'm told. The gossip rags were out for blood trying to get the scoop on the girl who took him off the market, then cheated on him with his new bandmate. It made headlines around the world.

"You can say that again…" Ryker trails off and shakes his head. "That's probably reason 647 million why I'm not dating anyone. I don't need *that* kind of attention from our fans."

"I don't know." Jax throws his arm around Sloane and pulls her close. "I kinda like being with my fiancée."

"You'd better like it," Lanie cuts in, leaving no room for arguments. "As Dad would say, the moment you put that ring on her finger, the warranty was null and void—no take backs."

"Speaking of Dad." Sloane releases on a heavy breath. That sigh alone says she's delivering unwanted news. "He's postponed his trip out this week. He didn't go into details, but I'm certain he's spinning up."

My stomach clenches, like it does every time I hear he's out on a mission. Don't get me wrong, I love that he's dedicated his life to being a pararescue pilot. But it doesn't mean I like knowing he's in harm's way. I prefer getting the details—after he's home safe and sound.

"Did he sound like he'd be gone long?" Lanie asks.

"Naw." Sloane shakes her head. "I think it's fairly routine, from what little he could say."

We know Dad can't share all the details of his "trips," as he calls them. As we've gotten older, we've learned not to hound him. It's no use—he can't talk about it. However, he's taken to using specific phrases only us girls understand to explain his upcoming mission is a routine procedure and not to worry. It's an impossible request—let's face it, what he does is dangerous. I know he's one of the best and will fight like hell to come back to us safely.

"He'll let us know when he's coming," Lanie assures us. "He's got two weeks of leave during the festival. Aunt Mable is coming out, too."

"Ohmigod. I sure hope she doesn't play matchmaker," I groan, being the only singleton in the family.

Sloane chuckles at the reminder. "You're still safe... for now. After graduation, I'd assume all bets are off with meddling Mable."

Great. Just great. That's the last thing I need.

When the waitress arrives with our drinks, all thoughts of Dad and Mable disappear. Before I know it, Raven and Finn join us from the dance floor, and drinks are passed around the table—somehow, mine finds me last.

Just as mine is placed in front of me, my family lifts their glasses in the air, as if on cue. Not wanting to be left out, I do the same.

"Cheers, Lizzy! Happy Birthday!" Lanie starts, and my family joins with various toasts of "Happy Birthday, To the birthday girl, and Here here," but the one that registers when most settle is, "Drink up."

This may be my twenty-first birthday, but it's not my first cocktail.

Bringing the salty rim to my lips, I quickly get some on my tongue before sipping my margarita through the straw.

Damn, this tastes incredible! It's the perfect blend of sweet and sour.

Cheers erupt, and they burst out singing *Happy Birthday* to me.

Scratch that. Apparently, our commotion stopped the band, and now, the entire bar is singing to me.

Holy shit, it's loud.

When the song comes to an end, I swear my ears feel hot as fiery coals in a campfire. I typically avoid attention like this, but—it's my birthday. I shouldn't expect otherwise.

As the band resumes, thankfully, the chaos around me settles. Now that I'm no longer the center of attention, my body relaxes onto my stool.

Resting my elbows on the high-top table in front of me, I do one of my favorite things in public—watch the crowd. The band is on fire, and couples are living it up on the dance floor in front of us. My family animatedly talks with one another about something that happened the last time they went out, and I'm just sitting here, taking it all in. Pop's is busy, and I finally get what the hype is all about.

God, I love my family. It's rare that we're all in one place. As the youngest, I've witnessed them all go off and find their own lives. I'm happy for them, I truly am. But watching from the sidelines doesn't mean I haven't missed them like crazy. Who knew Seaside would be the place to reconnect us? If Nana hadn't made this feel so much like home, I'm not sure where we'd all be.

When I finish student teaching and graduate next spring, I could end up anywhere. Hopefully, my next adventure won't take me far from my sisters.

Speaking of adventure—I wonder what Cameron's up to tonight.

A smile plays at my lips as flashes from our one and only date fly through my thoughts. Being with Cameron was hands-down the hottest night of my life. If given the chance to go back in time, even knowing our current connections, I swear I'd do it all over again. No questions asked.

I have zero regrets.

Hell, I'm certain that one night with him has ruined me for all others.

Sure, he's my boss, and nothing can happen again, but a girl can daydream, right?

"Hey, man. How's it going?" Jax stands and walks around the table, greeting someone behind me, but I don't pay any attention. He's often recognized, especially being a local in Seaside.

However, when Ryan stands, grabs a chair from another table, then places it beside me, I finally pay attention. "Have a seat. Have you eaten?"

"I could eat," a sexy familiar voice replies, and my eyes practically pop out of their sockets, as it registers who's standing next to me.

"Cameron?" His name comes out as a question because my brain can't process the fact he's here.

His sexy smirk makes my belly flip and a shiver runs up my spine.

God, this man is gorgeous.

Leaning in, he pulls me in for a side hug and kisses me on the cheek. "Happy Birthday, Beautiful," he whispers so only I can hear. "I hope you don't mind me joining you."

All I can do is stare with a dopey smile on my face as three things hit me at once.

First, the man I was *just* thinking about is here.

Did I conjure him? How is this even possible?

Second, he kissed me on the freaking cheek—in front of the world to see.

Third, he called me beautiful.

With my eyes locked onto his, I watch as his handsome face morphs from playful to concerned in a nanosecond. "Elizabeth?"

"W-what?" I sputter.

Way to play it smooth, Lancaster.

When he leans in and whispers, "Is it okay that I'm here?" I'm assaulted by his mouthwatering cologne.

As he steps back, my hand involuntarily clenches his shirt, effectively halting him in place. "Don't..." That one word falls off my lips, and I plead with my eyes, saying the rest.

Don't go.

He darts his eyes between mine, and I'm not sure how long we stare at one another.

"Everything okay?" Ryan pipes in, breaking our trance.

Then, I realize I'm fisting his shirt, so I unclench the fabric and pat him on the chest, twice for good measure.

Clearing my throat, I plaster on a smile. "Yep. It's all good."

To Cameron, I sincerely admit, "I'm glad you're here."

"All right then... Have a seat and let me get you something to drink. What are you having, Cameron?"

Looking around the table, Cameron says, "I'll take a Puckering Pear or whatever stout they have on tap if they don't have it." Reaching for his wallet, he pulls out a card. "I can get it."

Ryan waves his hand in the air. "I'll get this round. You can catch another."

Settling onto the stool next to me, I'm hyper aware of Cameron's every move. His leg brushes against mine, and my entire body hums with excitement. I have no idea what it means that he's here, and frankly, I don't care.

I'm happy he came.

As the conversation flows around me, it's clear no one is surprised to see him. They carry on as if this is something we do every day.

All is good, until my sister Lanie catches my eye and raises a brow, clearly asking, *what's going on?*

No one would think anything of her gesture, but I simply shrug, sending the message, *I have no idea.*

Nana used to say never kick a gift horse in the mouth, and I'm taking that advice. I truly didn't know I was missing Cameron, until he arrived. Now that he's here, my energy soars and somehow, I feel grounded at the same time.

It's crazy what this man does to me.

When the waitress brings our meal, Cameron orders a burger and fries.

While he waits for his food, I offer my fries. "Want some?"

Snagging one, he grins. "Thanks. I'm starving."

"Me, too," I admit, picking up my mushroom burger. The moment I take a bite, I moan in appreciation. "Mmmmm... This is delicious."

"Pop's does make great food," Cameron agrees. "I haven't had a meal here I didn't like."

Curious, I ask, "How's your kid-free weekend going?"

Rolling his eyes, he sighs. "Of course, I miss her, but it's mostly been filled with one firestorm or another at work... but now that I'm here, celebrating you, it's improved."

My body heats as his eyes pin me in place.

When he brushes a piece of hair behind my ear, my pulse skyrockets.

What this man does to me is beyond insanity.

He's my boss, I shouldn't be thinking like this.

But apparently, my body doesn't get the message.

When his food arrives, my drink is empty. Cameron leans in and asks, "Want another or something different?"

"Sure. I'll take another margarita."

He hands the waitress his card to start a tab, then turns to me with a wicked grin. "So, what kind of trouble have you been up to?"

"Hmmmm..." I tease. "This is Seaside; there's only so much to do..."

Slowly running his tongue along his lower lip, as if he's heavily contemplating, he adds, "I'm sure you can think of something..."

"The night's just getting started, and I'm only one drink in... It's pretty mellow for a twenty-one-run."

Looking around my family, he shrugs. Then he leans in and lays down a challenge, "I don't know... the night's still young. A lot can happen. For the record... alcohol shouldn't have anything to do with it."

I swear the mood between us shifts when he lifts his glass to mine, raises a brow, and promises, "Let's make this a night to remember."

Chapter 18
Cameron

I'm not sure what came over me, but the second the words come out of my mouth, a life-altering decision is made, and the tightness in my chest loosens.

I like this woman.

Period.

I'm tired of denying it.

I know I'm her boss, and I'll follow her lead on how she wants to navigate this summer but fuck if I'm not shooting my shot.

We're both adults.

Surely, we can figure something out.

"You good?" I ask, hoping she understands the double meaning of my words. If not, I'll gladly spell it out for her—when the time is right.

Never losing eye contact, she tilts her head to the side and slowly nods.

I'm not sure what her family knows about us, but the only opinion that matters when it comes to us is the beautiful woman's beside me. To reassure her things are good on my end, too, I reach under the table for her hand and give it a squeeze. As I pull away, she surprises me by gripping my palm tighter, then resting our linked hands comfortably on my thigh.

Naturally, my body shifts closer to hers, and this simple gesture gives me hope that we might once again be on the same page.

*****

When the band plays a cover of "Shut Up and Dance" by Walk the Moon, Raven jumps up from the table. "Hey, birthday girl, let's get your ass on the floor." To her sisters, she puts up a finger in warning. "Don't even think about sitting this out... as the song says, shut up and dance with me."

That's all the prompting they need. The next thing I know, every Lancaster is on the dance floor, having the time of their lives. Bouncing to the beat, hips swaying, and hands waving in the air, they sing along with the tune. Each spurring the others to step up their game.

I'm vaguely aware the guys are talking around me, but I couldn't tell you what they're saying. My focus is on Lizzy.

Damn, she's stunning.

I love seeing her so carefree and living her best life with her sisters.

Just as she should.

From our conversations over the past month, I know spending as much time with them as possible is her goal for the summer. Being a father myself, I could only hope that someday Emilia can bond like this with future siblings or at the very least friends if that isn't in the cards for us.

Until this very instant, I've never considered having more kids.

But then again, I've never met anyone I could see myself with long-term.

Hands down—no one compares to Elizabeth Lancaster.

When the song switches to "Moves Like Jagger" by Maroon 5, Ryker says something that catches my attention, "You really think you can get away with that?"

Wait... what's he talking about?

"Hmm... I don't know," Finn muses mischievously. "It could happen..."

"Only if you want your ass handed to you by Mark," Jax warns. "He's a pretty chill dude, but don't forget, he's also a freaking colonel in the Air Force. If you think he doesn't know how to hide a body, you've got another thing coming. Hell, I'd be just as scared of your mom if we're talking about hiding bodies. She literally told me as much when we played in Charlotte. That poor woman's probably been waiting for years on your sorry ass."

"Uh... I'm not sure who'd be worse," Ryan pipes in. "I've seen Lanie react when her sisters have kept things from her. This isn't a little secret—and that twin talk is real. She and Sloane will *both* have conniptions."

"What's going on?" I finally ask when curiosity gets the better of me.

Ryan points his finger suspiciously at Finn. "This guy over here is hoping to run off and get married just weeks after proposing."

"What?" Finn asks defensively. "Raven's not into big extravagant weddings... and now that she's said yes, I don't wanna give her a chance to draw this out forever."

"Bro... you just bought a house *here* in Seaside," Jax points out. Looking out at the dance floor, he adamantly shakes his head, then shivers. "My money's on Sloane stringing you up by the balls—not their dad—if you don't find a way to include the girls in this. You don't have to wait or plan anything big, but for the love of all that's holy, *do not* sneak off and get married."

Ryan leans back and steeples his fingers under his chin as

he gazes at Finn. Finally, he leans forward and asks, "Is there a reason you think she'll bail?"

"No, man. It's not like that... but..." he starts, and his eyes flit to find Raven on the dance floor. "You *all* know how afraid she was of commitment before I came along." Shaking his head, he returns his focus to the guys at the table. "No... I'm not afraid she'll leave me in the slightest. I just don't wanna let *anything* get in the way of me keeping my promise of forever to her."

"So... what's the rush then?" Ryker draws out. "Is this like a shotgun wedding?"

"For the love of fuck, Ryker," Finn chastises and looks around to see if anyone is paying attention. "No, it's not!" he hisses. "For the record, it would be the biggest blessing in the world *if* that were the case. I made her a promise, and I plan to keep it. We don't want to let mundane things like waiting on venues, photographers, and things like that getting in the way. We also want the focus of it to be on us, not the fanfare."

"Makes sense," Ryan muses. "I know I'm not a *rockstar* or anything..." A smirk plays on his lips before he finishes, "But after all the hype of the two of you getting together last summer, I'm sure if word got out about you getting married, it would be utter chaos."

Finn's eyes bulge out, almost comically. "Exactly." Looking to me, he says, "Don't get me wrong, I love my job and have only ever dreamed of this level of success, but I've put my life on hold for years, focusing on music. I found the one woman I want to spend the rest of forever with, and I don't want the chaos of anything extravagant."

"Look at you, getting all lovey-dovey," Ryker mocks. "What's next? You gonna write a banger love ballad, or something?"

"Not the point," Finn growls and throws a fry at Ryker, hitting him square in the forehead.

"Hey now," Jax says on a laugh. "I'm not sure we want *that* kind of attention tonight. The girls will kick *all* of our asses if we get thrown out of Pop's. Besides, if you dumbasses ruin Lizzy's birthday, we'll *all* be in the doghouse, and I for one ain't havin' it."

My job is to make people famous. I've personally been responsible for taking several to the top in this industry and keeping them there for as long as possible. As big as Ruby Frax has become, I'm grateful to see it hasn't gone to their heads. They've got grit, which will take them far in life, but as I think about it, they're also among the humblest musicians I've worked with. They've got their priorities straight—and I admire it both personally and professionally.

"Speaking of dumbasses," Ryan interjects as he stands. "Finn, I love ya like a brother... And you know my two cents... I'm certain this discussion is far from over..." To the rest of us, he thumbs over his shoulder. "Fellas, my wife wants me to join her, and from the looks of it, so do her sisters. Y'all can sit here and bicker among yourselves, but I've got better things to do."

It takes Finn and Jax all of two point four seven seconds before each are up and walking toward their fiancées. The girls light up when they see their significant others join them on the floor. I'm not much of a dancer, but as I watch Lizzy dance among her family, it takes everything in me to remain seated.

When the song turns to a slow one, and the couples pair up, Lizzy turns in my direction.

She barely makes it two steps before Ryker knocks the breath from my lungs when he clears his throat and claims, "I'm not sure what's going on between you and Lizzy, but I'd bet my best guitar there's only one of us that girl is interested in at this table, and it sure isn't me."

Chapter 19

Lizzy

The moment a slow song starts, and couples pair up, that's my cue to exit the dance floor. After weaving around the crowd, I spot Cameron popping up from his stool. In long, determined strides, he rounds the table, his fists clenching and unclenching as he turns toward the dance floor.

Uh-oh, what the hell is going on?

When his head lifts, and our eyes meet, I'm frozen in place. His stony expression is unreadable and makes my nerves fire off like live wires. As his determined strides close the distance between us, my stomach ties in knots. I've never seen this look from him, and I have no idea what's going on in that head of his.

The moment he's directly in front of me, chills run up my spine. The sudden tension between us is palpable, and I see a heat in his eyes I finally recognize.

Ho-ly fuck, this man wants me.

"Wanna dance?" The invitation comes out deep and gravelly, as he reaches for my hand.

Between the want in his eyes and the sexy timbre of his voice, I'm certain I'd follow this man anywhere.

One nod is all it takes.

In a well-practiced move, he simultaneously rests our linked hands on his chest, as his free hand splays across the center of my lower back, pulling me close. The moment we start swaying to the music, my entire body melts into him.

Leaning my head against his chest, I inhale deeply.

Holy hell, this man smells utterly divine. It's a spicy mixture of cinnamon, sandalwood, the ocean breeze, and something I can only determine as Cameron himself all rolled up into one.

Squeezing me tighter, Cameron exhales heavily. "I can't believe how much I've missed this."

We sway for a few beats before my brain needs confirmation. Hating to break away from him, I pull only my head back to look him in the eye. "You've missed dancing?"

A smile plays at his lips. "No. You sexy adorable woman. I've missed you."

There's no way he's saying what I think he is saying, is he?

"I've seen you almost every day for the last month."

"Yes, and in that time, it's been hell keeping my distance."

Pressing my body closer to his, I raise a brow and hedge. "You don't seem to be keeping much of a distance now."

The hand on my back grips me tighter, and his voice is thick when he says, "I was *trying* to be good. I was *trying* to do what's right for Emilia, and I was *trying* to do right by you."

Grinding my hips into his, I innocently ask, "How's that workin' out for ya?"

"Jesus Christ, Elizabeth. Are you *trying* to get me killed?" he spits out.

Well, that's not what I was expecting. "Killed?"

Pursing his lips, he glances over my head, then back to me.

"Right now… there are three disgruntled guys who look like they might kick my ass if I hurt you."

"Oh, please," I huff, and then turn to see for myself.

Oh, shit. He's right. Ryan, Jax, and Finn are *all* glowering at Cameron.

Obviously, they think he's taking advantage of me.

Fuck, I need to prove them wrong before they cause a scene.

Turning back to Cameron, I ask, "Do you trust me?"

By the way his brows pinch together, I can tell he's not following where I'm going with this. But once his eyes meet mine, he whispers, "Of course, I trust you."

"One last question… Do you still want to keep your distance?"

"What do you think?" he says, gripping my back tighter.

That's all I need.

Throwing an arm around his neck, I reach up and run a thumb along his cheek with my free hand. Guiding his face closer, I press my lips to his and kiss the ever-loving hell out of him. The chemistry we've been concealing all summer explodes between us, and I can't get enough.

I may have started this kiss, but Cameron quickly takes over.

When his tongue sweeps against mine, I know I'm a goner.

He deepens our kiss, and I cling to his body with all my might.

A tidal wave of emotion swells within me. I've been denying my feelings for this man for way too long.

Here, at this moment, I'm done.

I want Cameron Kruse in every way possible, and it's time I let everyone know it.

Thank God, Cameron has the sense to remember where we

are. Before I can get too carried away, he breaks our kiss, leaving me breathless and panting.

A sexy smirk plays on his lips as he watches me catch my breath. "For the record, I will *never complain* about you kissing me like that, but what exactly was I trusting you for?"

Glancing toward my family, I see an assortment of expressions on each of their faces. Most are stunned, some are confused, while others are in awe of what they just witnessed, but none look like they want to kick Cameron's ass.

Mission accomplished.

"For allowing me to save you from an angry mob."

Chuckling, he challenges, "So, this was all for the sake of safety?"

"That... and I'm showing them this is *my* choice. That you aren't taking advantage of me... Because... I want to be with you, too."

"Thank fuck that's settled," Cameron mumbles. "I wasn't sure how I was gonna convince you to change our arrangement when I walked in tonight or how we'd tell your family about us, but with a kiss like that, I'm certain they'll figure things out for themselves."

Nuzzling his face into my neck, he whispers, "I know we have a lot to talk about, but for the record, birthday girl, plan on going home with me tonight."

"I can't think of anything I'd want more," I admit, and then kiss him once again.

Chapter 20
Cameron

Knowing she's coming home with me tonight is the only thing keeping me rooted in this bar. Since we're celebrating her birthday, I'm determined to make it a night she'll remember. She and I have the entire night ahead of us, and I won't cut short time with her family on her special day.

As we dance to a few more songs, it hits hard just how much I've missed having her in my arms. Holding her close is one of the best feelings in the world. I can't tell you how many times I've dreamt of this possibility but given our situation, I've always held back.

She's like a ray of sunshine after the gloomiest of storms. Putting things on hold since the start of summer has been torture. Now that she's made her feelings public, I'm determined to find a way to keep her.

Eventually, we return to the table, and I order us all another round of drinks. This time, I order a Coke, and Lizzy chooses water for now. When we've all got a drink in front of us, Raven clears her throat and addresses the elephant in the room.

"So... exactly how long has this been going on between the two of you?"

"It's not what you think," Lanie jumps in, and Raven throws daggers her way.

"What do you mean?" Sloane interjects.

Sighing heavily, Lizzy states, "It's truly a long story... so before any of you get your panties in a wad, or decide you need to defend my honor... you should know Cameron and I actually met last semester in Portland. No... he's not taking advantage of me. Nothing's happened since we've been in Seaside, until tonight... which as you saw... I initiated."

"But... you work for him!" Sloane interjects.

"Uh... we kinda all do," Ryker muses, clearly wanting the inside scoop.

A beautiful smile forms as her eyes meet mine. "When we met, we had no idea how small our worlds would be. Trust me... It's way smaller than you think. We cut things off when we left Portland, neither knowing we'd end up in Seaside of all places."

Before Lizzy says another word, I reach for her hand on the table, link it with mine, and show them exactly where I stand.

"I had no idea any of you were connected to Lizzy. Hell, I got the shock of my life when my mom picked her of all people as the top candidate to be Emilia's nanny. At the time, your sister and I made an arrangement to put our feelings aside for the summer... and I swear on Emilia's life... Nothing nefarious has happened between us since she started working for me."

"Look," Lizzy says, regaining control of the conversation. "I really like him. Sure, Cameron and I have a lot to work out, but *nothing* needs to be settled tonight. Seriously... you know as much as we do about where this is going... you can give me the tenth degree *after* Cameron and I have figured things out... but give us time to do that... Okay?" she trails off.

"Does Emilia know?" Sloane asks.

"Not yet," I admit. "But when the time is right, she will."

"That makes sense," Lanie agrees.

"Look, I know this is an extremely unusual situation... Given you all work with me in one way or another. But I give you my word... *I will always* keep our professional lives professional. I won't treat any of you any differently, and the decisions I make at work will reflect what needs to be done for the sake of the job."

Inhaling deeply, I search for the right words to explain everything adequately. "From the day I met Elizabeth Lancaster, my life has flipped upside down. She's not only captured my heart but has completely stolen my daughter's, too. I've tried like hell to deny my feelings, but now that she's let hers be known, there's no way I'm letting her go."

"Point taken." Jax nods in understanding. "I'm, by no means, speaking for the rest of her family, but I for one appreciate your directness."

Finn adds, "If Lizzy's happy, then I'm happy... but I'll give you the same warning I got when I started seeing Raven. It's not the colonel you should worry about should shit go sideways... these sisters are a force to be reckoned with, and you can officially consider yourself warned."

This makes the entire group burst into laughter, and any remaining tension dissolves instantly.

Grinning from ear to ear as she shakes her head, Lanie demands, "Enough with the heavy talk... we've got a birthday to celebrate!"

*****

"I thought we'd never make it home!" I growl between kisses as we fumble through my front door.

"No... kidding," Lizzy pants as she claws the hem of my shirt, pressing her lips to mine. "Mmmm... Need... You."

Running my hands along her back, I kiss along her jaw to

that spot under her ear that drives her wild. "You've got me," I promise on a deep exhale.

From the moment she claimed me with that kiss on the dance floor, an undercurrent of pent-up tension has been building between us. By the time we left the bar, I'm wound so tight, I might explode. I need this woman more than I need my next breath.

I nip, suck, and lick along her collarbone as her hands roam my body. Her silky-smooth skin makes me burn with desire. When I feel my shirt tug against my back, I reluctantly break our connection and hastily pull it over my head, then toss it to the floor.

Heat flows through me as I watch her eyes widen with hunger. My dick jumps in my jeans when I catch her tongue sliding along her lower lip.

Fuck, that's sexy.

Memories of just how talented that tongue of hers is makes my cock grow even thicker. The vixen catches the movement and smirks in the most seductive way.

"If you're gonna ogle, it's only fair I get a show, too..." I warn.

"Wha...?" she starts, but I cut her off.

"Strip..." I challenge, toeing off my shoes. After I've kicked them aside, I add, "I wanna see that sexy ass of yours... naked. Start with your shirt."

Forcing myself to remain frozen in place as she crosses her hands over her waist is torture. My pulse races when she reaches for the hem of her blue V-neck and slowly drags it over her head, revealing the sexiest royal-blue bra I've ever seen.

It's the perfect contrast to her sun-kissed skin. It's satin and lace and forms to the contour of her curves perfectly.

When she tosses her shirt on the floor beside mine, she stops and stares.

God, her tits are fucking perfect.

They're round and full and heave with every breath she takes.

The longer I stare, the harder her nipples pucker through the sheer lace.

Groaning, I run a hand down my face.

When I can't take it any longer, I step closer. "Fuck, you're gorgeous, Elizabeth."

A slow smile spreads across her face, and she darts her tongue along her lower lip, driving me wild. "You're not too bad yourself, Cameron."

The way my name rolls off her lips sends tingles racing up my spine, and my muscles contract in anticipation. No one in this universe holds a candle to the woman before me. Not only is she hot as hell and makes my cock turn to steel with just a simple look, her beauty shines from the inside out. I know for a fact she gives as good as she gets, and I can't wait to spend the night with her in my arms.

It takes everything in me to hold my ground and not devour her right this very instant. For the longest time, we just stare at one another, letting the tension between us grow so thick, I can barely breathe.

I'm one second away from throwing my patience to the wind and undressing her myself when she lifts a brow and challenges, "You gonna drop those pants of yours?"

Fuck, this woman might be the death of me.

But if it's a game she wants, I'll play along.

Slowly, I reach for the fly of my jeans and pop the button free.

I don't miss the way her breath hitches as I torturously lower the zipper in a measured pace. My pulse thunders in my ears as I push the dark denim over my hips and let them drop to the floor. In only my boxers, I step out and challenge, "Your turn."

After kicking off her shoes, she seductively mimics my motions, giving me the hottest strip tease imaginable. Her jeans hug her curves. She adds the sexiest shimmy to get them over her hips before dropping them to the floor. Standing there in her black high-cut cotton underwear and lacy blue bra, she grins adorably and takes my breath away.

All willpower disappears as my eyes roam over her.

"You're fuckin' perfect."

But she's still too far away. Reaching for her hip, I pull her closer.

The moment our lips touch, an inferno ignites.

Her arms fling around my shoulders, she fists my hair, and her lips crash onto mine. Standing to my full height, I pull her up my body until her legs wrap around my waist. Then, I kiss her back for all I'm worth.

She feels fucking incredible, and I can't get enough.

I need more.

I want to devour her right here in the entryway, but the thought of licking every square inch of her on a soft bed has me hightailing it to my bedroom. Once we're at the foot of my bed, I lean forward and lay her on the mattress, then stand to take this moment in.

Holy fucking hell, she's breathtaking.

Splayed out on my bed, her soft, brown hair fans around her face, and her freckled cheeks are flushed. In this light, her hazel eyes look greener than I've ever seen before, and I'm mesmerized by the sexy smile playing at her lips.

When she starts shimmying up the bed to make room for me, I reach for her legs and stop her. "Not so fast, sweetheart," I murmur, dropping to my knees. "I've waited way too long, not to taste every inch of you."

Running my hand down her silky-smooth leg, I lift it slowly and kiss, lick, and suck my way to her inner thigh. She squirms in anticipation when I reach her center, and it drives me wild. I swipe my tongue along the edge of her underwear but skip right over the place I know she needs it most. She drags out my name as a plea just before I reach for her other leg and repeat the process.

"Cameron... please..."

When my mouth drags along her apex once again, she rocks her hips, fisting the comforter beneath her as if her life depends on it.

Her skin heats, and her hips buck wildly when I run a finger along the edge of her panties. Wanting to draw out her pleasure, I return my focus to her legs by trailing kisses along her inner thigh. She arches higher, and a strangled moan escapes, making my dick strain in my boxers.

"Cam... I... Oh, fuck... that feels good."

Slipping a finger under the fabric, I slide effortlessly through her slick folds.

She's soft, warm, and oh so wet.

"Damn, you're soaked, Elizabeth."

"Need... These... Off," she pants, thrusting her hips into my hand as she pushes at her underwear.

Taking the hint, I quickly help her slide them off. "Been dying to do this forever," I groan in anticipation as I widen her thighs and settle between her legs.

I fucking love how she relaxes and lets me in, rather than being shy. Her confidence is a turn-on, and my dick twitches in appreciation.

But I ignore it and focus on her.

With her beautiful bare pussy on full display, I moan, "Mmmm... Liz... You're fucking beautiful."

Sliding a finger along her slick heat, I'm rewarded with a guttural cry, "Oh, Cam... so good."

Her back arches into me as I circle her outer lips, purposely skipping her clit. I know it's sensitive, and I want her begging with need before she falls apart on my face.

"More, Cam... I... Fuck... Oh...My..." Her outburst becomes a gargled slur of words the moment my tongue traces the same pattern as my finger.

"I love this sexy cunt of yours," I say between flicks of my tongue. "Soft and sweet and oh so perfect."

After one taste, I'm certain I didn't spend nearly enough time between her legs the last time we were together. I'm for damn sure making up for it tonight. She tastes like heaven, and the way her body responds makes me want to feast on her for days.

Every few strokes, I slide my tongue along her clit, and she bucks in appreciation. Needing to milk out every ounce of pleasure from her, I shallowly insert a finger and rim her opening. I'm rewarded with her fist clenching my hair and pressing my head right where she wants me.

"C-Cam... I...Oh my... Fucking god... More..."

After a few more circles, I add a second digit and press further into her tightness. In and out, around the rim, and as deep as I can go, I fuck her with my fingers as my mouth focuses on everywhere but her most sensitive spot. When I add a third finger, her hips thrust wildly. Needing to keep her in place, I press my other hand on her lower abdomen and devour her completely.

By the time I give into her needs and finally suck her clit into my mouth, she practically levitates from the bed. My pride soars as a slur of her curses fill the room.

Fuck me, she's turned on.

Her grip tightens on my hair, and her body stiffens.

She's so fucking close, and I'll be damned if I can't push her over the edge.

It's a painful pleasure, and I'm certain I'll be bald before the night is over.

But who needs hair?

I could eat her for breakfast, lunch, and dinner and never tire of her taste.

When I point my tongue and rapidly flick her clit, her thighs tighten around my head.

Massaging her g-spot, I press harder.

"Cam... I'm..." is all the warning I get before her once wild body stiffens, and I feel tremors start deep from within.

"Ohmigod... Cam... I'm..." is the last thing I comprehend before her legs become a vise grip on my head and screams of ecstasy fill the room.

Her coming on my face is hands down the hottest thing ever.

Pulse after pulse, I stay with her. Making sure I milk every last ounce of pleasure, I relentlessly maintain my rhythm.

When her trembling subsides, I stand and slowly kiss up her body. She barely moves a muscle until our eyes meet. Then, a lazy smile slowly spreads across her face.

"You good?" I ask when she doesn't reach for me.

"I'm wrecked... In the best possible way..." she says on a whimsical sigh.

Leaning in, I kiss her tenderly.

She feels like heaven came to earth. I'd stay here all night, if it weren't for my legs hanging awkwardly off the end of the bed.

This just won't fucking do. Reaching for her, I suggest, "Need help getting further up the bed?"

She remains lifeless but whispers, "Probably..."

Chuckling, I capture her lips once more before dragging her like a ragdoll to a more comfortable position for the two of us. When her head rests on the pillow, I snuggle in beside her on my side.

Her warmth against my body brings a sense of peace I never expected.

Tucking a hand under my head, I prop myself up and stare down at her beautiful face.

God, she's fucking gorgeous. Her skin is flushed and radiates blissfully in my arms.

Tracing small circles along her torso, she doesn't flinch. The only movement I can clock is her eyes and even that seems to be an effort. Smiling at her dazed expression, I tease, "Did I break you?"

A sexy smirk slowly forms as she sighs, "Broken... No... Wrecked me for life... Possibly. I have *never* experienced anything so intense."

Yeah, my ego soars with that one.

A triumphant grin spreads across my face knowing I did this to her.

"I don't know..." I tease, gently circling her areola through her bra. "It's your birthday; I still might have some tricks up my sleeve."

"Thank God you're almost naked," she huffs out on a laugh. "I'm not sure I can handle more tricks."

As if my dick has a mind of its own, it chooses this moment to bob against her thigh, drawing her attention. An infectious grin spreads across her features, and she rolls onto her side to face me.

Sliding her hands into my underwear, she cups my balls and squeezes them lightly before dragging her hand along the length of my cock. "Hmmm... I think he's ready to play."

"Oh, he's been ready all night, but it's not *his* birthday. We're here to pleasure *you*, birthday girl."

Raising a brow in challenge, she asks, "Does that mean I can do *anything* I want with you?"

"Your wish is my command," I promise.

"In that case... We've got far too many clothes on."

In an instant, her energy returns, and she pops onto her knees beside me.

Reaching behind her, she unclasps her bra and tosses it to the side.

My mouth dries as I take in her beautiful tits. Her pebbled nipples hang inches from my mouth and beg to be played with.

Reaching out, I run a thumb around one, and it gets even harder. "Why do I feel as if it's *my* birthday?"

Pulling her closer, I run my tongue around her dark pink areola, then suck her nipple into my mouth.

"God... I'm so sensitive," she warns.

"Is this what you want..." I ask between kisses along her cleavage to give her other one the same attention.

"Only if you let me ride you while you're doing it," she says, straddling me. "Sit against the headboard."

She doesn't have to tell me twice.

As I move up the bed, she tugs at my boxers.

I lift, and she has them off me in an instant.

The moment her silky thighs straddle mine, my cock bobs between us, begging to get in the action.

Christ, this woman is a wet dream come to life.

Sitting face-to-face, she reaches for my hand and places it on her breast. Then, she squeezes her hand around mine and doesn't let go. Her chest heaves at the sensation. With our eyes locked, she cups her other tit with her free hand and simultaneously squeezes my hand in hers while she uses her thumb to play with her other nipple.

Moaning in pleasure, she rocks against my lap.

"Fuck me…" I groan in appreciation.

This is hot as hell.

Every nerve in my body is on fire for this woman.

"I thought you'd never ask." She grins triumphantly.

The next thing I know, her lips are on mine, and her slick heat grinds against my straining cock. "Ah… that's it… use my cock how you need it," I encourage.

And use my cock she does.

Fuck, her slick heat has me panting with need.

My dick thickens as she rides along my ridge.

When tingles spark at my spine, I warn, "Fuck, Liz… I'm not gonna last long like this… You feel *too* good."

When she grips me in her hand, I'm sure she's gonna stroke me, and I'll be done for.

But instead, she lifts up and uses the head of my cock to trace around her clit.

Once, twice, three times.

Holy shit, she's wet.

"Take me, Liz…" I demand, wanting her fantasies to come to life.

On her next thrust, she aligns our bodies and slides her glorious heat onto me.

"Fuuccckkkk." Roars from my chest erupt as she bottoms out.

My brain short circuits, and I'm filled with so much need, I can't wait for her to adjust. She feels too good.

The moment her hips rock into mine, all bets are off.

Her fingers dig into my shoulders for balance as she grinds onto me. She's tight, wet, and feels so fucking phenomenal. For the longest time, we get lost in one another as she takes what she wants.

Eventually, she breaks the silence with a pant. "I want…"

"What... What do you need, baby?"

When she doesn't say anything, but picks up the pace, I demand, "Tell me what you want, Elizabeth."

"Nipples... Please... Play with my nipples. Play with them, Cameron, while I fuck you senseless."

My body hums in delight by the way she's taken charge.

Her full beautiful tits bounce mere inches from my face, and I waste no time giving her what she wants... scratch that— what she needs.

Reaching for the closest one, I run my thumb over the pointed peak before pulling it into my mouth.

Fuck me—her moan of pleasure will be burned into my memory for eternity.

It's loud, feral, and full of need.

I will die before disappointing her.

Sucking and teasing with my mouth, I roll her exposed nipple with my thumb and pinch it lightly.

"More, Cam... Harder..." she demands.

When I comply, her movements become frenzied. I'm rewarded by her cries. "Fuck, Cam... I'm... So close."

Her grip on my shoulder tenses as her tight pussy clenches me like a vise.

I can tell she's close but needs help tipping over the edge. Simultaneously, I suck her tight pebbled nipple further into my mouth and flick it fervently with my tongue, while rolling and pinching the other. She cries out as her body suddenly stiffens, and I feel wave after wave of her pleasure crash through her.

Gripping her hips, I take over and top her from the bottom. The moment my balls tighten, I swear I barely thrust once more before my release explodes through me.

My orgasm bursts through me faster than lightning, burning me up from the inside out. My legs go numb, my vision goes black, and I'm fighting like hell for my next breath.

As she collapses against me, the last thing I remember is wrapping my arms around her and holding on for dear life.

"If I die, this is how I wanna go."

Chapter 21
Lizzy

I have no idea how long I've stayed plastered against Cameron's chest. I'm wrecked beyond belief. I couldn't move if I tried. My arms feel like heavy weights, my spine's nonexistent, and my legs are Jell-O. My eyes may as well be glued shut, and I don't want to even think about opening them.

My first orgasm of the night had me sated.

This one... well, it might have killed me.

Is this what heaven feels like?

All I can do is breathe in and out, matching my breaths to Cameron's as my heart rate slows.

I'm certain I've never been this blissed out in my life.

I'm vaguely aware when my body shifts, and there's a burst of cold air against me. But it's quickly replaced with warmth, and all is forgotten as I snuggle into the softness that surrounds me.

*****

The next thing I know, my head rises and falls with every breath Cameron takes. He's drawing lazy circles across my back, and I'm snuggled into his side. There's no place I'd rather be.

"Hey there, sleepyhead," Cameron greets when I finally force my body to move and make eye contact.

Stretching, I ask, "How long have I been out for?"

"Uh... It's almost six... So, a few hours," he says quietly.

"Holy shit. Have you been awake this entire time?"

Pulling me close to his chest again, he kisses the top of my head. "No... I woke up about twenty minutes ago."

"Why aren't you sleeping?" I ask.

The moment the words leave my lips, his body tenses.

"I... Uh..." he hesitates, and I frantically dart my eyes to his.

Slowly, he pushes some of my hair behind my ear as his brows knit together.

"What's wrong, Cameron?" I ask, my chest filling with dread.

"I... Uh... Got carried away last night."

Unease washes over me, and I start pulling back, but he stops me.

Shaking his head, he quickly adds, "That didn't come out right... Let me try again."

"Okay..." I draw out, fear still not eased in the slightest.

His forlorn expression has my stomach tying in knots.

Why is he suddenly fumbling over his words?

Does he think this was a mistake now that he's had a chance to sleep on it?

Reaching for my hand, he squeezes it once.

"Fuck... I don't know how to say this... But... We... Uh... Didn't use protection. It was irresponsible of me, and I'm sorry. I've *never* not used a condom, and I haven't been with anyone since you."

Relief washes through me in an instant.

"What are you smiling about?" His question slowly comes out as if he's piecing together a puzzle he can't solve.

"First, I'm clean and on birth control. I *also* haven't been with anyone since you. So... We should be safe there."

When his brows knit together, confusion washes over me once again.

I replay his words in my mind and feel as if something's off.

"Wait... You've never gone without a condom..." That doesn't make sense. "But... what about Emilia?"

"Condoms are only 98% effective, even when used properly." he says gravely.

"Are you afraid that I'll get pregnant?"

It doesn't make sense.

Why isn't he looking at me?

"No... Not really. And even if you did, we'd deal with it *together*, I'm sure." He's quiet for moment, then his lips purse together. "Wait... If you weren't worried about getting pregnant, why did you look upset just now?"

"Uh..." Shit. How do I say this? "I thought maybe you were having second thoughts about us... You know... Since I'm Emilia's nanny and well... All my family's connections to you. A lot could happen while I was sleeping."

He's quiet for so long, I look away in fear of what he might say. His finger finds my chin and directs my eyes back to his. "Let's get one thing straight... I have zero regrets being with you, Elizabeth. Sure, we have things we need to talk about, but I'm certain we can figure out the minor details. For the record, this is between you and me and although your family is important when it comes to you... as far as I'm concerned, my connections to them professionally will not impact us being together."

Again, relief flows through me, but something is still off. As I replay his words in my head, a discrepancy hits. I have no idea what's happened with Emilia's mother, but I guess now's as good of time as any to get to the bottom of my questions.

"Wait... You said you've never gone without a condom... Does that mean Emilia wasn't planned?"

Cameron grunts out a laugh. "Oh, that's an understatement."

"If you don't mind me asking, what exactly happened with her mother? You never speak of her."

"It's kind of a long story. But you deserve nothing less than the truth."

He inhales deeply and releases his breath. Then he slowly adds, "I... Uh... Just hope you don't think differently of me once you know."

I can't imagine there'd be much he could say that would change my mind about him. I've seen how he is with Emilia. He's an amazing father and always puts her needs first. He's kind, thoughtful, and has never shown a single red flag.

Before I can say anything, he quickly adds, "Why don't I make you some breakfast, and I'll explain everything?"

As much as I don't want to leave the cocoon of his bedroom, if he thinks I won't take it well, maybe I should put some clothes on for this discussion.

Standing from the bed, he walks gloriously naked to his dresser and pulls a pair of boxers from his drawer, then tosses me a t-shirt. "Here put this on." Then with a sexy smirk, he shrugs. "I'm not exactly sure where your clothes are."

Thinking back to last night, I grin. "You and me both, buddy."

Once we're in the kitchen, Cameron goes through the motion of making blueberry pancakes. To pass the time, I cut some cantaloupe and make each of us a cup of coffee.

When I ask if he wants creamer, he shakes his head. "Just black coffee for me."

"You have peppermint creamer in the fridge; don't you drink it?" I point out, clearly confused.

"No..." he draws out, lifting his head to face me. "But you do."

He winks, and my belly swarms with butterflies. He's always putting others' needs first. I have no idea what he'll tell me about Emilia's mom, but I find it hard to believe my feelings for him could change because of it.

The next thing I know, we're sitting at the bar, half-naked for breakfast.

His black t-shirt hits me mid-thigh and since I didn't want to spend any time apart from him searching for my underwear, I settled for this. He's wearing a pair of boxers and nothing more. He's sexy as sin and if we didn't have more pressing issues to address, I might suggest skipping breakfast and feasting on him instead.

Grinning at the thought, I muse, "I could get used to this."

His navy-blue eyes smolder as he looks me over from head to my painted pink toes. "So could I, Elizabeth."

After a few bites, I break the silence by ripping the Band-Aid off the elephant stampeding in the room. "So where exactly is Emilia's mom?"

"I honestly don't know," he admits.

When my eyes widen, he quickly adds, "Like I said, it's a really long story that starts with a short beginning..." He darts his eyes to mine and back to his food before adding, "Which is why I... Think you might think differently of me."

"Okay..." I drag out. My mind is already racing with possibilities, but I'm hoping my silence prompts him to put me out of my misery soon.

Clearing his throat he starts, "I met Heather, Emilia's mom, in Boston. I was on tour, promoting Purple Flame, an alternative rock band. They were making a name for themselves and had quite a bit of groupies. I was fresh out of college and single as could be, living up the rockstar lifestyle. My life consisted of riding the tour bus, promoting the hell out of the band, and searching for new talent."

I cringe at that last bit; I know exactly what kind of lifestyle he was living. My sisters have spent months on tour buses, and the single guys are never lonely, or so I'm told.

Cameron takes a long drink of juice, then continues, "Heather had come to an after party with her friends. She wasn't interested in the band as it was her friend's favorite. She had never even heard of them and was just along for the ride. Apparently, from the moment they arrived at the party, she had her eyes set on me. She was on vacation from Salt Lake, attending college and was looking for an experience she'd never forget.

"I was young... Dumb... And... Well, you get it. Being part of management, I was never into groupies. But when we started talking, and she told me she wasn't into the guys in the band whatsoever, and her interest was only in me, it made her stand out from other girls I'd met on tour. As we talked, we quickly found we had more in common than I would've imagined... Not that it matters."

Sighing heavily, he shakes his head and looks to me. "I won't lie to you. You've seen Emilia. She's beautiful... And she gets a lot of that from her mom. Sure, I'm mixed in there... But keep in mind, I was twenty-four... Single and living what I thought was my best life touring with the guys from Purple Flame."

"Most guys that age would do the same," I admit.

"Heather and I literally spent one night together... Hell... I wouldn't even call it that. A few hours at best... But it changed my life forever."

Sighing heavily, he glances my way. "I swear to you, I never heard from her again until nearly eight months later. By then, I was back in LA, and she was long forgotten. Heather tracked me down via the label and made an appointment to meet with me."

My stomach clenches when he adds, "As awful as it is, I didn't even know her last name. When she walked into my office, round belly and all, I was shocked to say the least. I recognized her instantly but didn't understand why she'd track me down."

Holy shit, I can't imagine being a fly on that wall.

"At first, I'd thought for sure she was out for money... If the baby was even mine. Everyone would question it... Given our circumstances. But Heather didn't come to ask anything of me."

"What do you mean?" I ask, curiosity getting the better of me.

"She walked into my office and simply stated, 'Cameron, I know you don't know me, but you're the only person I've slept with since losing my virginity to Justin Ames my senior year of high school.

"The way she said it made me believe her. What drove her point home was when she told me she originally had planned to get an abortion. But her parents were extremely religious and convinced her to put the baby up for adoption instead. She told me there was a family picked out at her church, but she couldn't go through with the adoption without letting me know first."

The weight of the room is heavy as he takes in another deep breath and continues, "She already felt guilty enough walking away from her unborn child... But she'd made the choice and was determined to follow through with her decision. She had goals for herself and knew being a mom at her age wasn't what was best for the child."

"So, why did she come to you?" I ask softly.

"She couldn't go through with the adoption without at least letting me know I have a child in the world."

"Well... that's... commendable," I mutter.

Fuck, is that the right word?

Cameron ignores my comment. "I later found out that she'd been accepted into med school that fall. She had an eight-year plan in place... And one night with a stranger wouldn't ruin it for her. Since she truly didn't want anything from me other than to let me know of the baby's existence, I had no choice but to believe her."

He glances my way and answers the question on the tip of my tongue before I can even ask. "Of course, a prenatal paternity test was done. But long story short, I knew within a week the baby was mine. Before she could travel home, she went into labor. The next thing I knew, my daughter was born.

"Every doubt I had disappeared the second I saw Emilia. Not only were her eyes identical to mine, but instantly, I felt a connection I still can't describe, and I couldn't let her go."

He looks at the ceiling and shakes his head at a memory.

My heart aches for this man.

"What happened next?" I prompt.

"Immediately, I filed for sole custody. Thank God, I'd already consulted a lawyer and had everything in place. Heather wanted to have a sealed record of her birth. In that, she signed all legal and parental rights away. From the day Emilia was born, she's been mine."

Whoa, I'm not sure what I was expecting, but it certainly wasn't this. My head spins as I process everything. His words from before play through my mind, and it finally makes sense.

Why did he think I would think less of him?

I don't get it. If anything, hearing their story makes me fall harder for him.

I can't imagine my life changing on a dime and running with it as well as he's done. In less than a week, he went from single and carefree to a dad, doing it on his own. Most have nine months to prepare. Cameron had days.

"You're freaking incredible," I mutter as I think of all he went through for the sake of Emilia.

"I... Uh... Wouldn't say that. I've been faking it until I make it from the start... Trust me." A low chortle escapes as he admits, "Thank God for my mom. Without her, I'm not sure where we'd be."

"What I don't get is why would you worry I'd think less of you for any of this? Is there more you haven't told me?"

"You got the condensed version, but I'm not keeping anything from you, if that's what you're asking."

"Cameron, you're one of the most incredible humans I've ever met. What part of this could possibly make me not like you?"

Running a finger along his nose, his chin drops. "The part where I was a player... Hell, I didn't even know Heather's last name."

"Uh, last I checked," I draw out for emphasis. "Most guys in their early twenties are. Scratch that... We're *all* supposed to have fun in our twenties, not just the guys. Now, if you're in a committed relationship, that's different. Why would I judge you for living the single life to its fullest? Trust me... I've heard stories from Finn and Ryker about being on tour. Jax is an anomaly because he wasn't on tour until after he was dating Sloane."

His brows knit together, and his lower lip rolls under his teeth. Irritation rolls off him when he snidely asks, "Does this carefree single life apply to *you*?"

Of all things, he chooses to focus on *that*?

I quickly remind him, "I wasn't a virgin or anything when we met. You know that, right? But I..."

"Wait!" he cuts me off, then grumbles, "I don't wanna hear about you sleeping with other men."

A smile plays at my lips. "Good to know. But the truth of the matter is until I met you, I'd never slept with anyone I wasn't committed to."

Squinting his eyes, he barely looks at me when he asks, "Was there a lot of... commitments?"

"No, you jealous fool." I push at his shoulder and laugh. "There haven't been many."

Relief washes over his features, and he takes my hand in his. "For the record, Elizabeth, *you're* the first person I've pursued since Emilia came into my life...And if I have anything to say about it, you'll be in a committed relationship soon enough, and there will be *all the sex... Trust me.*"

God, this man.

"Good to know." I chuckle. He's adorable. "Speaking of Emilia, what does she know about her mom?"

"I don't intend to keep the truth from her, but it hasn't come up yet, so I haven't crossed that bridge. How the hell do I tell my daughter her mom didn't want her?"

"I have no idea," I admit. My chest squeezes tight at the thought of Emilia hearing those words.

"Since the day she was born, my goal has been to show her how loved and wanted she is. Hopefully..." he sighs heavily then continues, "when the time comes, and I tell her the truth, my love will be enough."

My heart aches for both of them.

"Oh, Cameron." I sigh, then stand, needing to squeeze him tight.

I'm a ball of emotions, and I'm just a bystander in this situation. I can't imagine what the last few years have been like for him.

Turning on the stool, he faces me and wraps his arms around my waist, pulling me to stand between his muscular legs. Then he hugs me back. It's one of the best hugs I've had in forever. It's fierce and filled with intense emotion. So many unspoken things pass between us, but I hope with all my heart, he knows he's an amazing dad, and Emilia is so lucky to have him in her life.

I can't imagine how hard this has been on him. Not only is he handling the roller coaster of being a single dad, but someday, when he least expects it, she'll ask about her mom.

How will he tell his sweet girl her mom didn't want her?

If put myself into Heather's shoes, I'm not sure what I'd do. I see where she was coming from—especially since she literally only knew Cameron for a few hours. How would two practical strangers have known they made a life-altering decision that day. For all I know, Heather could be on her way to being the best doctor who will save hundreds of lives.

As a broke college student, I can see Heather was putting her daughter's needs first. She knew giving Emilia up would give her a better chance at life. I also commend her for at least letting Cameron know about their child. She didn't have to tell him. She could've let the adoption go through, and Cameron would've never been the wiser.

But fuck, Cameron would've never known how amazing his daughter is. He wouldn't have held her as an infant, watched her first steps, or heard her first words. He would've missed out on all the firsts—Hell, he'd miss out on all the wonderment and joy that beautiful girl brings to this world.

As he holds me tight, something else hits me like a ton of bricks.

His love is enough—it has to be.

Pulling back to look him in the eye, I assure him, "Emilia's loved by everyone who meets her. I'm sure a part of her will be sad for what she could've had with a mom, but she'll never doubt your love for her. You'll be enough. I'm certain."

"I know, but it'll always remain my biggest fear," he admits solemnly.

The pain behind his eyes slays me.

How do I show him he's enough?

Running my thumb along his cheek, I stare into his navy-blue eyes until I can't take it any longer. His emotions are raw and even though he's not saying anything, I can see them bubbling on the surface.

"You're enough, Cameron," I whisper, bringing my lips to his.

One way or another, I will prove this to him.

Unbridled emotion burns between us as our kiss deepens.

Soon, he's leading us back to his bedroom.

Unlike last night, there's no sense of urgency. We're no longer frantic or playful. In fact, we're not even talking. Our passion is slow and sensual, but the heat between us burns just as hot.

When he enters me, I can only describe our connection as making love.

In all too short of time, my climax barrels through me like a freight train. The moment I stiffen, Cameron takes this cue and picks up the pace, chasing his own orgasm. Just as I tip over the edge, he plunges into me and stills.

"Fuck..." Cameron's roar fills the room.

Now that he's no longer moving, my focus is on his glorious cock pulsing relentlessly inside me. It's so intense, I can barely hold onto any thought.

The last thing I remember is him slowly kissing along my jaw to that place just below my earlobe. "You're so fucking perfect, Elizabeth."

"So are you," I remind him.

Then he turns my face to lock his eyes on mine. A slow smile spreads across his face as he claims, "You're mine."

Chapter 22

Cameron

By the time I return from the bathroom with a warm, wet washcloth, Lizzy's fast asleep. She's lying on her back, practically in the same position I left her just moments ago.

"Hey, Liz," I whisper, brushing loose strands of hair from her face.

"Hmmm," she moans but doesn't open her eyes.

"Let me wash you up," I suggest, leaning in and kissing her cheek.

Having no barriers between us is fucking phenomenal. I've never gone without a condom, but I think our intense connection has everything to do with my feelings for Elizabeth, rather than being without one. Unfortunately, the aftermath of letting myself come inside her is much messier. I need to take care of this.

"Babe?" I ask, hoping she'll wake, but it's no use.

When she still doesn't respond, I quickly use the warm washcloth between her legs.

"Hmmmm.... Thank you," she moans, then curls in on her side once I finish.

Glancing at the clock, I'm relieved to find I've still got hours until my sister's due with Mills. There's plenty of time to crawl in with her and take a nap.

Reaching for my phone to set an alarm, I realize it's nowhere in sight.

Fuck, where did it go?

Hopefully, I didn't miss a call from my sister.

Hell, it had better not be dead.

Quickly retracing our steps from last night, I search for my phone.

God, that strip tease was one of the hottest things of my existence.

As I make it to the hallway, I can't help but laugh at the scene we left behind in our haste to get to my bedroom.

"Holy shit, it's like a reverse scavenger hunt."

I make quick work of picking up our discarded clothes. There's a sock here, a shoe there. Eventually, I get to the foyer where I find what I'm looking for—my jeans.

With an armload of laundry, I fish through my pocket and drop my keys and wallet in the bowl where I usually keep them. When I finally get to my phone, I'm relieved to see the battery is at eighteen percent and most importantly, I haven't missed a call.

When I finally return to my room, I'm relieved to find Lizzy hasn't moved a muscle. I quickly pick up the clothes from in here, putting mine in the hamper and neatly folding Lizzy's, then placing them on the dresser.

Before climbing into bed, I set my alarm and place it on my charger.

Pulling back the covers on my side, I slide into bed behind her.

My bed smells of her. Sexy and sweet with a hint of vanilla spice.

Her warmth makes the soft sheets even more inviting.

I can't remember the last time I just snuggled with a woman.

Sliding an arm under her pillow, I pull her against my chest.

Her soft, silky skin feels heavenly against mine.

Instinctually, she slides closer, grabbing my free arm, and snuggles into it.

I swear, I'm not trying to be sexual, but our bodies fit as if she was made for me. She pulls my hand until my elbow rests comfortably over her hip, and my forearm lays between her perfect breasts along her sternum. She's hugging my arm, and my hand rests with ease, cupping her cheek.

I'm not sure I'll be able to sleep, but feeling her breath against me, my body relaxes. Closing my eyes, I focus on matching my breathing to hers. She's so soft and warm. I don't ever want to let her go.

*****

The whir of a garage door opening has me bolting up in bed.

Frozen in place, I take a moment to process what I'm hearing.

Yes. That's the garage door.

But who's here?

"What's wrong?" Lizzy croaks.

Ignoring her, I reach for my phone.

"Shit, I've missed three calls."

Swiping it open, I find they're all from my sister, along with a few texts. Apparently, my phone's been on silent.

"Fuck, Emilia's home," I say, bolting from the bed as if my ass is on fire. "We need to get dressed."

Rushing to my dresser, I quickly grab a pair of sweats and

hastily pull them on, then grab the first t-shirt I can get my hands on.

"Where are my clothes?" Lizzy whisper shouts frantically as she stands and looks around the room. It would almost be comical if I weren't in pure panic mode.

There's no way I want Emilia, or my sister for that matter, finding out I'm with Lizzy by walking in on us naked in bed.

"Right here," I say, tossing them to her.

"Wh... what do you want me to do?" she says as she hops up and down, pulling her jeans on.

Pausing at the door, I grin. "Get dressed, Beautiful. I'll buy you a few minutes, but it looks like you're meeting my sister today. Oh..." I gasp when I fully take her in, "You... Uh... May wanna do something with your hair."

Frantically, she pats it down, but it does nothing to tame it. "What? Why?"

Triumphantly, my chest puffs out. "You look as if you've been completely ravaged in the best possible way."

Her jaw drops to the floor, and she chastises me properly, "Cameron!"

"Dadddyyy! I home!!!" I hear Milli call through the house, and the pounding of her feet follows.

Running a hand through my own hair, I grin. "I'll intercept my speed demon."

Lizzy's frozen in place, jaw hanging open.

Taking two quick strides to close the distance between us, I quickly pull her in for the briefest of kisses. "It'll be okay, Liz. Just take your time."

Pointing to the en suite bathroom, I teasingly pop my hand against her ass. "Go. Make yourself look less ravaged, woman."

With that, I quickly step out of my room, shutting the door behind me.

Emilia rounds the corner, just as I reach the end of the hall.

"Daddy!" Her eyes are wide as she launches herself into my arms. "I missed you!"

Pulling her in for a hug, I admit, "I've missed you, too, love bug."

Pulling back, she squishes my cheeks between her chubby hands. "Where were you?"

Walking further away from my bedroom, I say, "In the bathroom. What are you doing here?"

"We tried calling," my sister adds once she's in view.

"Sorry. I think my phone was silenced."

Looking me over, my perceptive sister smirks. "Obviously."

"Everything okay?" I ask when her eyes narrow.

"I should ask you the same thing," she says in return.

Shit. She knows something's up.

"Silly Daddy!" Milli shouts, shaking her head.

"What?" I lean in and boop her on the nose. "What's silly?"

Poking me in the chest, she states, "Your shirt's upside down."

"Upside down?" I ask, glancing at it for the first time.

"I think she means inside out," Megan deadpans as her eyes narrow perceptively. "What did you do, get dressed in the dark?"

Well, fuck. I was so worried about Lizzy, I never looked at myself. "I guess I wasn't paying attention."

"Obviously." She snorts like only an older sister can. Then her perceptive eyes look me over closer. "Having a lazy weekend?" Something behind me draws her attention, and her face turns into a wide grin, and she rolls her eyes.

Milli squirms in my arms, and excitement rolls off her in waves as she yells, "My Iz! You're here!"

The moment Milli's feet hit the floor, she races to Lizzy like she's the most special person on the planet.

Same kid. Same. I light up like that when she enters the room, too.

Lizzy bends just in time to scoop my daughter into her arms. Squeezing her in a tight hug, she asks, "Hey, Mills! Did you have a good time with your Aunt Megan?"

"I did. I saw the princesses on ice and went to the zoo!"

Lizzy's interest is genuine when she asks, "What was your favorite?"

"I love Rapunzel. Her dress is bea-u-ti-ful," She drags it out into several syllables.

"I'm sure it is," Lizzy agrees. "What about the zoo? What kind of animals did you see?"

"I saw the giraffes. They have loooong necks that go way up here." She reaches as high as she can into the sky. "It was *a lot* of walking. There were also otters, like here. You know... The ones that clap when we visit?"

"You mean the ones at the aquarium?" Lizzy clarifies. "I haven't seen any along the beach, have you?"

Milli's eyes widen in shock. "They live on the beach, too?"

Oh, how I've failed my child.

"Technically, yes. But it's rare," Lizzy quickly explains. "I think some were spotted in Cannon Beach last year, but I never saw them."

"Can we see them again?" Milli pleads, looking from Lizzy to me.

"Not today, Mills. Aunt Megan is here, and you've already had enough adventures for the weekend."

"She's not the only one who had adventures," my sister mutters so that only I can hear as she steps beside me.

I don't dare look at Megan, as I'd hate to draw attention to her comment and embarrass Lizzy.

"My Iz take me, Daddy?" Milli asks, drawing my attention back to her.

"I can take you after swimming one day this week," Lizzy promises.

Stepping around me, my sister approaches Lizzy. "Hi. I'm Megan. You must be Iz." My sister looks pointedly from Lizzy to me and back to her. "Milli's told me so much about your adventures together this summer."

Shit. I didn't introduce them—and she's obviously wishing I'd told her more.

"I'm sorry, Megan. This is Elizabeth Lancaster... or Lizzy as she prefers to be called. Mills claims her as My Iz, as you can see."

"It's nice to meet you, Lizzy." Megan reaches out and shakes her hand.

"Nice to meet you, too." Lizzy smiles, setting my squirming daughter on the floor. "Are you staying in Seaside long?"

"Just until tomorrow. I'm flying out of PDX on the red eye to JFK."

"Cameron said you were a pilot. Do you live in Portland, too?" Lizzy asks with interest.

"No. I live in Denver. But I like to see these two as often as I can. Though, it's much easier when they lived closer to a major airport."

"Not all of us have the luxury of being a jet-setter," I mumble. "I might be out in the sticks, but Seaside's not as bad as I thought it would be. In fact, it's growing on me."

"Oh, I'm sure it is." Megan smirks and glances to Lizzy again.

Yeah, I don't miss her double meaning.

She wouldn't be my older sister if she didn't pitch me shit. Even now, I'm relentless when I meet any guy she dates. I may be her younger brother, but I've always kept an eye on her and inserted myself when needed.

I will neither confirm nor deny an incident that involved

hopping over the back of a couch to separate my sister and her high school boyfriend while they were watching a movie. Megan was pissed for weeks and never lets me hear the end of it.

What can I say? She's my sister, and I'm the protective asshole brother when the role needs to be filled.

I'm brought out of my trip down memory lane when Milli shrieks, "I go potty!" then starts for the hall.

"Need help?" Lizzy offers out of habit, I'm sure.

"I got it," I volunteer, but Milli stops me.

Stomping her foot stubbornly, she demands, "I want My Iz, Daddy. I miss her."

"What am I? Chopped liver?" I grumble before thinking better of it.

Don't get me wrong, I love Emilia's connection with Lizzy, but it doesn't mean she should be on butt duty—especially on her day off. Turning to Lizzy, I assure her, "I can take care of this."

Lizzy waves me off. "No. It's not a problem. I've got this. Enjoy this time with your sister."

My heart squeezes tight in my chest as I watch Lizzy disappear down the hall, effortlessly chasing after my daughter. From the moment we met, I've felt a strong connection to her, and witnessing their bond only hits me in the feels harder.

"Bro, you've got it bad." My sister sighs once Lizzy's out of earshot.

"What are you talking about?" I ask dismissively.

"First, I've never seen you look at anyone the way you're looking at her. Not even Olivia, that girl in high school you were crushing on for years. I know for a fact Milli loves her with all her heart. She couldn't stop talking about her the entire weekend. Not to mention that Mom raved about her when you first hired her."

"But..." I draw out, waiting for the other shoe to drop.

"But..." Megan mimics, drawing it out longer for emphasis. "You need to be careful. You know you shouldn't shit where you eat."

"It's not like that," I quickly spit out.

"What's it like then, Cameron? I've never taken you as the *fall for the nanny guy*. You're smarter than that and more importantly, I'm not dumb. I'm sure you're not celibate, but since Emilia was born, you've *never* brought a girl around either."

"It's not what you think," I grunt out defensively. "Lizzy and I have a past—that I'll explain after Emilia goes to bed. But I swear on my daughter's life, nothing has happened again until this weekend."

"If shit goes sideways, it could be disastrous," Megan points out. "Mom told me how hard it was for you to find a nanny in the first place. Milli already thinks she walks on water. Are you sure you want to risk this for whatever is going on between the two of you?"

I love my sister, and I know she means well. But she can't be further from the truth with her assumption.

"Look, it's still new but rest assured, I'm not looking to fuck things up anytime soon. I know what's at stake for both Milli's and my heart. Trust me, *I've tried* to stay away but after reconnecting this weekend, that's just not an option."

"So, what's different, Cameron?" Megan asks, all sense of censure gone.

"That's a good fucking question," I muse more for myself than her.

Megan's eyes fill with concern as she waits for me to come to my own conclusion.

Sighing heavily, I admit, "Fuck, you're right. I was a player before Emilia. But you know as well as I do, the moment she entered my life, it's always been her needs above mine."

"You're an incredible father, Cam," Megan assures me, squeezing my arm.

"The thing is..." Shit, how do I put my feelings into words? "Elizabeth Lancaster is the first person *ever* to make me feel like I want more with someone."

"Cameron, she's *young*... And your *child's nanny*," Megan points out. "This could really end badly... For all of you."

"It could end badly..." I admit. "But the thing is, Megs, I don't think it will. Like I said, Lizzy and I have a history. But I swear, I didn't know the only person who's caught my attention in my entire adult life was the top person Mom chose to be Emilia's nanny."

"You like her," Megan states matter-of-factly. There's no judgement, just truth in her words.

"Megs, I'm pretty sure I *more* than like her. I've been falling for her for months, and it took her claiming me last night to finally act upon it. She'll only be our nanny through the end of summer. We have a lot to work through, but I'm certain she's worth it."

"Wow," Megan whispers in awe. "I never thought I'd see the day."

"You and me both, Megs." I sigh heavily. Then a new thought hits like a ton of bricks. "Elizabeth Lancaster is special. Even though I know the risks are high, I'm certain I'd have even more regrets if I *didn't* take a chance on her."

Chapter 23
Lizzy

By the time I arrive home later that evening, I'm exhausted. Cameron had asked if I'd go with them to show Megan around Seaside and of course, wanting to spend more time with him, I did. We went downtown, walked along The Promenade, and Milli got her wish of going to the aquarium, since we were right there.

Cameron and I were careful not to be affectionate in front of Milli. Sure, we held hands under the table at dinner and stole a few kisses here and there, but for the most part, we simply spent the day together, hanging out. Honestly, it wasn't much different than when he joined us on our daily outings. However, with his sister in tow, we did more touristy things.

When we went to get taffy at The Candyman Store for Megan, Milli saw the multi-person bike rental shop next door. Now that we had enough people to pedal the bikes she always sees around town, she easily convinced her dad and aunt to rent a three-person bike and explore. Of course, she rode in style being strapped into the front basket with a seat belt, while two of us adults pedaled like crazy around the touristy part of town. We quickly deemed Cameron as the permanent pumper and official navigator in our expedition, while Megan and I took turns pedaling when the other got tired. Milli's excitement as we spotted new things through the town was infectious.

It had been years since I'd ridden one of the bikes and soon after leaving the rental shop, I quickly discovered why. First, Seaside may feel flat to the ordinary walker, but it's not. Next, those bikes look magical to the average onlooker, but we quickly found they're hard to start and even more difficult to stop— don't even get me started on turning. Lots of laughs were shared as we came to high-traffic areas in town, and our cute little adventure quickly became a full team sport. By the time we finished, my face hurt from laughing, and my legs stung from pumping.

I'm certain Megan knows something is going on between us. She conveniently took Milli swimming when it was time for me to leave. Cameron insisted on driving me home and although I could easily walk, I couldn't turn down additional time with him.

I assumed he'd just drop me off, as he needed to get back to his family. But that crazy man parked, got out of his car, and walked me to the door. Then kissed the living hell out of me. When he pulled away, leaving me breathless and panting, he sexily teased, "I'll see you at seven tomorrow morning. I'm making breakfast, so come hungry. For the record, if my sister weren't here, I'm not sure I'd let you leave tonight."

"Promises, promises," I teased as butterflies took flight in my belly. I'm not sure how we'd manage it, but the thought of waking up in his arms again did sound promising.

As I sit on the couch reminiscing, I realize how easy it was being with him today. Sure, this could be a post-sex-induced haze, but I'm certain this thing with Cameron goes far beyond our physical connection.

It has from the start.

Last night only solidified just how much I like him.

What will happen when I return to school?

"Earth to Elizabeth... Come in, Elizabeth," Ryan says as he taps my foot and plops down on the couch next to me.

"Huh?" I ask, immediately returning to the present.

Thumbing over his shoulder, he says, "I started talking when I walked in. But you obviously didn't hear. You good?"

"Yeah." I stretch and nod. "I'm good. Just zoning out."

"Lanie's over at Sloane and Jax's place, helping her organize some new shelf. Mind if I watch some TV?" he asks, reaching for the remote.

"Not at all." He flicks it on and pulls up his favorite streaming service.

"Have you watched *The Night Agent*? I made the mistake of starting the series when Lanie was out with Raven the other night. Now I'm dying to find out what happens next. I'm only like two episodes in, so you haven't missed much."

"Between school and work, I don't really watch many shows," I admit. "But go ahead. I'm gonna head upstairs soon anyway. I need to shower and get ready for the week."

"Before you go, can you help me with something?" Ryan asks, starting the show, then immediately pausing it to keep it ready for him.

"What's up?"

"I wanna surprise Lanie with an anniversary gift, but I've been on the fence and could use your opinion."

"What did you have in mind?" I'm curious as to what he might have planned.

"I've thought about taking her away for the weekend, but

with the music festival in town and your dad and aunt coming right at the same time, that might not be a good idea."

"You can always give her the gift of a vacation and pick the date together," I offer, knowing my sister would simply appreciate the thought.

"True. I also thought about jewelry, though she doesn't wear much."

"What about a charm bracelet? It could turn into a tradition where you'd add something new each year. Oh... Last time we were out, I swear I saw her eying one the other day. It was in that shop just around the corner from Pop's. Maybe take her to a nice dinner and give her that, then go on a vacation when things slow down, or when she's on a break from school."

"Hmmm... I like that idea. Getting away after the holidays might be more enticing when it's drizzly and cold in Seaside... And she does have that break in February."

"Business is slow then, right?" Ryan's a project manager for his family's construction business. He and his dad do both renovations and new construction projects now that Ryan's onboard full time.

"True," Ryan muses. "I could make it more than a long weekend, if we wait."

"I'm sure no matter what you choose, Lanie will love it."

"I know you're working, and Milli keeps you busy, but is there any way we can meet up this week? Then you can show me which bracelet you're talking about."

"Of course. I'm not sure of my schedule tomorrow, but will Tuesday work? I'm usually back from Astoria by ten most days this swim session."

"Great. I'll double check my schedule, but I'm certain I'm in the office Tuesday morning, so I can meet you then?"

A long yawn escapes, and it's evident if I don't get off this couch, I'll be here until tomorrow morning. Forcing myself to stand, I stretch the slumber from my limbs. "I'm sure I'll see you tomorrow, but I'll text you when we get back to town."

Just as I'm about to leave the room, he stops me. "Hey... I forgot to ask... Did you enjoy your birthday?"

I couldn't stop the grin on my face if I tried. "Yeah..." I exhale heavily. "It was certainly memorable."

"I'll bet it was." He chuckles. "By the way, Lanie sort of had to fill us in on some of the details between you and Cameron, or you would've had unexpected company when you missed Sunday brunch this morning."

"Oh, shit," I gasp. "I'm so sorry. I totally forgot about it."

"We figured you were... ummm... distracted."

"Ohmigod, Ryan!" I laugh at his effort to remain diplomatic. "Distracted? You're sticking with that?"

"You may be twenty-one, but you're dealing with three older sisters and the protective guys who love them. There's nothing we wouldn't do for them *or you* for that matter. Maybe text us next time?"

"Point taken. I should've known better." Hell, if one of my sisters didn't show up, I'd be the same way. "But for the record. If I'm with Cameron, it's by choice, and we're likely... well... uh... distracted... As you said."

Ryan's deep laughter fills the room. "Good God, Elizabeth, there are just some things I have no business knowing."

"Just the perks of being married to my sister, dear Ryan. I seem to recall you and Lanie being *distracted* a lot when you first got together."

"As long as he's treating you well, he can *distract* you all he wants. We really don't care. But for the love of all that's holy, call, text, or hell, it's a small enough town, send a smoke signal."

"Okay, point taken." I laugh. "You're worse than Dad, I swear."

Cocking a brow dubiously, he says, "I'm worse than the

colonel? Your dad's pretty chill, but let's face it, he'd probably be cleaning his guns on the front porch when you returned if he knew you'd stayed out all night with a guy he didn't know you were dating."

"Touché! My dad would be so much worse."

Chapter 24
Cameron

I'm running on caffeine and pure adrenaline as I make breakfast. I have no idea how I'll make it through the long-ass day ahead of me, but as they say, there's no rest for the wicked. I'm on my second cup of coffee as I finish making omelets. Bacon is stacked on the plate beside the griddle, and Lizzy should arrive any time.

Emilia conked out immediately after getting out of the pool, and I'm not sure how long Megan and I stayed up talking last night, but it was far too late. After filling her in on everything with Lizzy, she encouraged me to pursue things—not that I need her permission. Apparently, I've never looked happier and after our outing, she is just as much in love with Lizzy as I am.

Love?

Did I really just go there?

Fuck, I think I did.

The sound of the front door clicking open has my heart jackhammering in my chest. Lizzy has a key, and we quickly learned that if she lets herself in, Emilia sleeps through her arrival. Milli plays hard and needs her rest for all the adventures she has with Lizzy each day.

Just the thought of seeing her again has me shutting off the griddle and beelining to the front door. When I round the corner, I find she's barely made it inside. Her back is to me, and she's balancing against the hall table as she toes off her Chucks.

Not wanting to startle her, I use this moment to take her in.

God, she's gorgeous.

Her hunter-green hoodie is warm and cozy for the brisk morning walk to my house. Her long, brown hair is hidden in one of those top-knot things girls wear. She's wearing the sexiest pair of jean shorts that accentuate her long, muscular legs and scrumptious curves. I can't tell you how often I've wished to peel those off her this summer. If my sister and Milli weren't somewhere inside the house, I'd gladly do it right now.

When she finally turns, her beautiful smile takes my breath away.

"Morning, Beautiful," I whisper, stepping closer and cupping her cheek.

"Hey, handsome. How are you?"

I've spent weeks keeping my distance, and I'll be damned if I waste another minute avoiding her. "Better now that you're here," I admit, lowering my lips to hers.

When her minty breath mingles with mine, everything I've been holding back lets loose. Our lips crash together, tongues tangle, and I get completely lost in Elizabeth Lancaster.

When the faint sounds of running feet catch my attention, I'm brought back to reality. At some point, Milli will learn about my feelings for Lizzy, but this isn't how she should find out. Reluctantly, I break the kiss, leaving us both breathless.

"Daddy?" Milli calls out from the other side of the house. "Where are you?"

"Right here, Mills," I answer. Then I squeeze Lizzy's hand reassuringly. "You good?"

Running her fingers along her lips, she nods. "I could get used to greetings like that."

"You and me both," I admit. "I thought you'd never get here this morning."

This earns me a beautiful laugh. "Hey now, I'm fifteen minutes earlier than normal. You *weren't* waiting."

Lowering my voice so only she can hear, I say, "Sweetheart, from the moment I drove away last night, I've been waiting to see you again."

The second her jaw drops, a low chortle escapes my lips.

This woman's adorable, and I think I might make it my mission to keep her on her toes. I love seeing how she reacts to the simplest of things.

Before she can respond, Milli enters the room. "I'm hungry, Daddy."

"Mornin', love bug. Did you sleep well?" I ask, scooping her into my arms for a hug.

"Uh-huh." She nods adorably.

"Breakfast is ready, but let's go potty first, then eat."

To Lizzy, I suggest, "Make yourself a plate. We'll be right back."

Milli and I make quick work in the bathroom. Since she was dry, I help her change into big girl panties from a Pull-Up. Once she washes her hands, she eagerly selects a purple star sticker for staying dry all night. She's working for a new book at the bookstore when she fills the chart. I'll gladly buy the entire bookstore if it means she's potty trained. Like most three-year-olds, she has good days and bad days, but as long as she's not too tired, she's typically dry if I help her first thing when she wakes up.

To further reward her potty-training endeavor, I grab her

special cherry-flavored ChapStick from the medicine cabinet and swipe it along her lips. Never in a million years would I have thought this tiny tube would work miracles. But alas it does—and it's all thanks to Lizzy and her brilliant suggestion.

A few weeks ago, Emilia was having a difficult day potty training. Lizzy offered her some of her ChapStick if she'd try using the toilet. Emilia thinks Lizzy walks on water most days, so of course she tried and was successful. Now, I can say my daughter will proudly poop on command if she knows she gets to wear her "Wipstick" as she calls it when she's done. I owe Lizzy everything for this little party trick, as my daughter is one step closer to being fully potty trained.

When we return from the bathroom, I'm pleased to find Megan and Lizzy both eating at the table. They're chatting away about their favorite places to hang out in Portland. When Megan opens her arms to Milli, she rushes to sit beside her. Megan's got a plate ready for her and once she's settled, Milli digs into those omelets like she hasn't eaten in a week.

"If you're shopping on Twenty-Third, you *have* to check out Salt & Straw," Lizzy suggests. "That's *the only place* my friends and I will venture out for late-night ice cream runs."

"It's rare I travel far from the airport if I'm only in town for an overnight layover. However, Cam's taken me there a few times when I've visited. I love their unique flavors."

"Really?" Lizzy looks from Cameron to me. "Have you tried their pear and blue cheese?"

"Uh, who eats ice cream with blue cheese?" I interject. "That sounds disgusting."

"I do." Lizzy proudly taps her chest twice. "Don't knock it until you try it, mister."

"I'll have to take your word for it." I chuckle, sitting beside her.

Warmth spreads through me when my leg bumps hers. "I take it you go often?"

"Only every chance I can. That's one of the things I missed most when my car went belly up last spring... No more Salt & Straw."

Even her pout is cute. How is that possible?

"That's terrible. I'm not sure I could go without a car," Megan commiserates.

Lizzy just shrugs. "Most everything I need is near campus, so it's not too bad. Lanie and Ryan come to Portland regularly, and she'll come get me if I wanna visit Seaside. The MAX isn't too far away either."

My stomach churns at the thought of her riding public transportation late at night. I know people ride it every day, but for some reason, this bit of information doesn't sit well. She lived close to campus when we met, but where will she live next year? Will she have to ride it often?

"What about you, Cam?" my sister asks expectantly.

Staring at her dumbfoundedly, I admit, "Sorry, lost in thought. What did you ask?"

Rolling her eyes, my sister repeats, "After breakfast, we're going to check out Painted Rock Beach. Mills painted some rocks last week with Lizzy, and she wants to contribute."

Shit. I'd love to go, but I'm already cutting it close for my first meeting as it is. "Unfortunately, I can't. I've gotta scoot as soon as I finish breakfast, or I'll be late." Turning my attention to Milli, I ask, "Can you show me what you've been working on?"

Milli nods excitedly.

Just as she's about to bolt from the table, Lizzy counters, "Let me wipe your fingers first."

The second her hands are clean, Milli's off to the races. She runs to the windowsill by the back door and picks up two large rocks I didn't even notice were there.

And the parent of the year award for most observant goes to... Cameron Kruse.

In my defense, she's been out of town, and I was rather distracted this weekend.

When she rushes back to the table, she points at me sternly. "We had to let them dry. See, Daddy." She proudly holds up a rock with what looks like a rainbow on one side and her name on the other. "I made this one..." Then she lifts the other into view, and it clearly looks like a ladybug. "And My Iz made this one."

"Have you been to Painted Rock Beach?" Lizzy asks as I inspect each rock with care.

"I can't say that I have," I admit.

"We can take Daddy when he's not working," Milli suggests.

"Most definitely, Mills. Maybe we can paint some rocks together for next time," I add.

My daughter barely contains her excitement. "Really? You paint with me and My Iz?"

Pulling her in for a snuggle, I kiss the top of her head and say, "I'd love nothing more, sweet girl."

"It's not too far from the house," Lizzy informs me.

"I, for one, am excited to see this rock beach," Megan says, standing to clear her plate from breakfast. "I need to move a little before making the drive back to the airport."

"Thanks again for coming, Megs. I know for a fact Milli enjoyed her weekend with you. I'm glad you could visit and see for yourself why I love this town so much."

The moment I stand, she walks over and wraps her arms around me.

"I wish I could be here for the festival and see all your hard work come to fruition. I'm so proud of you, Cam. You're doing an amazing job."

Wrapping her in my arms, I squeeze her tight. "Thanks, Megs. Let's make sure we get together again soon. I've missed you."

"Once the festival is over, I'm sure your life will be less chaotic."

I could only hope.

Chuckling, I add for good measure, "From your lips to God's ears, as Mom says."

"I hate to eat and run, but I've got a meeting. Give me a hug, Mills."

When she rushes to my side, I swoop her into my arms and hug her fiercely. God, this is the best feeling in the world. "You be good for Lizzy today, okay?"

Giggling with delight as I rub my cheek against hers, she squeals, "Okay, Daddy! Love you."

"Love you more, sweet girl. I hope you have the best day."

As soon as her feet hit the floor, she proclaims, "I dress for our walk," and off she goes to her bedroom.

My attention turns to Lizzy, "You got her?"

"Of course. Thanks again for breakfast. I'm spoiled when you cook like that."

Not caring that my sister's still in the room, I take this opportunity to pull her close. "Get used to it. I'll text you later and let you know my schedule. Do you have plans for dinner?"

"Yeah." She nods solemnly, and my heart sinks.

So she won't see my disappointment, I quickly look away. But she stops me by cupping my cheek.

A light laugh escapes as she returns my attention to her. "I've got a date with this hot guy I've been seeing."

"Is that so?" I play along.

"Yep! if he's lucky, I'll make *him and his daughter* their

favorite meal. It *might* include my infamous potato salad, asparagus, and quite possibly either steak or ribs."

"Mmmm... That sounds delicious. I'd better get to work, so I can hurry back and make that happen."

Leaning down, I brush my lips against hers. It's way too short but necessary as we have an audience, and I don't know how long Milli will be.

When I pull back, she pats me on the chest. "Go! Lord over your minions and make things happen today."

"Ohmigod." I crack up. "I can't even with you." This girl is too much. "Lord over my minions..."
*****

As I step out of my first meeting and head back to my office, I'm relieved to know things for the festival are on track. We've got spectacular talent lined up and an experienced staff who work together like a well-oiled machine when it comes to task management.

I barely get my ass settled in my seat when Merna buzzes in, scaring the shit out of me. "Cameron, I've got Marek on the line. He says it's urgent."

Marek Mindar is the CEO of Smashing Waves Records and more importantly, my boss. We have regular remote meetings as he is based in LA, but he rarely makes urgent calls. "Put him through."

The moment the line connects, he skips all preamble and pleasantries. "Hey, Cameron. I've got a situation here, and I need your help."

"What do you need?" I offer immediately.

"Tatum has a family emergency and will be out for the foreseeable future."

"Everything okay with him?" I ask, wondering why I'm not hearing this from him.

"Yes. He has some family things he must attend to and

can't make the meeting scheduled for tomorrow afternoon with the members of Sienna Flames. It's a potential multi-million-dollar deal, and I need my best on this."

"Okay, give me the details, and I'll get on the call."

"No can do, Cameron. I need you in LA tomorrow by noon. I'll send all the details to Merna. She'll make the arrangements to get you here and help get you up to speed on this deal."

"The festival is just weeks away," I remind him.

Clearly, I have things here in Seaside I need to be doing.

"Look, Cam, I know the timing sucks. But it'll be one, maybe two days tops, and you'll be back before you know it. I wouldn't ask if it wasn't necessary to meet in person. Tatum would be here, but his father just had a heart attack, and he needs to be there for his family."

"I understand. But I've also got Emilia to consider," I pointedly remind him. Tatum's not the only one with family responsibilities.

"I can have a sitter service available to you around the clock, if need be, but I need you here for this. If I weren't in our London office this week, I'd take this meeting myself."

Shit. "I'll make arrangements on my end and hop on the first available flight out of Portland."

"I'll send over all the details you need to know. I'll be in touch."

The line goes dead, and I'm left staring at my phone.

What the fuck just happened?

Needing to get my shit together, I buzz Merna.

"Yes, Cameron?"

"Hey, Merna, I need to be on a flight to LA this afternoon. Can you make that happen? I'm going to head home now to make arrangements on my end. Marek is sending you the details."

"His email just came through. With PDX being more than two hours away, I'll do my best to schedule one for this evening."

I hear typing on her end, then she says, "There's a four-fifteen flight, or six thirty. The latter is non-stop."

Glancing at my watch, I see it's almost eleven. "I'll catch the six thirty. Is there room on that flight for more people if needed? Emilia and her nanny will likely travel with me."

"It doesn't appear full," she offers. At least one thing is going right.

"Good. I'll let you know within the hour if I need additional arrangements."

"I'll be here, Cameron. Just let me know."

When I walk through the door to my house, it's silent. The car is in the garage, so I know they're either somewhere in the house, out for a walk, or Emilia's napping.

When I get to the family room, I see Lizzy in the backyard, reading on a lounge chair. As I walk through the sliding glass door, she looks up with surprise. "What are you doing home so early?"

"I had a thing at work come up, and I need to talk with you."

"What's going on?" she asks warily.

Where do I even begin?

"I have to be in LA tonight for a meeting tomorrow. Tatum had a family emergency, and Marek insists I handle it in his absence."

"Okay..." Lizzy draws out. "What do you need from me?"

"I know we didn't discuss anything like this, but I need someone to watch Milli while I'm in LA. I'll get a hotel and cover expenses, but would you fly out with me and watch her?"

"I can do that." She nods, then cocks her head to the side. "But... Won't you be in meetings the entire time?"

"Yeah," I say on a long exhale. "Most likely."

"Okay... hear me out. First, I'll watch Milli no matter what, so no need to worry about that. But how well does she travel? Will she do okay in a hotel?"

"I honestly don't know," I admit. "We haven't flown that much since she was born."

"Fair warning... She's been kinda grumpy today."

"Perfect! A grumpy toddler is just what I need when preparing for a multi-million-dollar deal. God, the universe must hate me."

Standing, she reaches for my hand. "Look, Cam, I want nothing more than to be with you. But hear me out. *What if...* I stayed here at your house and took care of her while you go to LA... Alone. This way, you could focus on work, and she'd get some rest. I think spending the weekend with your sister was fun, but Milli's exhausted."

"You'd do that for us?" I ask in disbelief. I've never had anyone besides my mom put Milli's needs above everything else.

"Of course, I would." She smiles at me. "For the record, I'd love to see LA someday, but being stuck in a hotel room while you're working all day doesn't sound much fun for me or Milli. That girl loves to run and play, and hotels aren't made for rambunctious toddlers."

My heart swells at her thoughtfulness.

Needing to show her just how much this means to me, I pull her close. All the pent-up stress I've been holding onto vanishes the moment my lips crash onto hers. She's soft and warm and everything that's right in this world. The way she's put Milli's needs first makes me fall even harder for her. I can't believe I let her walk away this spring. She's everything I never knew I needed.

My phone buzzes in my pocket and as much as I'd like this

to continue, I know I'm on a time crunch. Reluctantly, I break our kiss, then lean my forehead onto hers as our breathing steadies.

"You sure you're okay with staying here? It might be a few days."

"Yeah, Cameron. Milli and I'll miss you, but it's what's best for her."

"But what if you need a break?" I ask, knowing how much I need them sometimes. I'm sure she's never been around a child twenty-four-seven. It's exhausting.

Taking my hand in hers, she squeezes it reassuringly. "I've got my entire family nearby. They'd come running if I even hinted of needing help."

"I'm sure they would... In fact, why don't you invite them over so that I know you're not alone the entire time. You can make use of my pool."

"We'll be fine, Cameron. Go, get ready. You don't want to miss your flight."

Leaning down to kiss her once more, I admit, "You're one special lady, Elizabeth Lancaster. I don't know what I did to deserve you, but I thank my lucky stars our paths crossed again."

Chapter 25
Lizzy

Milli is either under the weather, missing her dad, or perhaps both. I can't quite put my finger on it, but she's been off all day. Maybe she's just exhausted from her weekend with Megan, and I'm reading too much into it.

I don't know what she's like after I leave each day, but she chose snuggling with me on the couch and watching a movie over going for a walk with Lanie and Ryan when they stopped by after dinner. I even offered to push her in the stroller, and she asked to stay home instead. She barely ate and was fast asleep before I even got two pages into her book.

When my phone buzzes in my pocket, I extricate myself from her bed and exit her room quickly.

It isn't until I'm in the hall that I see who's calling. Then, I can't swipe at my phone fast enough.

"Hey, Cam," I answer, breathless.

"Hey yourself, Liz. Is this a bad time?"

Plopping onto the couch, I snag the blanket we'd left earlier and snuggle into it. It smells faintly like Cameron, and it makes me miss him that much more.

"No, I just had to extricate myself from a sleeping Milli."

"She's already asleep?" Surprise is evident in his voice. "I was hoping I'd catch her to say good night."

My heart aches for him. I remember how much I missed my dad when he was deployed. "Sorry, she was out within two pages of *The Princess Wears Hiking Boots*."

"You must work miracles. I can barely get her down before nine."

"No, she's been really tired all day," I admit. "Lanie and Ryan even stopped by to go for a walk, and she asked to stay home and finish the movie instead."

"Hmmm... That *is* strange," he muses. "I hope she's not coming down with anything."

"Me, too," I admit. "I promise I'll let you know if things change."

"I hate being away from her," he exhales heavily.

"I know you do."

My heart aches for him. From what I can tell, he truly didn't want to leave her. After all, his first response was to take us all with him. I also know firsthand what it's like having your dad gone from Emilia's perspective. My dad didn't have a choice and frankly, neither does Cameron, so I remind him. "You'll be back in a day or two."

"I know. When I'm busy working, it flies by, but when I'm sitting here alone in a silent hotel room, it hits a little harder."

"You're an incredible dad, Cameron. Never doubt that."

"If she's caught a bug or something, maybe it's best that you two stayed home."

"Speaking of home, with Mills not feeling well, I never made it to pick up my things. Mind if I use one of your shirts for bed?"

"I should've made time before I left for you to get your things."

"Cameron, you barely made it to the airport in time as it was," I point out sternly, then add, "It's not like you planned this. Stop worrying about me. I'm fine. Hopefully, Milli feels better tomorrow. If not, Lanie will bring things over. In the meantime, can I grab something of yours?"

"Hmmm... The thought of you sleeping in my bed with my clothes on is something I could get used to."

"What makes you think I'm sleeping in your bed?" I tease.

Honestly, I've been so focused on Milli, I hadn't even thought about sleeping arrangements.

"This isn't the time to be difficult, Elizabeth," he warns. "I just want you comfortable. Though teasing aside, if Milli needs you, it's the first place she'll go."

"Fair point."

But my sass just won't stay hidden.

Sighing heavily, I quickly add, "It'll be such a hardship sleeping in a huge, comfortable bed that smells like you. But rest assured, it's a sacrifice I'll gladly take for the team."

His deep laugh comes through the phone, and my heart warms. "Oh, Elizabeth... What am I gonna do with you?"

"I can think of a few things... But you'll have to be here in person."

"Ms. Lancaster," he gasps. "What are you suggesting?"

"Well..." I draw out for emphasis. "You do have nice... Hands."

"Anything particular you like... About my hands?" I can hear the smile in his voice, and my stomach dips, remembering just what he did with those magical hands of his.

"Hmmm... It's a toss-up between how they feel against my skin and what they feel like deep inside me."

"Fuck," Cameron groans in the sexiest tone. "You're making me hard just thinking about it."

"Really?" I ask, surprised. "Just one little comment will do that?"

"All it takes is thinking about you, Elizabeth... Throw in how you explicitly want to be touched and fuck... I'm done for."

"Hmmm... Maybe I could *help* you with that problem."

"If only you weren't three states away."

Standing, I make a split-second decision.

"Switch to Video."

The moment his sexy smile comes onto the screen, I know I'm making the right choice.

"Hey, Beautiful. This is much better."

Holding the phone close so he can't tell what I've got up my sleeve, I casually say, "So much better."

"I think this just might be my new favorite view," he says, leaning his head against the headboard in his hotel room.

Shutting and locking his bedroom door, I prop my phone on his dresser.

"Favorite? I can think of a few things that might make it better."

The way his brow arches and the phone is suddenly brought closer to inspect what I'm doing causes heat to flood through me. His voice is sexy and rough when he says, "And what might that be?"

Trying to keep him in the dark until I'm ready to reveal my plan, I keep my face close to the screen as I undo the fly of my shorts and drop them to the floor. "Oh, you know... Maybe if I show you some of the places I love you using those sexy hands of yours most... You'll know what to do next time we're together."

"Hold on," he warns, and the screen suddenly goes black as if he's dropped it on the bed.

I use this moment to rip my t-shirt over my head and quickly take off my bra.

"You okay, Cam?" I ask when I see movement through the darkened image on the phone.

"I'm... just getting more comfortable."

God, I love being on the same page as this sexy man.

Shivers run through me in anticipation of what's to come. Cameron is more than all my hottest fantasies coming to life.

When he returns to the screen, he takes my breath away.

Damn, he's fine.

He's propped the phone so I can see his entire chest on display, and I'd give anything to run my tongue along his stacked muscles.

"See something ya like?" he challenges when I have yet to say anything.

"Just thinking about what I'd do to you if you were here... But to answer your question... Yes... You're freaking hot, and you know it."

Thumbing the waistband of my underwear, I quickly slide them off.

Tipping his head to the side, his eyes narrow speculatively. "Why is that beautiful face of yours suddenly so flushed?"

Stepping back from the dresser and resting my ass on the edge of the bed, I let him finally get a glimpse of my plan.

"Holy fucking hell, you're gorgeous."

"I thought maybe this would help you with your little problem you had before."

A low chuckle escapes as he scoots back onto the bed further. "He's not so little at the moment. Fuck, if I thought I was hard before, I'm a fucking steel rod now. Touch yourself, Beautiful."

"Where?" I ask playfully.

"Hmmmm... Where to begin? Roll your nipples in your

fingers and run your palm down your stomach but stop right before you reach that beautiful pussy of yours... I want to make sure you're good and primed before flicking that sensitive clit."

My breath hitches as I do exactly that. "Mmmmm. I wish this was you. Your hands know just what I need."

"You and me both, babe. Trust me," he growls.

As he leans back, his hands disappear off screen, and I won't have that. "Reposition your phone. I need to see your straining cock on screen. I want to fantasize about licking you from root to tip as I touch myself."

"Mmmmm... I'd like that," he murmurs as he repositions his phone. His voice is rough and strained when he demands, "Run your fingers along your slick heat. Let me know if you're wet."

"I'm drenched," I pant. I have no idea what it is about this man, but I've been soaked since the moment he mentioned being hard.

"Fuck me, you're beautiful."

"Free your cock, Cam," I beg, finding a rhythm that will have me flying over the edge in no time. "Need to... see you."

Pushing his boxers down, his beautiful thick cock springs to his belly button.

My mouth waters at the sight. "Swirl your thumb along the head and give it a squeeze for me with one hand, while you cup your balls with the other. I wanna see you lose control."

My breath becomes ragged as I rub myself and take him in.

"It won't take much," he warns. "Watching you pleasure yourself is the hottest thing in my existence.

"Damn... Elizabeth, you're so fucking beautiful. God... I wish it were my fingers gliding along your slick wet cunt.... I want my thumbs rolling your pert nipples against my palm, and I need to feel my rough stubble marking your inner thighs as I feast on you. Tasting you..." he exhales heavily. "God... I don't want to just taste you. I fucking need to devour you. Hell, licking your sweet pussy is the first thing I'm doing when I see you again."

Electric sparks prickle along my spine at his words.

"Oh... Shit... I'm so fucking close..." I warn. "Keep talking, Cam... I need your sexy voice to push me over."

"I want you so fuckin' bad, Elizabeth. Next time we're together, I'm also gonna prop you up on all fours and slide into you from behind."

"Oh... That sounds so good," Just the thought of him entering me from that position has me slick with need. "I want that..." I encourage.

"You're gonna hold the headboard while I use my hands and my thick cock to pleasure you until you pass out," he promises.

The tingles up my spine morph into bolts of lightning tremoring through my entire body when he continues, "I'll squeeze your nipples just the way you like it with one hand, while I play your clit like a fiddle with the other. I'll be relentlessly slow... As I slowly slip in and out of you... Until you fall apart on my cock."

"Ohmigod, Cam... I'm... Right there," I beg for him to continue.

"So am I, Beautiful... Pinch yourself," he encourages, and that's all I need.

A slur of curses fall from my lips as I come—hard. Wave after wave of pleasure rockets through me, making my toes curl, and every fiber of my being lights on fire. Flopping back onto the bed, I ride out my orgasm.

"Fuck, Liz... You're so hot." I hear the sound of Cameron coming, but my vision is blurred, and I can't focus on anything of substance.

When my body returns to earth, I force myself to finally focus on the screen. Cameron's wiping at his chest with a tissue, and an enormous smile plays on his lips when his eyes meet mine.

"I think I've found a new favorite hobby."

"Really? What's that?" I ask, curiosity piqued.

"My goal is to make you come like that every fucking day."

"That's a lofty goal," I muse, shaking my head.

This man is ridiculous.

"I think it's a worthy one."

"And what if I die in the process?" I tease.

"There are worse ways to go," he deadpans.

I burst out into laughter as I stand on wobbly legs. "Okay, Mister King of Orgasms... Where are your shirts?"

"Hmmm... I like the sound of that... King of Orgasms."

Cutting him off, I quickly add, "Who knows when Milli will wake, and I need to be dressed when she does."

Reaching for my phone, I study his dresser. I wasn't paying attention when he pulled one for me, and I don't want to snoop.

"Second drawer from the top. Not sure my pajama bottoms will fit you, but they have drawstrings, so they might. You can find those in my bottom drawer. You're welcome to anything I have. Get comfortable and get into bed. I'm not ready for my time with you to end."

Once I'm dressed and snuggled into bed, I inhale deeply. "Ahhhh, this smells like you. Fair warning, Cam, your bed is so comfortable, I may never leave."

"I can get on board with that." He grins wickedly.

Chapter 26
Lizzy

I bolt out of bed when I hear the distinct sounds of Milli crying, "Daddy!"

"I'm coming, sweet girl!" I holler, rushing to her room.

Just as I open her door, she wails, "My tummy hurts."

I barely make it two steps into the room, and the distinct sound of retching fills the space between us. Milli may be tiny, but her stomach muscles are mighty as she proceeds to projectile puke all over her blankets.

Knowing there's nothing I can do but let it happen, I rush to comfort her. Rubbing her back, I assure her, "You're okay, sweet girl. I'm right here."

Once her stomach is empty, she looks to me with watery eyes and weakly whispers, "Sorry, Iz."

"Oh, Emilia, you have nothing to be sorry about." Not wanting to make an even bigger mess, I ask, "Do you think you're done puking for now?"

She slowly nods. "Uh-huh."

I quickly spring into action. "Don't move. Let me get you cleaned up."

In one fluid motion, I grab all the corners of her comforter and get the mess away from her as quickly as possible. Rushing to the spare bathroom down the hall, I drop it into the tub—I'll deal with that later. When I return, Milli looks so tiny in her twin-sized bed. She's sitting up, and her shirt is soiled as well as the sheets around her.

"Let's get you into the tub. Do you think you can walk?"

"Too tired," she moans.

Scooping her into my arms, I walk her to the bathroom just off her bedroom. "Let's get you in the tub, and I'll finish cleaning your bed."

The moment her body sinks into the warm water, she perks up and plays with her bath toys. This brings me hope. Turning off the water when it crests her thighs, I ask, "You okay for a minute? I wanna finish cleaning up your bed."

"Uh-huh. My bed is yucky."

Yeah, kiddo. That's an understatement.

I make quick work of grabbing her pajamas and sheets and throwing them in the wash. With the laundry room right across the hall from her bedroom, I'm able to check in on her often as I hastily clean up. Unfortunately, the smell keeps following me and when I look down, I see why. Rushing to Cameron's room, I find another pair of pajama bottoms and t-shirt to sleep in.

When her bed is stripped, and the washer is started, I return to the tub. Then I quickly wash and condition her hair. As I rinse off her hair, I ask, "Do you know where your daddy keeps your extra sheets?"

She adorably shakes her head and offers a weak, "No."

"Okay, kiddo. You ready to get out?" I offer, holding up a towel for her.

"I'm tired," she yawns heavily.

"Let's get you into some fresh jammies, and then I'll get a big bowl for you to use, in case you get sick."

"You stay with me?" she asks, hopeful. My heart melts for her when she squeezes my leg in a hug.

"Of course, sweet girl. Let me see if I can find some extra towels and blankets so we can set you up and not ruin any more bedding tonight."

As quickly as I can, I help her into pajamas and run a brush through her hair. Then I quickly pull it back into a braid, like my mom always did for us when we were sick as kids. Hopefully, it'll stay out of the way should she get sick again.

Once she's dressed, I rummage through the closets in the hall, hoping to find where Cameron keeps the spare blankets. When I can't find any, I realize desperate times call for desperate measures.

Rushing to the extra bedroom where Megan slept, I pull the blanket from between the comforter and sheets and bring it into Cameron's room. It's warm and will be easier to wash if she gets ill again. Folding the blanket in half like a sleeping bag, I spread it on the side of the bed closest to the bathroom. Then I open it up and lay towels on the pillow and across the mattress where she'll sleep. It may seem excessive, but it's what my mom and Nana would do for me as a kid, so they didn't have to wash every stitch of bedding multiple times.

Lifting the unused portion of the blanket, I help her onto the bed. "Hop in, and I'll cover you up."

"Will you hold my hand?" she asks when I've got her snuggled in tight to the blankets.

"Of course, Mills. Just let me turn off some lights."

She waits patiently for me to return. As soon as I lie down on my side of the bed, she reaches for my hand and squeezes it. "Night, My Iz. Love you."

Emotion clogs my throat, but I manage, "Love you, too, Mills," as I squeeze her hand in return.

It takes her no time at all to fall fast asleep.

Once I'm sure she's out, I reach for my phone to update Cameron. Hopefully, he's sleeping at three in the morning, but he deserves to know what's going on.

> Me: You were right. She did get sick. Poor girl (Sad face emoji)

> Me: Don't worry. I'm taking care of her. Puke is cleaned up. She's had a bath, and she's back to sleep. I'll let you know if anything changes.

*****

A miserable moan startles me from my sleep.

Registering what it means, I jump into action and place the bowl in front of Milli just in time for her to be sick once again. This time, the blankets are spared, but the girl in front of me looks miserable.

"I want my daddy," she moans.

Seeing that it's after seven in the morning, I offer, "Let me take care of this and when I get back, we'll call him."

When I return from cleaning the bowl, I see he's already texted.

> Cameron: Oh no. I'm so sorry. Call me when you wake up.

Pressing the call button, it barely rings when Cameron's concerned voice comes through the line. "How's she doing?"

"Can we switch to video? Milli wants to talk with you."

Within seconds, Cameron appears on my screen. "Hey, love bug. I heard you're not feeling well."

Milli nods in agreement but doesn't say anything, so I add, "She just got sick again."

"Oh, Mills. I'm so sorry."

Running a hand along her forehead to push her hair out of

her face, she feels warmer than usual. Not wanting to make a big deal of it in front of Milli, I ask, "Do you have a thermometer?"

Blowing out a deep breath, he closes his eyes. "I think there's one in the medicine cabinet in my bathroom. If not, it's in the drawer in the kitchen by the dishwasher. My mom helped me move, so I'm not sure where it is."

"I'll look when we get done with this call."

"If you can't find it, I can have one delivered for you. I'll get some saltine crackers and 7-Up, too."

"Where are you?" Milli asks, touching the screen of my phone.

"I'm in my hotel room."

"Can I see it?" she asks, burrowing into her blankets beside me.

Cameron quickly flips the camera around and shows her his bed, the bathroom, the couch, and the table. Milli nods but isn't nearly as energetic as she usually is when they video call.

Once he finishes his tour, his face returns. "When are you back?" Milli asks, running her finger along his face on the screen.

Running a hand through his hair, he tells her. "Hopefully by tomorrow night."

"How many sleeps is that?"

Oh, this girl. She melts my heart over and over again.

"Just one more night," Cameron reassures her.

Yawning, she tells him, "I sleep in your bed with My Iz."

"I thought you were in my room. I see you've got a mountain of blankets."

"My Iz didn't want your bed yucky. I'm like a bird, and this is my nest. There's soooo many blankets. She even put towels on the bed."

Cameron's lips twitch, and I can tell he's fighting like crazy not to smile. Milli hates it when people laugh at her adorableness. Somehow, he manages to maintain a straight face and points out, "At least you're cozy."

"Can I nap, Daddy?" she says on a long yawn. "I'm sleepy."

"Get some rest, love bug. I love you."

"Love you, Daddy," she whispers and hands the phone to me.

When he sees my face on the screen, he asks, "Can you take me off speaker?"

Flipping to a regular call, I hold the phone to my ear. He quickly points out, "She's really wiped out."

"She was sound asleep until she got sick again. I think it took a lot out of her."

"I feel horrible being here when she needs me."

"I can only imagine how you're feeling. Hopefully, it's just a twenty-four-hour flu, and she'll be back to her bubbly self in no time."

"I can see if I can get on the next flight home."

"I know it's not the same, but I'm here with her. She's already back to sleep," I assure him. "When she wakes up again, I'll get her to drink some of that Pedialyte you have in the cupboard. She's only been sick twice in five hours. We have both the urgent care and hospital here in town. If it'll make you feel better, I'll reach out to my mom. As a nurse, she'll know exactly what to do."

I hear the stress in his voice as he processes my words aloud. "Hmmm... It's only been five hours. Let's let her rest some more, and I'll check in with you a little later. I've got another meeting soon, so let me know if we need a thermometer. I'll get the crackers and soda delivered within the hour."

"This is Seaside, Cameron. Nothing delivers," I pointedly remind him.

"My assistant will get it. She's due into the office soon. I'll text her and have her drop things by. Just let me know what her temperature is as soon as you get it."

As much as I hate bothering others, this isn't about me. "Thank you, Cam. I'll call you if anything changes. I promise."

"Thanks, Elizabeth. I'll talk to you later."

"Talk to you later," I whisper, staring at his sleeping daughter.

Just as I'm about to hang up, he shouts into the phone, "Wait! Please know I have full confidence in you. My issue is with me not being there... Nothing else. I can't thank you enough for caring about Emilia like you have."

"She's easy to love, Cameron. Go to your meeting, and we'll talk later."

Chapter 27
Lizzy

"My tummy hurts," Milli moans. She's thrown up off and on throughout the entire day. I've given her Tylenol and tried to push fluids a little at a time, but nothing is working. Cameron and I have been in touch all day. I've assured him I've got things handled, and I'm doing everything we collectively can think of.

"I'm sorry, Mills. If I could, I'd take all your pain away. Do you wanna try taking another sip of this?" I offer, holding up the Pedialyte. "It should help you feel better."

"No, my tummy hurts," she groans quietly and curls into a ball on Cameron's bed. She's exhausted, and I've tried everything I can think of to help her.

Picking up my phone, I call my mom.

"Hey, honey, how's Milli doing?"

"She's not getting any better, Mom. She's got a low-grade fever of one hundred point seven, and I can't get the medicine to break it. She can't possibly have anything left in her stomach, and I've tried to push a small sip of Pedialyte every half hour or so. But she keeps saying her stomach hurts. Maybe she's pulled a muscle? I don't know what more I can do. Nothing I'm doing is working, and she's miserable."

"I think it might be time to take her to urgent care, Liz. They'll make sure she's not dehydrated and give her some anti-nausea meds to make her stop vomiting. If something else is going on, they'll get to the bottom of it."

Glancing at the clock, I see it's past six. "I think urgent care is closed."

"Then take her to the emergency room." Mom's tone is no-nonsense, and I quickly stand to gather the things I'll need.

"Okay, Mom." I nod, decision made.

"I'm gonna pack a few things for Milli and get her into the car. I also need to call Cameron and let him know what's happening."

"Are you okay to drive?"

Trying to keep level-headed and not freak out, I tell her the truth. "Yeah, I'll be fine."

"Want me to call Lanie and have her meet you there?" Mom offers.

"Yes, please. Who knows how long I'll be there, and I could use the company."

"Okay, sweetheart. I'll do that. Please keep me informed. I'll be waiting to hear from you. I love you, and I'm so proud of you."

"I love you, too, Mom. I'll be in touch."

With that, I hang up the phone and call Cameron.

It rings four times, then goes to voicemail.

Crap. He's probably at the concert and won't be available for hours.

When his message beeps, I take a deep breath and fill him in.

"Hi, Cameron. I've just gotten off the phone with my mom. She thinks it's time I take Emilia to the hospital to get checked out. Hopefully, they'll give us some anti-nausea meds and make sure she's not dehydrated. I'll text you when I know more since you won't be able to hear this over the music."

The moment I hang up, I text him the same information, then go into action. Grabbing her diaper bag, I walk to Milli's room and restock it. I pack a change of clothes and her favorite blanket that's now clean from the wash. I also grab a stuffed animal to snuggle with, should she feel scared.

Then I find my purse and slip on my hoodie and shoes from the hall. Making sure I have my charger and wallet, I rush to the kitchen and grab the medical form from the bulletin board Cameron's signed, giving me permission to have Emilia treated should we need it. I've never been more thankful for being prepared in my life. In all my years of watching kids, I've *never* needed this form—until now.

Loading everything in the car, I return to Cameron's room to wake a now-sleeping Milli. Lifting her from the bed, her hot little body clings to mine. "Where are we goin'?" she softly whispers.

"Let's get you to the doctor. Hopefully, they'll get you some medicine, and you'll feel better soon."

"My tummy hurts, Iz," she whines as I buckle her into her car seat.

"I know, sweet girl," I say, brushing her hair from her face. "The hospital is only a few minutes away, and I'll get you the help you need."

*****

When I pull up to the emergency room, my sister and Ryan are waiting at the door. I don't think I could love my family more than I do in this instant. I no sooner pull up to the curb than Ryan comes around and reaches for my keys. "Here, let me park for you. Get Milli inside, and I'll be in as soon as I can."

When I lift Milli out of her car seat, she clings to me once again. "My tummy hurts, Iz."

"I know, sweet girl. We're here to get you some help."

Being in a small town, the emergency room can either be crowded or fairly empty and usually no in-between. I'm relieved to only find a few other people in the waiting room when I walk up to the intake desk.

The man at the desk asks, "What brings you in today?"

I explain as succinctly as possible what's been happening with Milli and give him the permission-to-treat form with all the relevant information. He makes a copy. Then he takes her vitals and asks her a few more questions. Eventually, we're sent to the waiting room to be called back for triage.

As Lanie, Ryan, and I wait for Milli to be seen in a quiet corner of the hospital waiting room, a loud commotion can be heard from the entrance. When I look up, I find Sloane and Raven frantically walking toward us with Jax and Finn not far behind them.

"Wh... what are you doing here?" I ask when they sit down beside us.

"We heard Milli's sick," Sloane says as if it should explain everything. I should've known better when Mom called Lanie, they all would come—what I didn't expect was all the guys in tow.

"How are you doing, kiddo?" Finn asks when Milli looks his way.

"My tummy really hurts, and I keep getting sick," Milli croaks miserably, and my heart continues to break for her.

Looking at everyone, I point out the obvious, "You know they're not gonna let us all back there, right?"

Raven shrugs. "Where you go, we go. We can't let you go through this alone."

"Besides, we can't just sit around twiddling our thumbs, knowing you're here," Finn interjects.

"No kidding," Sloane adds. "I'd feel utterly useless sitting at home. Besides..." She reaches out and pats Milli's leg next to her. "We can't let this sweet girl go through this alone."

"We'll stick around until we know what's going on with Mills," Jax assures me. "Do you need anything, Liz?"

Shaking my head, I pull my phone from my pocket. When I see my message to Cameron is still left as delivered, I sigh. "Only for the concert to end, so my message can be seen."

I choose my words carefully because there's no way I want to draw attention to Cameron in front of Milli. I know he'll get here as soon as he can. Besides, until we know what's going on, there's nothing any of us can do but wait.

Jax winces, then looks to Milli. Reaching for his own phone, he stands and says, "I'll see if I can do something."

Jax steps away, and I assume he's reaching out to someone at the label, but the moment Milli moans again, my focus is on her.

Rocking her in my arms, I brush the hair from her face. "I'm here, sweet girl."

"It hurts, Iz." Her voice is weak and miserable and utterly heartbreaking.

"We should be seen shortly. Just a little longer," I promise.

My family talks around me, but my focus is on keeping this poor girl calm and comfortable. She's got her blanket wrapped around her and although she's like a personal radiator in my arms, I just rock and do my best to soothe her.

Relief washes through me a few minutes later when we hear, "Emilia Kruse?"

"Right here," I say, attempting to stand, but my feet don't feel steady, so I sit down and readjust her before trying again.

Finn offers, "Want me to carry her?"

"I've got it. But could you get her bag?"

"I'll get it," Lanie says, catching up to me. "I'm going back with you."

"Right this way," a man in his early thirties says as I approach. "I'm Daniel. I'm a pediatric nurse. I'm gonna get you into a room where we can further assess what's going on. Can you tell me what's wrong?"

Milli's voice is weak, and my heart aches as she explains, "I'm sick. My tummy hurts *really* bad."

"Can you tell me what's been going on?"

I quickly go through her symptoms, starting with when it happened and how long she's been sick. By the time we get to the room where they'll examine her further, he knows the entire story.

"Let's get her lying on the bed. Can you show me where it hurts?"

With one hand, Milli reaches for mine as the other rubs along her lower abdomen. "Right here."

"Mind if I have a look?"

As Daniel goes through the motions of completing his exam, I feel utterly helpless. Milli's cooperative and answers his questions. That is until he presses lightly on her stomach. Instantly, her tiny body contorts, and I'm sure my family can hear her cries from the waiting room.

"I'm so sorry." He quickly pulls his hand back. "I won't touch you there again. Is it better now that I've stopped?"

Milli nods but keeps her grip on my hand tight.

"I need to start an IV and get some blood work started. I'll also page the pediatric doctor on call to get things rolling."

In a well-practiced move, he pulls things from the cabinet beside us and says into his radio clipped to his shoulder, "Page Pediatrics. I need Dr. Wilks to room seven, STAT."

Holy shit. This is more serious than I thought.

Glancing to my sister to ensure she heard the same thing, panic sets in when her wide eyes meet mine. Needing to keep my reaction under control for the sake of the precious girl beside me, I force myself to close my eyes and breathe slowly.

"Emilia?" Daniel says, reaching for an iPad on his cart and handing it to her, "I need to place an IV in your arm so we can get you the medicine you need. Do you want to watch a show while I do this?"

The iPad is loaded with various cartoon icons. Seeing one of her favorites, I point out, "Do you want to watch Bluey?"

Emilia nods and presses the icon herself.

"Great," Daniel says. "I'm going to spray your arm to numb it. Then I need to step out for just a sec to grab a smaller needle. It seems they don't have one for someone her size in this room. While I do that, would you mind changing her into this?" He holds up a pink hospital gown.

"Okay," Milli says quietly, already interested in the show.

Before Daniel leaves, he hits us with another hard truth. "I'm going to personally make sure Dr. Wilks is on her way. Once I get the IV started, she'll likely have some tests she wants me to run."

"Do you know what's wrong with her?" I ask desperately.

"I can't say for certain, but please note I will make sure Emilia's considered a priority until we find out."

The moment he steps out, my sister steps to my side and wraps around me. In a quiet whisper, she says, "It's gonna be all right. We'll get through this."

*****

I'm stuck in the worst game of hurry up and wait of my life.

The last few hours have been a blur. Milli's been poked, prodded, and given a series of tests. She's had both a CT scan as well as an ultrasound, and we're waiting on the results so the doctor can tell us how to proceed.

The worst part of it all—I still haven't heard from Cameron.

Since I still don't have any concrete updates, I've held off on calling again. I know him. He's already going to freak out. He felt guilty enough leaving her here. I can't imagine how he'll react to knowing we're at the hospital.

Glancing at the clock, I realize we've been here for less than three hours, though let's face it, it feels like three years. It's agonizing waiting like this. Every nurse that comes in to check on her has me jumping in my seat, hoping they'll bring us something substantial to proceed with. Now that Milli's pain is managed, and she's currently napping, sitting here is almost bearable.

"I'm going to use the restroom and check in with everyone. Do you need anything?" Lanie asks, standing near the door.

"No. I'm good." I sigh, leaning my head back against the wall behind me. I close my eyes and do my best to remain relaxed.

Lanie's been my rock through this. She's held my hand and asked questions I didn't even think to ask the doctors. I don't know what I'd do without her or the rest of my family for that matter.

I'm startled by the door sliding open.

When I see Dr. Wilks instead of a nurse, I'm simultaneously relieved to know I'll get answers, yet on edge for what's to come. Her grave expression doesn't help. She doesn't examine Milli or look at any charts. Instead, she grabs the rolling stool and sits down in front of me.

"I've just gotten the results for all her tests and there's no doubt in my mind Emilia's appendix is the culprit. From what I can tell, it hasn't ruptured... yet. But I'm not willing to take that chance much longer."

"Her dad's in California..." I start but don't know where I'm going with it.

"I understand that. But this truly is an emergency situation. If her appendix ruptures, it'll be far worse for Emilia and her recovery. Thankfully, the paperwork you brought in allows you to make the decision for him in his absence. But in this emergent situation, the hospital would operate on her regardless of any paperwork. I'd like to get her prepped and into surgery within the hour if possible. It could very likely rupture at any time and the sooner we get it out, the less complications we'll have going forward."

Handing me the papers she has in her hand, she points to the place where I would sign for consent.

Fuck, what do I do? Cameron should be the one making this decision.

She needs this, Elizabeth. Get your shit together. Stop freaking the fuck out and sign the damn paper.

Taking a fortifying breath, I reach for the pen in her hand and scribble my signature across the page.

"Okay, we can let her rest for now, but in a few minutes, a slew of people will be in here to care for Emilia. I find it's easier if the parent, or in your case caregiver, stays with their child until they go under. This means we'll have you get gowned up and have you join us in the operating suite. Once she's under anesthesia, a nurse will lead you to the waiting room for family and visitors."

Holy shit. This is happening so fast.

"Ms. Lancaster?"

Shit. She's waiting for a response. "Okay. I'll do that."

"I promise the moment the surgery is over, I'll personally come to tell you how it went. I know this is scary, but it's necessary. I've successfully completed this exact surgery dozens of times. She's in good hands. I assure you. Do you have any questions for me before I leave to get prepped?"

"Uh... how long does it typically take?" I ask, trying to get all the pertinent information for when Cameron finally calls.

"It typically takes about an hour. If for some reason it goes longer, I will send someone from the OR to update you."

I nod in understanding. God, this is so much to take in. "Okay. Thank you."

The door opens, and a determined nurse comes in, pushing buttons on monitors and unhooking cords from Emilia. I feel so helpless just standing here watching them. But not wanting to get in their way, I stay seated beside Milli's bed.

When a second nurse comes in, Milli stirs. "Where's My Iz?" she says, sleepy.

Reaching for her hand, I squeeze it reassuringly. "I'm right here, sweet girl."

She darts her wide eyes around the room, then they meet mine. "I want my daddy!"

"I know, Mills. He loves you and will be here as soon as he can."

"What are they doin'?" she asks, watching the nurses in full action mode.

What the fuck do I even say?

How do I tell her she's going into surgery?

Does she even know what surgery is?

She's three for fuck's sake. Why would she know?

"We found out it's your appendix that's making you sick. The doctor is going to make you better by taking it out."

With wide eyes, she looks around at the chaos in the room. "Will you stay with me?"

"I'll be with you as long as I can." I won't lie to her, but I'm not telling her the entire truth either. I can't do that to her. Needing her to understand what's happening, I quickly explain, "They're going to make you really sleepy, then when you wake up, your appendix will be gone, and I'll be waiting for you."

She nods but doesn't say anything.

The next forty minutes is a complete blur. When my sister comes back from the bathroom, I fill her in on everything. With everything happening so fast, she assures me she'll wait with me when Milli goes into surgery.

When it's time, I help Milli get transferred to a gurney and hold her hand the entire way to the operating room. Once inside, I couldn't tell you any of the details of the operating room, other than it was bright, cold, and so sterile.

It took everything in me to just be there for Milli. To stay strong and not show her just how scared I am for her.

Just as she's about to be transferred to the table, the doctor says it's time to say goodbye.

Hugging her, I promise, "Love you, sweet girl, I'll see you when you wake up."

"Love you, Iz."

The doctor tells her to count as high as she can.

I'll never in my life forget her sweet little voice echoing through the room.

"One... two... three... four...fff..."

My heart breaks into a million pieces when it's time to walk away.

Chapter 28
Cameron

My heart has been frozen in my chest from the moment I read those words on my screen.

> Lizzy: I've just gotten off the phone with my mom. She thinks it's time I take Emilia to the hospital. Hopefully, they'll give us some anti-nausea meds and make sure she's not dehydrated. I'll update you when I know more.

> Lizzy: We're at the hospital, and they're running tests now. Won't know for an hour or so.

It was nearly three fucking hours before I saw either of those texts.

I'd closed the deal with Sienna Flames and decided to celebrate by attending their sold-out concert. It was great to relax after all the stress of the deal that has consumed the last three days of my life was settled. Lizzy and I had been in contact all day and although I've felt torn from the moment I learned Milli was sick, there wasn't anything I could do about it. If she has a virus, it needs to run its course.

I met up with a buddy of mine from when I lived in LA. We grabbed a drink before the concert and caught up. Nick is still living the single life and enjoying the music scene to his fullest. I've never felt so old or out of touch. Don't get me wrong, I like the guy and wish him the best, but the moment Emilia came into my life, all thoughts of living that single life he's still thriving in sailed.

It wasn't until I got back to my hotel room and went to charge my phone that I noticed it had been on *do not disturb*.

Fuck. My. Life.

The moment I changed the setting, notification after notification blew up my phone.

Seeing a missed call from Lizzy, Jax, and even my assistant Merna made my blood turn to ice.

Only one mattered, so I instantly connected a call to Lizzy.

It rang once.

Twice.

Three times.

Then it went to voicemail.

Knowing Jax would be close by, I call him next.

He picks up on the first ring. "Hey, man. I'm glad you called."

"What's wrong? Is Emilia okay? Lizzy? My fucking phone was on do not disturb, and I'm just now getting notifications."

Frustration flows through me. I can't believe I was so stupid. My daughter's sick for crying out loud. I should know better.

"Okay, man, take a breath. I need you firing on all cylinders so we can figure out how to get you here as soon as possible."

"What's going on, Jax?" I spit out. My nerves are wound so

tight, it's taking everything in me not to snap. "Lizzy's not answering her phone."

"That's because she's back with Milli at the moment and probably can't pick up. Please sit down and take a breath. I promise I'll fill you in on everything."

Sitting on the edge of my bed, I inhale deeply and demand, "Please just spit it out. I'm on the verge of losing my shit. If I don't get answers... well I... fuck, I don't know what I'll do."

"First, you need to know Emilia's in good hands. We're at the hospital, and it's been determined she needs an appendectomy. At the time of her last scan, it hadn't ruptured, but we won't know until she comes out of surgery for sure."

What. The. Actual. Fuck?

This cannot be happening.

Surgery? Did he say surgery? As in she's in surgery now?

"I need to get to her," I mutter as I gather my things from the hotel.

"That's what I'm trying to help you with. I've been looking at flights. If you can get to the airport, there's one that takes off in about an hour, but it's a long shot. If you can't make that one, you might have to wait 'till morning. The first flights leave around five."

"You've already looked into this?" I ask in disbelief.

"Look, man, I'm trying to bring you solutions, not more problems. Tell me what you need, and I'll make it happen. If you need me to come pick you up so you're not driving like a crazed lunatic, I'll leave for Portland now."

"I've got my car," I mumble, zipping the last of my things into my overnight bag.

Making one last sweep through the hotel room, I'm out the door and bolting to the lobby.

"I've gotta check out and get to the airport. I'll let you know if I make the flight. Have Elizabeth call me."

"Will do, man. We're here for you and that precious girl of yours. Just let us know what you need."
*****

The airport gods are in my favor.

I manage to get on the last flight leaving LA and although I can't talk to Lizzy, I'm able to text her.

> Me: I made the flight just as they were closing the doors. Any update on Mills?

> Lizzy: No. She should be out of surgery soon.
> I promise I will keep you updated.

Waiting is agony. I've only known about Emilia's condition for less than an hour. I can't imagine what Elizabeth is going through.

> Me: How are you doing?

> Lizzy: Not gonna lie—I've never been more terrified in my life. But she's in good hands, and the doctor assured me it's a routine procedure.

> Me: I can't thank you enough for being here for her when I couldn't.

> Lizzy: Cameron, do not even for one second beat yourself up over this. There is nothing either of us could do. My mom has assured me of this more than once tonight, so I'm passing that message along to you.

Logically, I know she's right.

But guilt holds no bounds when it comes to your children and their safety.

Lizzy: Cam, what's going on in that head of
yours? Talk to me.

She's had a shit day and still above everything, she's worried about me. What did I ever do to deserve her?

Me: I don't even know what to think. I'm just
trying to hold it all together and not lose my
shit completely.

Lizzy: Same.

Me: I can't thank you enough for being here
for Emilia.

Lizzy: You never need to thank me.

Lizzy: I think I see the doctor. BRB

The nervous energy ripping through my veins could fuel this entire flight. I want nothing more than to rip the doors off the cockpit and force them to fly to Seaside rather than Portland. No matter what happens, I still have a two-hour drive ahead of me once I land.

I swear, this is the longest fucking day of my life.

Nearly twenty minutes later, I finally get the text I've been waiting for.

Lizzy: She's out of surgery. Everything went
as planned. It did not rupture. She's in
recovery. I'll send you a pic when I see her for
myself.

Relief washes through me, and I can finally breathe again. Before I can respond, another text comes through.

Lizzy: If I don't answer, it's because I'm with Mills until she wakes up in the recovery room.

This woman thinks of everything.

Here she is—scared shitless—but she still puts my nerves at ease.

Me: Thanks. I'll let you know when I land.

*****

When I land at PDX, I have one thing in mind. Getting to my daughter. I'm so focused as I enter the main part of the airport, I almost walk right past Jax Cartwright in my haste.

"Wait up, man." I hear as a man who's been leaning against the wall approaches.

"Wha... What are you doing here?" I ask in disbelief when I recognize him.

He's wearing a black hoodie with a baseball hat covering most of his face, but it's clearly him. Surely, he'll get recognized in a place like this. Especially with his bandmate Finn standing next to him.

"We couldn't let you drive in this condition," he admits as he points to the exit. "Where's your car? The girls dropped us off, and it's only a matter of time until we're recognized."

"Girls?"

"Raven and Sloane insisted you not drive or be alone for that matter. They're already on the way back to Seaside. No sense in all of us waiting."

"You *all* came?"

"Dude, you don't get it, do you?" Finn laughs.

"What don't I get?" I ask, making my way to the parking garage.

"There's nothing those girls won't do for their family."

"But... I'm not family," I say, pressing the elevator button.

"But Lizzy is... and by the way every single one of us was at the hospital within minutes of hearing about Emilia arriving, I'm pretty certain you're a part of us... whether you like it or not."

"I'm right here." I unlock my car and pop my luggage in the trunk.

As I walk around to the driver's side, Finn stops me. "Look, man, I can't imagine the trainwreck of emotions you've been through today. Let me drive. I promise, I'll get you to your daughter."

Realizing how frazzled my nerves are, I relinquish my keys, then go to the passenger side, as Jax climbs into the back seat.

We ride in silence as Finn maneuvers his way out of the parking garage.

Once we're on the freeway, Jax hits me with another truth bomb.

"Look, I'm not exactly sure what your *summer arrangement* is with Lizzy being Emilia's nanny. But after witnessing her actions tonight, I'm certain that girl loves both *you and your daughter*. I hope like hell for your sake you know just how special she is."

Chapter 29
Cameron

Jax's words roll through my mind the entire drive to Seaside. I know Lizzy's special. If I have my way, I'll turn this summer arrangement into something permanent. She's it for me. She has been since that day in the coffee shop.

I was stupid and let her go before, but I won't make that mistake twice.

As soon as I get the chance, I'm gonna tell her exactly how I feel.

But first, I need to make sure Emilia's okay.

It's barely five in the morning when I finally walk through the door of the hospital room. The lights are off, and the sound of monitors beep in the distance. I'm surprised to find Lanie resting on the lounge chair beside the bed.

Where is Elizabeth?

I can't imagine her leaving Emilia's side.

Maybe she's in the bathroom?

As I look around the room, it hits hard—the guys were right.

Without a doubt, the Lancasters do love my daughter.

Not only did they drive all that way just to make sure I know I have a support system, Lanie's spent the entire night at the hospital. Hell, the entire family's gone out of their way to be there for both Emilia and me. I don't know how I'll ever thank them or let them know how much this means but somehow, I'll find a way.

When I turn the corner in the room, and my daughter's hospital bed comes into view, my heart combusts on the spot. There's Lizzy, lying on her side, barely staying on the bed, with her arm wrapped under Milli's head. Milli's snuggled up next to her, holding Lizzy's arm like a security blanket. Milli has covers on her, but Lizzy's on top of the blankets. She's wearing my pajama bottoms and her green hoodie.

The brevity of what she's gone through hits me like a ton of bricks. She literally dropped everything and put my daughter's needs above all else. Despite the chaos of the last twenty-four hours, both look so peaceful and perfect—minus the hospital bed and monitors in the room. I almost hate to disturb them, but my need to be near them is unbearable.

Walking beside Milli, I brush the hair back from her face and kiss her forehead. She smells sweet and innocent. Suddenly, all is right in the world. Now that I can see for myself that she's okay, my legs almost buckle from the weight I've been carrying.

God, I've missed her. I don't know what I would've done if something worse had happened. I can't imagine what she's been through. It kills me that I wasn't here for her.

When I pull back, the movement wakes Lizzy.

"Hey, you," I whisper, leaning in further and brushing a kiss over her lips.

"When did you get here?" She blinks, looking around.

"Just a few minutes ago," I admit. "Sorry I couldn't get here sooner."

"You got here when you could. That's all that matters," Lizzy assures me, then tries to extricate herself from my octopus of a daughter.

Personal space is nonexistent when it comes to sleeping beside Milli.

By the time Lizzy's standing, I'm already at her side.

Pulling her into my arms, I hug her fiercely. It feels like forever since I've held her, and I can't get enough. Inhaling deeply, I'm finally able to relax. She feels like a warm spring day after the storm. I'm not sure what I would've done if she hadn't been here with Emilia. I have so much I need to tell her, but that can wait. For now, I just need her in my arms.

When Emilia moves, Lizzy breaks our hug and replaces the bedrail behind us. This simple gesture makes me fall even harder for her. Here she is sleep deprived and exhausted beyond belief, but she still makes Milli a priority.

The click from the bedrail stirs Lanie. She darts her eyes around and when they meet mine, she gasps. "Oh, you've made it."

"Yeah, thanks to Jax and Finn. I can't thank you all enough for being here. It means the world to me having you all step up like you have. I don't know what I did to deserve you all in my life, but I'll be forever grateful."

Words can't even express how I feel for the entire Lancaster family. No one has ever been in my corner like this, and I'm still unsure how to process it.

Lanie stretches and stands. "It's not a problem. There's nothing I wouldn't do for Liz or Emilia for that matter. Now that you're here, and they won't be alone, do you mind if I head out? I could use some good sleep."

Lizzy reaches for her sister and pulls her into a hug. "Thanks so much for everything, Lane. I love you."

"Love you, too, Liz. I'm only a phone call away. Let me know if you need anything."

The moment the door clicks shut, I hear the one voice I've been going out of my mind over. "Daddy, is that you?"

Rushing to her side, I reach for her hand. "I'm right here, sweet pea."

"I had an owiee, and they fixed it," she says, pulling at her hospital gown. "See, I have a mark."

Her mark is covered by a bandage, but I'm sure I'll see it soon enough. Feeling utterly useless for not being here, I ask, "How are you feeling? Can I get you anything?"

"I'm thirsty," she croaks out.

"Let me get a nurse and ask what you can have," Lizzy says, jumping into action.

"I can do that," I offer, but she shakes me off. "Just stay with her. She's missed you."

Again, this woman puts Emilia first.

If I weren't already head over heels in love with her, I certainly would be now.

Emilia draws my attention when she moves, and a little grunt escapes.

"Hey now, Mills. You gotta take it easy."

"Help me get my blankie?"

I get it and cover her up. Leaning in, I kiss her forehead once again. "I've missed you, sweet girl."

"Me, too, Daddy. Will I go home today?"

Shit. I have no idea. "I'll have to talk with the doctors first. We want you to be strong and healthy before going home."

"My Iz will know. She takes care of things," Milli states matter-of-factly.

Guilt flows through me. I should know this. Hell, I should've talked with the doctor. With everything happening so fast, I never got the chance. I've been so focused on getting here, it never crossed my mind to reach out to the surgeon.

Before I can respond, Lizzy pushes through the door. "They'll bring us something as soon as they can."

"Good. Have you heard anything from the doctor since her surgery?"

"No, they'll do rounds at seven. I'm sure we'll hear more then." Walking straight to Milli, she squeezes her hand. "This little sprite was so brave and strong last night. She's on antibiotics and if all goes well, she'll likely go home later this evening or tomorrow."

"Did they mention how long it typically takes to recover and what her restrictions will be?"

"She just needs to rest and take it easy for a few weeks. We should cancel her swim lessons until her doctor releases her. Milli, it's really important you don't lift anything heavy or ride your bike for a few weeks. It could hurt your tummy."

"I'm too sleepy to ride." Milli yawns.

Running a hand along her hair, Lizzy smiles lovingly at Milli. "Get some rest, Mills. We'll be here when you wake up."

"K, Iz. Love you."

"Love you, too, Mills," Lizzy whispers and leans in to kiss her forehead.

I knew they shared a bond from the moment they met. But witnessing how easily they express their love for one another takes things to an entirely new level—for all of us.

A sudden burst of emotion rips through me and nearly brings me to my knees. Gripping the bedrail beside me for strength, I blink back unshed tears. These two are everything to me. My life may be crazy and chaotic, but one thing has never been clearer than in this instant. I'm one thousand percent without a doubt in love with Elizabeth Lancaster.

Chapter 30
Lizzy

After staying through morning rounds and hearing from Dr. Wilks herself that Milli's making great progress, Cameron convinces me to go home, get some rest, and freshen up. As much as I hate leaving him because he's had just as much sleep as I have, I admit I do feel disgusting and in desperate need of a shower. It's been more than two days since I've bathed, and I'm certain my deodorant expired many hours ago.

I drive through the quiet streets of Seaside to Nana's house on autopilot, all the while reliving the events of the last twenty-four hours. The moment I park in our driveway, all the emotions I've kept tucked away burst to the surface like a flash flood. Big, fat, ugly tears blur my vision, and I finally let all my fears flow out of me. I've never been more scared in my life and now that I've had the chance to think about what could've gone wrong. Fuck, it terrifies the living hell out of me.

Leaning my head against the steering wheel, my tears flow freely. My chest burns as sobs wreck me. I'm so thankful I called my mom when I did. Who knows what would've happened if I hadn't listened to her. Milli just kept puking and crying, and I couldn't do anything for her.

I'm so lost in my misery, I barely register when the door opens and strong arms wrap around me and squeeze me tight. Jax doesn't say anything; he just squats beside me and holds me as I lean into him and unload every emotion I've been holding in. Feeling his warmth and security just makes me cry even harder.

Eventually, he pulls back to look me in the eyes and asks, "What's wrong, Liz? Did something happen to Milli?"

Swiping away at my tears, I sob, "No... She's... fine. The doctor says..." Hiccup "That she'll make a full recovery."

"Then what's wrong?" His eyes fill with more concern than he had for Milli at the hospital last night.

"I... she... I don't know if I can do this." The words rush out, and I can't even make sense of what I'm trying to say. I have so many thoughts swirling through my head, and I can't keep any of them straight.

"Let's get you inside, and we can sort it all out," Jax suggests.

I'm sure he thinks I've lost my mind and will be calling for reinforcements soon.

Maybe I have?

I don't know.

I just hurt so much. I can't imagine going through anything like this ever again in my life. I felt so helpless, and nothing I did worked.

Sobbing the entire way, he helps me from the car and ushers me to the porch steps. "Let's sit out here. Everyone else is likely still asleep."

As soon as we're seated on the top step, he puts his strong arms around me and pulls me close. "Take a breath, Liz. Tell me what's going on."

"I'm..." I snort. "I'm getting snot all over you."

"Least of my worries," he assures me. "Talk to me, Liz."

"I'm so scared," I admit. "We could've lost her. So much could've gone wrong."

"But they didn't." He pats my back softly. "Shhh... You're okay. I've got you."

"What business did I have thinking I could care for a three-year-old? If I hadn't called Mom when I did, it could've ruptured. And then what? Call Cameron and tell him sorry, I don't know shit... and may have irrevocably harmed his sweet innocent daughter."

"Liz, you can't—" he starts, but I continue with my rant.

"She loves me. She told me as much. How can I let her love me when I can't even be sure I can care for her the way she needs?"

"Elizabeth." His voice raises, and his tone is dead serious. This causes me to pause and take notice.

"What?" I ask, wondering why he's so upset.

"First, you did everything right last night. It's *because of you* Emilia's safe right now. You were calm and decisive and only had her best interests at heart. Fuck, you were cool as a cucumber when the rest of us wanted to freak the fuck out. Why are you falling apart now? What's this really about?"

I take a moment to consider his words.

What is this really about?

"Seriously, Liz... What's going on?"

"I'm..." *When I take stock of my emotions, only one sticks out.* "I'm scared, Jax."

"She's safe," he whispers and squeezes my shoulder tight against him.

"No... That's not it. I'm scared of losing them."

Fuck, is that really it?

"Losing who? You haven't lost anyone."

Yes. When I look deep down, that's the crux of my issue.

"I'm scared of losing Cameron and Milli. They've come to mean so much to me in such a short time. I know without a doubt I love them. But who am I to think I even deserve to be with them? Hell, I can't even support myself. I'm still in school and won't even have a paying job until I finish my student teaching. How is that fair to them? Cameron deserves to be with someone his own age who has their shit together. And that sweet, innocent girl... as much as I'd do anything for her, I certainly have no business stepping into the role of being her mom. She's the most amazing thing ever. She's smart as a whip, and I swear, half the time when I make a decision for what I think is best for her, I'm totally fucking winging it."

When I finally take a breath, Jax just cocks a brow and smirks.

"What?"

"Hmmm..." he draws out, and the jerk has the nerve to smile at me.

"Hmmm what? Just spit it out, Jax. My nerves are frazzled, and I'm clearly already losing my shit."

"There's so much to unpack in that word vomit of yours, I'm not sure what to tackle first."

"Why are you smirking at me? What's going on?"

He should know better than to hold back like he is. Sloane's my sister after all; I'm sure I'm not the only Lancaster to freak out on him.

"I think..." he starts to say something then narrows his eyes on me. "I think there's one sentence you need to focus on, and.... the rest... well, it'll work itself out."

Replaying my words, I'm at a loss for what he's getting at.

"Gah, Jax... you expect me to remember what I just said. Apparently, I just *word vomited* all over you. I'm running on empty and obviously, I'm on an emotional roller coaster. Help a girl out."

"You said you love them," he draws out.

"Of course, I do. What's your point?"

His brows rise to his hair line. "Do you hear yourself?"

"Grrrr..." I growl. "What's your point, Jax?"

"Elizabeth, you're one of the smartest people I know." He shakes his head and has the audacity to laugh. I seriously might rip his arms off his chest and beat him with them. "You literally just said it. Why isn't it sinking in?"

"What are you talking about, Jax Cartwright? My patience is thin and unless you want *my crazy* unleashing on you... spit it out!"

"Elizabeth Renee Lancaster... I love you like a sister, but you're gonna be the death of me. You. Love. Them. Plain and simple. Nothing else should matter. Yes, you just went through an extremely traumatic experience, so of course you're scared. But focus on what you just said. You. Love. Them." He punctuates each word as if he wants to slap me across the face with them.

Replaying his words, I repeat, "I. Love. Them."

"Don't you?"

"Yes, but that doesn't mean I should be with them."

Jax's arms flail out between us. "Why the fuck not?"

"So much could go wrong. What if I'm not ready?"

"Liz, you could walk across the street and get hit by a bus tomorrow. Nothing is guaranteed. The bigger question you need to ask yourself is can you handle *not being with them?* Can you seriously say you'd be okay if he moved on? Our paths are bound to cross; will you be okay watching him be in love with someone else?"

"He... he hasn't said he loved me," I quickly point out.

"Oh, you didn't ride with him for two hours this morning.

He was equally worried about *you and his daughter*. Trust me. That man loves you just as much as you love him. I'd bet my best guitar on it."

Jumping to my feet, it hits me like a bolt of lightning. "I... I need to see him."

"Maybe take a minute and shower first. No offense, but your eyes are puffy, and you're a bit ripe at the moment."

Chapter 31
Lizzy

Just as I get out of the shower, I receive a text.

Thinking of the state I left his house, I pick up my pace. There isn't a bed that's ready for Milli or Cameron for that matter. I'm sure they must be exhausted. I washed all the blankets while taking care of Milli yesterday but never got around to making any beds.

As I rush downstairs, I find Lanie in the kitchen. "Great news, Milli's being discharged this afternoon. I'm going to head over to their house and make it so they'll have beds to sleep in."

"Liz, you're exhausted. Have you even slept?"

"A little at the hospital this morning," I admit.

"Here," she says, grabbing her purse. "I'll head over there

and help you. Who knows how long they'll take, but I don't want you running yourself ragged."

I'm seriously dead on my feet, and only the thought of finally telling Cameron how I feel is what's getting me through this.

"Sure. Wanna take your car since I have Cam's?"

"How about I drive? I'm well rested, and you're clearly running on fumes. I'll walk back or get Ryan to pick me up... Oh, don't give me that look. I'm not negotiating with you. I'm driving."

Rushing to her, I hug her fiercely. "I love you, Lanie. You're the best."

My sister lives up to her word. She and I make quick work at getting Cameron's place ready for their return. We make all the beds, she does the dishes, and I put another load of laundry in the wash. She even has the forethought to order takeout for us before heading back home.

With nothing left to do, I sit on the couch to wait for them.

Who knew a couch would be my kryptonite?

Well, that and the remote being on the counter in the kitchen.

The couch is soft, inviting, and I'll be honest, I don't even remember closing my eyes.

The next thing I know, I'm being lifted into Cameron's arms.

"Wha-what are you doing?" I mutter, still half-asleep.

"Putting you to bed, beautiful," Cameron says, walking to his room.

"But you just got here," I protest. "Where's Milli?"

"She's resting on the chair in the living room. We've been home for a bit, and you haven't budged."

"I... I need to talk with you," I say on a long yawn when he sets me on his bed.

"We have *all of forever* to talk, Elizabeth. For now, let's get you into some pajamas and into bed. You need sleep more than any conversation."

Walking to his dresser, he snags a t-shirt and pajama pants for me to wear.

I want to protest, but my body still feels like lead weights have been anchored to each limb. It takes everything in me to just remain seated and stare at the clothes he's set beside me.

"Here," he says, helping me lift my shirt. "Let me take care of you for a change." He grins adorably. "You really are out of it, aren't you?"

"Mmm-hmmm," I moan.

In no time at all, he has me changed into pajamas and under the covers. Leaning down, he kisses me softly on the lips.

"I really do... need to talk with you." I yawn heavily again.

"Get some rest, Elizabeth. Milli won't be up for long. She's due for some medicine, and I'll be back to join you shortly. I'm beat."

Kissing me once more, he heads for the door and turns off the light.

Just as he's about to leave, I remember. "The baby monitor is in the kitchen."

I can hear the laughter in his voice. "You always do think of everything."

The moment the door shuts, and my head hits the pillow, I'm out for the count.

*****

As I drift into consciousness, I'm vaguely aware of the wall of heat cocooning me. It spreads along my back, over my hip, and up my sternum. I feel safe and protected and never want to break this bubble of bliss.

That is until I feel a light tap on my nose. Instantly, my eyes bulge open, and I'm greeted by two large navy-blue eyes staring at me from the edge of the bed. Her eyes barely reach over the top of the bed.

Seeing me awake, a beautiful smile spreads across her face as she whispers, "Hi, Iz."

"Hi yourself, Mills," I whisper back.

She cups her hand over her mouth and attempts to whisper, "There's no room on Daddy's side. Can I snuggle with you?"

Shit. This is one of the things I should've stayed awake and talked to Cameron about.

When I don't answer, I suddenly hear, "Climb in, kiddo. Daddy needs five more minutes." He lifts the blankets and reaches an arm for her.

Within seconds, she's snuggling into me, and he's got his arm around both of us.

"Hmmm... best morning ever," Cameron says, squeezing his arm around us both. "I've got both my girls and nowhere to be until tomorrow."

Milli's voice is filled with wonder when she innocently asks, "My Iz is your girl, too?"

"Yep. Elizabeth's pretty special. What do you think, Mills? Should we keep her?"

"I love My Iz," she says matter-of-factly, and my heart melts into a giant puddle of goo.

Looking at Cameron to see his reaction, I'm greeted with the most dazzling smile. His navy-blue eyes pin mine as he says, "I love Elizabeth, too. You okay with that?"

My response bubbles out of me before I can contemplate whether he's asking me or her the question, "I love you, too."

Leaning down, he presses a kiss to my lips. "What do you say, Elizabeth? Wanna start forever with me?"

My body stiffens as the meaning of his words hit me right through the chest.

Holy shit. What is he saying?

Laughing, he leans down to kiss me once more. When he pulls back, a devilish grin spreads across his face. "You don't have to answer just this moment. But you should know... that's where I'm going with this. I love you and knowing you love me back is all the answer I need... for now."

Epilogue
Lizzy

Five Years Later...

"Wait up, Mills," my dad says as we walk toward her third-grade classroom. It's just across the hall from mine, and we're heading to officially meet her teacher on back-to-school night. She's already met Angela, my co-worker, several times over the years, but this is the first time she'll be a student in her class.

"Papa," she chastises. "You're walking way too slow. You should just pick Embry up and carry him. His tiny little legs are never gonna get us there."

"Mills, we've got plenty of time," Cameron says, shaking his head as he holds my hand. "It doesn't start for twenty minutes, and your mom still needs to get to her classroom."

"*Dad*," Milli huffs, exasperated. "If we're on time... we're late. You know that."

Chuckling, my dad mumbles, "Gee... wonder where she got that from."

"Hmmmm... I don't know, Colonel," I tease as I hip check him, making us all laugh.

He's retired from the Air Force and is currently living in Seaside, not far from Lanie and Sloane—or any of us for that matter. It's Seaside after all. Now that my sisters and I all have started families of our own, he claimed he'd missed enough of our childhood, and he won't miss out on time with his grand-children.

"I'm surprised she's not in your class, Liz," my dad states, guiding our youngest to Milli's classroom. He's almost three and is as independent as Milli was at that age.

"I love that girl to the moon and back, but I'm choosing to be her mom, not her teacher. Everyone deserves *some* independence as they grow up."

When Cameron said forever that morning, he meant it. It was only a matter of time before he was down on one knee in front of my entire family. He, Emilia, and I all went back to Portland that fall so I could finish my degree. When it was time for my student teaching, he purchased the home he'd been renting in Seaside, and we were married that next summer.

To our surprise, I also found out I was pregnant with our daughter Everett, the week we returned from our honeymoon. She's starting preschool and will be in kindergarten next fall.

"Daddy, are we going to see Vivian and Savanna's class, too?" Everett asks as we walk through the door to Milli's class-room. Vivian and Savanna blessed us with their presence liter-ally nine months after Raven and Finn were married. Raven freaked out of course, but Finn was over the moon. Now they couldn't be happier.

"We'll see if we have time," Cameron says, then adds, "We're supposed to meet up with Josh and Jason when they finish touring their kindergarten class. Sloane and Jax said they'd meet us in Mom's classroom."

"What about Candace and Carter?" Everett asks excitedly.

Carter's also starting first grade, and Candace is the same age as Everett, so she'll start school officially next year.

"Yep. Lanie and Ryan are coming, too. They wouldn't miss it for the world." Cameron beams.

It's a tradition. After back-to-school night, we always go to ice cream as a family. Not only do I deserve the break after meeting my new families each year, but It's something special we started when Milli began kindergarten. My family rolled with it, and now, the whole herd of us gather at the local ice cream shop or at one of our houses to celebrate the start of a new school year.

"Did I tell you that I've finalized next year's tour schedule for Ruby Frax?" Cameron asks nonchalantly.

"No. My sisters will flip their lids if you send them away for too long, though."

Cameron puffs out his chest. "I just so happened to coordinate it with the kids' summer break. What do you say, beautiful? Wanna join them all in Europe next summer?"

"Seriously?" I ask in disbelief.

"Well, it is our fifth anniversary, and you've always said you wanted to travel."

"But what about the kids?"

"Last I heard, everyone's going. The guys don't wanna be away from their families, and I've even convinced Lanie and Ryan to join us for a few weeks."

"Were you planning a concert tour or a family vacation?" I ask in disbelief.

"With this crew, it's more like the National Lampoon's Family Vacation I'm sure." Dad chuckles.

"A little of both." Cameron shrugs. "When I told you I wanted forever with you, I meant with all of you."

Leaning in, he kisses me chastely on the lips.

One kiss is never enough with Cameron, and he knows it.

With an impish grin, he reaches for my hand and says on a sigh, "I love this beautiful, crazy, and chaotic life we've built, Elizabeth. Who knew that magnificent summer arrangement we agreed to would end up like this?"

THE END

I HOPE you've enjoyed reading Cameron and Lizzy's story in the *Summer Arrangement*. This story holds a special place in my heart. If you'd like to stay up to date on all things Amanda Shelley, please join my newsletter https://geni.us/AmandaShelleyNL

OH, here's a tidbit of information I'll bet you weren't expecting... While writing the epilogue for this book, it hit me that ***their dad needs a story***. So of course, I had to write it.

You'll be happy to know Mark Lancaster get's his own story in The Summer I Found Home. You can start reading it today: https://books2read.com/SISFOUNDHOME

You can also see how Ryan and Lanie's story began in *The Summer Dare*. It is now available, and you can grab your copy today: https://books2read.com/SummerDare

If you missed Sloane and Jax's story, *The Summer Ultimatum*, you can grab your copy today and start reading: https://books2read.com/SummerUltimatum

You will also find Raven and Finn's story, The Summer Proposal, is available to read now as well. Grab their story today: https://books2read.com/SummerProposal

. . .

AUTHOR'S NOTE: If you like reading books set in one world, you'll be happy to find several full-length stories for several of the characters mentioned in *The Summer Proposal* already written and available on my website www.amandashelley.com.

**Ryan is a character included in both *Vince* and *Damien*.

Fair warning—Jules will surely win your heart in these full-length, stand-alone stories. **

ACKNOWLEDGMENTS

First, I would like to thank you the reader, blogger, and reviewer for taking the time to read this book. There are so many stories to choose from, and I'm humbly honored you've chosen to read mine. I hope you enjoyed Lizzy and Cameron's story. If you want more from the from their word, be sure to check out the Summers in Seaside Series.

I'd love to hear from you and your thoughts about Lizzy and Cameron. You can find me on social media, my reader's group *Amanda's Army of Readers*, or at www.amandashel ley.com. If you care to share your thoughts on this book with other book lovers, please consider leaving a review at any of the retail sites or on Goodreads, BingeBooks, and BookBub.

I'd like to thank C.L. Collier for being my partner in crime and making the Summer in Seaside Series come to life. She helped make this random thought I had one day, turn into an amazing multi-author collaboration.

I'd also like to thank the authors in this series for taking a chance on us as collaborators and taking this journey with us. I couldn't be prouder of what we accomplished together!

Next I'd like to thank Sue Soares at SJS Editorial Services. You are amazing to work with. I appreciate your patience and flexibility. I simply love working with you. My books wouldn't be what they are without you.

To Julie Deaton at Deaton Author Services, thanks for making my book pretty and talking me off a ledge. I appreciate knowing your proofreading is exquisite, and my worries disappear. I know that if I make you feel all the feels, I've met my mark. Your eagle eyes are spectacular, and I don't know what I'd do without you.

To the people who have supported me along the way, I'm humbly grateful to have you in my life. Whether you've read my books, asked me about my progress, listened to me talk about my fictional characters as if they're a part of my family, plotted with me, or been my cheerleader, I appreciate your continued support. Please know it hasn't gone unnoticed.

Last but certainly not least, to my four beautiful girls who have had to wait patiently when I said, "Just one more minute," when I obviously meant a lot more than one. I love that you get that I have deadlines and will sometimes keep me on task with your not-so-subtle reminders that "Mom... you should be working" during my designated times. I appreciate your support more than you'll ever know. Even though you can't read this book—because that might be *weird*—for both of us, I love that you keep asking. I love you all more than words can express. You're the reason I continue to strive and reach for my goals each day.

ABOUT THE AUTHOR

Amanda Shelley writes romantic stories you can escape into. Some are steamy, others are sweet but all have strong characters with a little bit of sass.

When not writing, Amanda enjoys time with her family, playing chauffeur, chef and being an enthusiastic fan for her children. Keeping up with them keeps her alert and grounded in reality. She enjoys long car rides, chai lattes and popping her SUV into four-wheel drive for adventures anywhere.

Amanda loves hearing from readers. Be sure to sign up for her newsletter and follow her on social media. Join her reader's group Amanda's Army of Readers to stay up to date on her latest information.

Readers group:
https://www.facebook.com/groups/AmandasArmyofReaders/
Goodreads:
https://www.goodreads.com/author/show/19713563.Aman
da_Shelley
Newsletter:
https://geni.us/AmandaShelleyNL
www.amandashelley.com
Website:
www.amandashelley.com

Facebook:
https://www.facebook.com/authoramandashelley/
Instagram:
https://www.instagram.com/authoramandashelley/
Tik Tok:
https://www.tiktok.com/@authoramandashelley
Amazon:
https://www.amazon.com/author/amandashelley
Book Bub:
https://www.bookbub.com/profile/amanda-shelley

ALSO BY AMANDA SHELLEY

If you enjoyed this book, you will be happy to discover Amanda Shelley primarily writes in one world. For a complete list of the series reading order as well as a chronological time line, please visit:

https://amandashelley.com/reading-order/

The Summer Dare

Leave it to Nana to think of everything.

After a grueling semester, I'm ready for a peaceful summer in Seaside with my sisters.

Imagine my surprise, when I'm woken by the screeching sound of a saw coming through my wall, the first official morning of break.

Not only did I come flying out of bed swinging, but I gave Ryan, the unsuspecting carpenter the surprise of his life, when I came wielding my killer coat hanger and all.

Too bad, I was only in a tank and undies and it wasn't nearly as effective as I'd hoped.

Of course, he insists he's only doing his job.

Since it's Nana's last request to care for us, I can't refuse.

However, I won't let a tall, pesky, sexy as sin, know-it-all get in my way of my summer plans. I pretend I ignore him - that is until my youngest sister pokes her nose in my business and throws down a dare I can't back down from.

Kiss the next single guy who walks up to the bonfire - or explain to my sisters why I get riled up over the contractor.

When Ryan suddenly appears, I know I'm screwed in more ways than one.

Not only will my sisters learn my secret, but from the determined look on Ryan's face, I'm afraid he's eager to reveal it to the world as well.

What have I gotten myself into?

As I walk toward him, one thing is certain - *this summer dare will either make or break me.*

https://geni.us/AmandaShelleyBooks

The Summer Ultimatum

Watching my sister fall in love last summer gave me something I hadn't expected—hope. It gave me hope that there might be someone out there for me and hope that I might get past my misguided fears and finally let someone in.

With my help, Ryan's planning the most epic proposal. I just have to get the know-it-all musician I work with to fall in line to make it work.

Jax is wicked smart, extremely talented, and sexy as sin. But he can't see the forest for the trees when it comes to his potential. He'd rather keep playing in dive bars along the coast than take a real shot at success.

When the Seaside festival has a music competition, I present Jax with an ultimatum that will either make or break both our careers.

I've laid it all on the line, but can he?

https://geni.us/AmandaShelleyBooks

The Summer Proposal

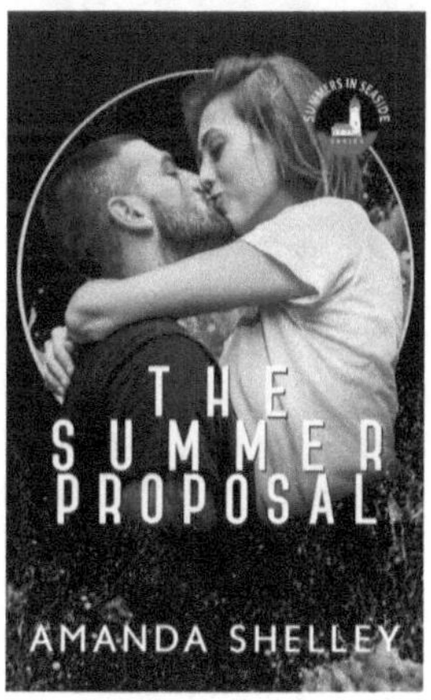

My sisters are dropping like flies.

They're falling in love and having the time of their lives.

Don't get me wrong, I'm ecstatic for them. I love seeing them happy.

But I'm not ready for that type of commitment.

I can't even keep a plant alive, let alone find someone worthy of getting past a third date.

As the only sister done with school and single as a pringle, I have to do something fast, or I'll be my matchmaking aunt's next victim.

When Jax's drummer joins him for the summer and needs some help with his image, I make him a deal he can't refuse.

All is perfect—until I realize my summer proposal has one minor flaw.

Our relationship may be a sham, but there's nothing fake about my feelings for Finn.

https://geni.us/AmandaShelleyBooks

The Summer I Found Home

Being a pilot is all I've ever known.

I served my country and I'm damn proud of my career.

But sacrifices were made, especially when it came to family.

I've missed first steps, first days of school, and first dates to name a few.

My kids grew up. They're having families of their own.

Was it worth it?

When an opportunity brings me to Seaside, I jump feet first no questions asked.

It means experiencing all those firsts with my grandkids.

With family as my focus and my guard down, I don't even see Faye coming.

She's a force to be reckoned with and has me holding on for dear life.

I thought our ship had sailed, but now that I'm home for good—I just might get more than one second chance.

arrangement?

https://geni.us/AmandaShelleyBooks

Zander: A Perfectly Independent Series Novella

(Available for free on All Retailers)

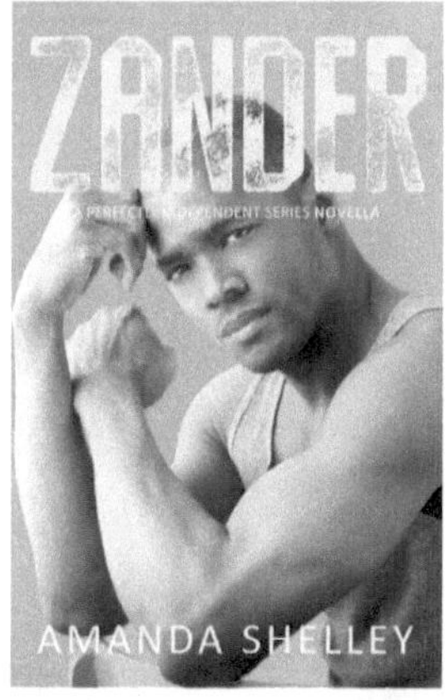

Zander's known for being a player both on and off the court. When his name shows up as my next client, my heart stalls, and not in a good way. There's no way I'll survive the semester with him. I just don't have the patience.

However, when I need help, Zander makes a proposal I can't refuse. He'll be my fake date to my best friend's wedding so I don't have to face my ex and his new girlfriend alone.

The weekend goes off without a hitch as we effortlessly pretend to have the time of our lives.

All is perfect... until I realize my feelings for Zander are no longer an act.

What will I do when our arrangement comes to an end?

https://geni.us/AmandaShelleyBooks

Drew: Book One of the Perfectly Independent Series

Of all people, why him?

He didn't EVEN bother introducing himself, just assumed I knew him from his fame on the court.

I nearly died on the spot when our professor announced we were permanent lab partners. Between his arrogance and the constant interruption from basketball groupies, there's no way I'll survive this semester.

Sure, he's hotter than anyone I've ever seen in a science lab with his sexy blue eyes, cute dimple, and muscles for days - but I can't afford *his* kind of distractions.

Okay. Deep breath.

I can do this.

After all, it's only one semester.

Just when I think my self-control is in check, he does something to show me that he isn't the egotistical, self-centered jerk I thought he was.

How can his stupid smile suddenly make my mind melt, heart race, and palms sweat?

If I take this chance on Drew, will my perfectly laid out plans disappear?

https://geni.us/AmandaShelleyBooks

Vince: Book Two of the Perfectly Independent Series

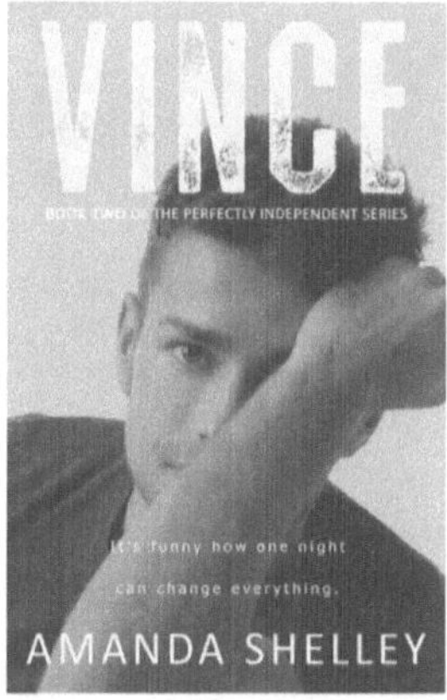

It's funny how one night can change everything.

As a bartender near campus, I'm certain I've heard it all. Rarely a shift passes without some guy taking his best shot, hoping I'll end my self-proclaimed dating diet.

Of course, this is exactly how I meet Vince.

Except, he isn't the one running his mouth.

No, he simply shuts down his idiotic friend, then stops my heart with the simplest of smiles and walks away.

Just when I force myself to forget him, he bumps into me on campus.

Our connection is consuming, and my world is knocked off kilter. It's far beyond physical attraction. He's smart, sexy, and feels like—home?

Wait, that can't be right...

Whatever it is, Vince has me breaking my rules to spend time with him.

My entire life I've prepared for meeting the wrong guys.

What the hell should I do when I find the right one?

https://geni.us/AmandaShelleyBooks

Damien: Book Three of the Perfectly Independent Series

Beautiful girls are not hard to find at Columbia River University.

The coeds on campus are great to look at but I was over that scene after graduation three years ago.

These days, outside of being part of the largest civil engineering job on campus, all I'm searching for is a decent meal and some peace and quiet. It's why I'm happy to have found what I consider a hidden gem in the diner I frequent.

All I need to do is finish this job and move on to the next by year's end.

Should be easy enough. Only when Vanessa walks up with a sexy smile and a mouth full of sass, she does more than take my order. She completely takes my breath away.

Next thing I know, I'm here every morning, making every excuse to dine with this intriguing woman. Not only is she smart and sexy, but she's laser focused on reaching the goals she's set for herself.

The more I get to know her, the more I'm convinced she's the one. I just have to find a way to get her to deviate from her perfectly laid plans and take a chance on me.

Making The Call

Dani

As a bestselling romance author, most assume my life's glamorous, filled with combustible chemistry, and most of all, romance. Ha! I can only wish. With a deadline looming, I've escaped to my family's cabin on Anderson Island to free myself from distractions. My plan's great, until a man, who could pass as a cover model on one of my books, comes to my rescue. Is there chemistry? Sure. Is he everything I'd look for in a guy? Absolutely. But will my career be at risk if I give into my desire?

Luke

For a player, women line up outside the locker room. For coaches, we're lucky to get in the game. As the youngest NFL coach in the league, I live, eat, breathe, and even sleep football. To gear up for this season, I return to my home on Anderson Island for a much-needed break. When Dani literally crashes into my life, my mind's suddenly on the sexy brunette with a sailors mouth, rather than my team's next play. She has me dusting off another playbook entirely, making me wonder, did I make the right call?

https://geni.us/AmandaShelleyBooks

The Boy Upstairs

I ran into Derek while trying to escape the neighbor from hell.

Instantly, we hit it off. Since he's only here for three months and the microbrewery leaves me little time for commitments, it's the perfect setup for a fling.

He's adventurous, challenges me, and he just gets me from the inside out.

With our expiration date quickly approaching, I'm left to wonder… Will my heart ever be the same without the boy upstairs?

https://geni.us/AmandaShelleyBooks

He Saved My Boy

Davis is the first guy to catch my attention since... hell, I don't even know.

Instantly, he makes me think and feel things I've forgotten existed. It has been forever since I put my needs first, so I take the chance and let him light me up from the inside out.

Our night is the kind that will ruin me for all others.

But then I get the dreaded call.

I rush out without a second glance, knowing I'll likely never see him again.

My son will always come first—Always.

Imagine my surprise when Davis walks in, and I find he's the only one who can save my boy.

This cannot be happening—*I guess it's time to pull up my big girl panties and see what happens.*

https://geni.us/AmandaShelleyBooks

The Vegas Pitch

This pitch could make or break my career.

Not only will it set a personal record for the biggest account I've ever landed, but it could set my newfound company three years ahead of schedule for expansion.

Thank god I've got Nate Bellinger on my team.

Even though I had my reservations hiring the sexiest man I've ever laid eyes on – he more than meets my expectations with his hard work and determination. Together, we've formed a solid team and play off each other perfectly.

As we wait for the final verdict, I begrudgingly take Nate up on his offer for a night on the town. After all, this is Vegas and I need to let the chips fall where they may.

Imagine my surprise when I wake up the next morning to find we've not only won the campaign, but I'm apparently married to the man I've only ever let myself fantasize about.

The kicker of it all – he has no intentions of letting me go.

But what will it mean once we leave Vegas?

https://geni.us/AmandaShelleyBooks

Resilience: Book One of Resilience Duet

Resolution: Book Two of Resilience Duet

Samantha never saw Enzo coming.

As the dust settles from her divorce, her life is full. She doesn't have time for distractions. She's too busy running her own company and checking off numerous items from her kids' demanding schedule to have a life of her own.

Then he walks into her kitchen with his breathtaking green eyes and a mischievous grin. He's there to surprise his father - her contractor, but his presence makes everything off kilter.

Enzo's perfectly content with his adventurous life as an elite rescue pilot, until a harmless prank turns on him. Instead of surprising his father, he finds his world thrown off course by the beautiful woman with a sexy smile, wicked sass and the mouthwatering ability to keep him on his toes.

With his limited time on leave, is she worth the risk to his heart?

https://geni.us/AmandaShelleyBooks

Collide: A Sweet Romance

Falling head over heels was the last thing I expected.

Literally.

Coffee is everywhere – and more than my ego is bruised.

When the handsome stranger I plowed into calls me by name, mortification sinks in.

He rushes off to class. I run home to change, hoping to forget the whole incident.

If only I could be so lucky.

I quickly find it's a small world and Gavin Wallace is completely unavoidable. Everywhere I turn he's there. In my classes. Hanging with my friends.

I've got his full attention and I have to admit, I like it a lot more than I should.

https://geni.us/AmandaShelleyBooks